Robert Parker is a married father of three, who lives in a village near Manchester, UK. The author of the *Ben Bracken* books *A Wanted Man* and *Morte Point*, and the standalone post-Brexit country-noir *Crook's Hollow*, he enjoys a rural life on an old pig farm (now minus pigs), writing horrible things between school runs.

He writes full time, as well as organising and attending various author events across the UK - while boxing regularly for charity. Passionate about inspiring a love of the written word in young people, Robert spends a lot of time in schools across the North West, encouraging literacy, story-telling, creative-writing and how good old fashioned hard work tends to help good things happen.

Praise for *A Wanted Man*:

'A stunning debut thriller filled with brutal, breakneck action and seductive, brilliant prose combined with a compelling, credible hero – simply unputdowanable!' – Danielle Ramsay, bestselling author of the *DI Jack Brady* series

Also by Robert Parker:

A Wanted Man (*Ben Bracken* series book one)

Crook's Hollow

MORTE POINT

Robert Parker

ENDEAVOURQUILL

AN ENDEAVOUR QUILL PAPERBACK

First published in 2018 by Endeavour Quill

This paperback edition published in 2018 by Endeavour Quill

Endeavour Quill is an imprint of Endeavour Media Ltd. Endeavour Quill,
85-87 Borough High Street, London, SE1 1NH

ISBN 978-1-911445-73-9

Typeset by Ana Marija Meshkova

Printed and bound in Great Britain by Clays Ltd, Elcograf S.p.A.

www.endeavourmedia.co.uk

Contents

For grandparents everywhere, not least my own...

Freda, Edmund, Sylvia and Bob,

and Uncle Selwyn.

Love you always.

Author Acknowledgements and Notes

To Dr Helen Collins, Dr Lewis Collins and my sister-in-law Dr Susie Parker; the smartest people I know. We had a lovely chat about botulism one day, and this was the result. Helen's assistance in the factual accuracy of the book has been invaluable, fascinating and extremely generous. Thank you all.

To the main man, Wayne Coghlan, at The Jube in Woolacombe. Thanks for looking after us all these years. And to Dougal... the best pub dog of them all.

To everyone at Endeavour Media, but most notably my ace publisher Alice Rees, who has always backed me and I couldn't be more grateful. Also special mentions to

Matthew Lynn, Jasmin Kirkbride, Rufus Cuthbert, James Faktor and Hannah Groves. Thanks to you all.

To my agent and guardian, Linda Langton, constantly scrapping for me, always driving me on - thank you. And to Linda MacFadyen, Alan McDermott, Peter Beck, Roger A. Price and Paul Finch, thank you for all your kind words and encouragement.

To Mum and Dad, Jonny, Susie, Charlotte and Abigail, Lauren, Matt and Max, and Graham, Joy, and Dru - thanks for all the love and support. And huge thanks to each and every wonderful person in my extended family.

And of course, to my gang, Becky, Avalyn, Sylvia and Robin. Love you - always. Xxx

The wreck Ben finds off Morte Point, is a genuine vessel that sadly sank and was never recovered. All that is known is that on May 23rd 1868, The Seabird came into difficulties off the coastline during a storm, and the entire crew was sadly lost. The Seabird might still be down there.

APEX (ey-pex)

noun , pl.: apexes , apices

1. the highest point; vertex;

the pointed end or tip of something

a pinnacle or high point, as of a career, etc.

Retrieved from Dictionary.com website: http://dictionary.reference.com/browse/apex

Prologue

There he is. My enemy, my target, my polar opposite. Leathered skin, red and blotchy, peels at the edges of his fleeing hairline like parchment. The luminous green drink he holds in his left hand, the heavy gold chain weighing down the wrist on his right. The sheer entitlement in his stance. The entire package makes me grimace.

But somehow… I smile. The mere fact that he is like this, only makes things easier for me.

I sit in a McDonald's, nursing a long-melted McFlurry, peering through the plate glass windows out into 24-Hour Square. It's a malaise of excess in flip-flops, a sweltering southern Spanish day having lazily made way for a humid evening, and with that the neons of 24-Hour Square have blinked into life. The clubs line the square like so many ant hills, sending their workers out to bring back recruits with the promise of cheap booze and girls.

I've been hanging out in this place for a few days, blending in without too much trouble. Just another soul, hunting endorphins and pheromones.

He takes her hand, and I know it's on. He walks her across to the taxi rank, an urgent potter to his step, darting through the stop-start traffic.

Nkeoma. She trots behind him in scuffed Nikes, which I felt when I met her was an odd choice for a street corner prostitute. She throws a look back at her friends. I'm not sure if they are actually friends or mere acquaintances. They seem to look out for each other but only to a point — it's all weary smiles and oft-trod conversation, until a trick comes along. Then the lucky girl is on her own.

They are in the taxi in a flash, and with that, I'm up and out the door. I know exactly where they are going, and I'll be there, waiting.

*

He's certainly laid it on thick. In the distance, the marinas of Torremolinos glow with promise before being swallowed abruptly by the darkness of the sea, while on the terrace coffee table sit some pills, a baggie of cocaine and a bottle of red. From my spot on the patio roof, eight feet above them, I can see it's a Shiraz. What a smoothie.

He sits there in his underpants, his wiry body and pot belly, like a fat stick insect with a leer at full wattage. She is now in a swimsuit he had out waiting for her.

'Come on love,' he says in a crackling Cockney gargle. 'Do the dance you know I like. Do it right here.'

My teeth itch, hearing him talk like this. Nkeoma stands about a foot away from him, and starts a half-hearted grind.

'Not that one,' he says. 'The other one. The one that makes that arse jiggle.'

My fists are balled now. Nkeoma turns and shakes her rear at him rhythmically, near hopping up and down on the spot, in a bored music video twerk.

I feel voyeuristic and dirty, knowing I could stop this and I'm just watching. But I need to learn. I need to know the signs. I need to know what makes these bastards tick.

'That's the one,' he says, adjusting himself. He reaches out and smacks her backside, causing her to yelp. He sighs in obvious delight. It's all foul. I hold fast as best I can.

He throws an arm around her waist and pulls her close, before reaching for the pills.

I know I won't stand for that.

I drop into their midst, and land with the skill only my training could provide. She springs out of the way and I'm on him in a heartbeat. He doesn't even have time to stand. I clamp the rubber clown mask over his face — it's the best I could come up with from the marketplace in Fuengirolla earlier in the day. He struggles, but I hold him firm, pinning him into the seat with my hands against his elbows and a foot up into his swollen abdomen.

The interior surfaces of the ill-fitting mask are covered with rags, soaked in chloroform. Once it's over his head, like now, all I have to do is keep him in place. His confusion will be massive, and he's already losing his control. I turn and sit on his belly while he slips away. I face Nkeoma.

We met yesterday. She is a beautiful, soulful young Nigerian, who came here to find work, knowing full well that the sex trade was her likely destination. She was prepared to take the risk that there might be another way. Now she is corrupted, warped and wayward, contorted by the demands of her industry. Yesterday, I offered her a hot dog. She offered me a series of sexual options by way of gratitude, each one more crude and carnal than the last.

Our conversation today couldn't be more different.

'Thank you,' she says.

'You're welcome. Do better for yourself, Nkeoma,' I say. I take the glass of red from the table, and give it a sniff. Smells cheap and not necessarily cheerful, like a jockstrap full of old fruit.

'I'll try,' she replies, grabbing her fallen clothes. She looks at the table with a half glance, but it's enough for me to catch it. I know the plight these girls face. For girls like these, drugs and booze become anchors in a sex trade storm. I'm realistic enough to know that my saving Nkeoma from one nasty trick isn't going to be enough to steer her away from addiction.

'Try harder,' I say, before standing up briskly and sliding the table roughly to the edge of the balcony. Nkeoma just watches with sheepish futility, as I hoist the whole lot up and over the railing, raining the booze and contraband down into the swimming pool below. She drops her eyes to the floor.

'On your way,' I tell her, before looking back to my stricken prey. He's out for the count, but his mask stares back at me. One of the rubber eyes has folded in on itself into a dark slit. He could be winking at me.

Right back at you, slick. You won't be harming anyone, any more.

1.

Thursday

I stare at the sky, the fierce cerulean prickling my eyes, and it forces them to squeeze shut — as does the pain, of course, because what I am doing really bleeding hurts. I try to focus on something else.

Why, as humans, are we so obsessed with the sky?

It is fickle, changeable, treacherous...

But it is also a vast harbinger of hope. As long as there is a sky, much as when there is a will, there is a way.

It's a thought-process that seems oddly paradoxical, since I am lowering a cheap pine coffin into a giant wooden freight crate. A shipping plane is leaving Malaga

Airport in an hour, stacked with export goods bound for Great Britain... and I want this crate to be on it.

The coffin is bound tight by a security seal, the key to which I have posted back to England, a couple of days ago. By now it should have reached Jeremiah Salix, an Officer in the National Crime Agency's Organised Crime Command. He alone can open the coffin, and it's up to him what happens to the contents.

Just as I feel the weight begin to overtake me, I hear the clunk below and my shoulders release. It's amazing how heavy a wooden casket is when it contains a grown man.

I take out my phone, the trusty Samsung I have become so familiar with, and load my favourite app. Custom built by a third party for one user, designed by a promising young fellow in the Philippines. It allows me to call a number direct, but it builds a firewall around the call itself, rendering it untraceable and unidentifiable. You can't call me back. No caller ID. You can't get my number. You just get my call, and, for the purposes of my relationship with Officer Salix, that suits me just fine.

We call it Cryptocall, and it takes over the phone screen, which is barely visible in the harsh afternoon sun. I access Jeremiah's number within the app, and make the call. Safe. Neat. Secure.

I look back towards the airport terminal, a dusty couple of building blocks backed by mountain peaks, and Jeremiah picks up almost immediately, as if he has been camping by his phone handset.

'Hello?' he says, reaching out across the static void, his voice sure but searching.

Our relationship is set, established. Pleasantries have been left by the wayside.

'Did you get the key?' I ask.

'I most definitely did. What it opens has been the topic of a fair amount of office debate. There's even a pool going.'

'Do you want the inside track?'

'Is it the one we discussed?'

'Yes. Wes Finnegan. Remind me what he did again, so I don't feel so bad about what happened to him.' I know vague snippets, and detail will only add to my resolve, strengthen my backbone.

'He had a nasty habit of marching into quiet village post offices with a sawn-off shotgun and a balaclava.' My gut tightens.

'What a lovely specimen. You sure you want him back on home turf?'

'Sadly, yes. He's been on the UK's most wanted top ten for three years, and this is as close to catching him as any authority has got. The Met's own Flying Squad have been after him for double that time.'

'Top ten most wanted? For robbery?'

'Well, he has got forty-two robberies attached to his name, and two of those ended up with dead post office owners. Messy.'

Helplessly, I fix a stare upon the grain of the wood that forms the casket below me, almost boring a hole right through it, to Finnegan himself. What a piece of shit. It irks me, that. He took the piss, this guy — out of everyone who tries to make an honest living. Everyone who holds a pen, taps a keyboard, is on their feet or on the road all day.

This particular costa is a honeypot for those fleeing British shores in the name of something criminal. Lives left behind. Criminal charges abandoned. Bail terms abused. With kilos of cash from organised crime, they head to the costa to seek escape… and a sunny corner to enjoy their ill-gotten gains. An example of the type is in the coffin below me, respiring heavily and sleepily with breathing apparatus nestled between his knees and connected to a mask over his face. He is securely held in place, and should be comfortable enough. He'll probably piss himself, but you can't have everything.

For the last five months, I have existed in a comparable way, with my own secret cash keeping me afloat, my own nefarious deeds left behind, my own fabricated identity sheltering me. My passport, a slick, solid forgery, says that I am Sean Miller. It was a parting gift from an avuncular old criminal mastermind, right before I put a bullet through his cranium.

I could give Finnegan similar justice right here, right now. Justice he deserves. But I won't. I made a deal. If I'm going to do good, *real measurable good*, I need him to get home.

'Let your superiors know he's on his way. Tell them it's from that source of yours. I'm sure you have everything you need at your end already. From there —'

'Keep you out of it, I know,' Jeremiah interrupts.

It is a relatively new routine, but homely, like a fifteen-year-old sweater. Jeremiah uses the NCA resources to feed me information on targets, and I have a little look-see. I answer to nobody but myself. I am trained and motivated. I am doing Great Britain's dirty work, even though it doesn't know it.

I am Ben Bracken.

Five months back, I pulled the biggest fish out of Manchester's criminal pond and he wasn't safely returned to the water. It ended bloodily, in Manchester Airport's baggage reclaim, and since I was holding all my worldly possessions when the deed was done, I decided to grab the next cheap flight out of there. Jeremiah suggested the Costa del Sol might hold some interest for me, thinking of the likes of Finnegan. So I hopped on a 9.00 am budget airline flight to Malaga, and was the soberest person on the plane by some distance.

'Is there anything else?' I ask. The line goes quiet for a good few seconds. 'Jeremiah?' I prompt him.

The beat of silence is as revealing as any word. There is more.

'I'm not sure,' says Jeremiah, after a couple of seconds. 'My team... we were monitoring something that was potentially very urgent, but we were suddenly called off, by powers much higher up the food chain.'

'Sounds delicate.' The National Crime Agency is not just some corner-shop, ten-a-penny security outfit. It is the institution to which the safeguarding of the British people is entrusted. For the NCA to have been called off by someone bigger than itself...

'It is. Very much so. I just... Something about it doesn't sit right with me. I've never known this kind of interference on an active investigation before. I mean we ruffle feathers all the time, sure, I'm really used to pissing on other investigative bodies' chips by now, and they're rarely too happy about it, but this... This is something else.'

'You sound suspicious.'

'I am.'

'I don't know where I can fit into this for you.'

'To tell you the truth, I don't either,' replies Jeremiah. 'Save for the fact that I think a man operating outside an official channel may have more of a chance to get to the bottom of things than would be the case for one of us here, fumbling about in the dark, doing something we've been specifically asked *not* to do. Plus, I get the distinct impression that the powers that be have their eyes on us.'

That has snagged my interest a little. Jeremiah simply wouldn't mention it if it wasn't important. He is very well placed, considering his position in the National Crime Agency's hierarchy. And that's without considering what are as far as I can tell, his purity of motive and loyalty to his cause. He is sharp as lemon juice on an icy blade, and is just as switched on, and he will embrace the unconventional to ensure the job gets done. That's why I like working with him, for I *am* that very sprinkling of the unconventional.

'Can you elaborate?' I ask.

'This topic is extremely sensitive. It's not been made clear to me, but… I think the pressure is coming from Westminster.'

Government. Interesting, but even more reason to steer clear. The tendrils of our democracy creep deep into the length and breadth of the country, and entangling myself in *that* would be mission suicide. I broke out of prison last year, and I suppose I'm still on the run. So... keep away from authority, that's my current motto.

'Again, I don't think I can help you,' I say.

'What we were working on had huge implications. We were working on the basis that it concerned national security.'

The words *national security* strike a chord that echoes in my head.

'I'll be back on home soil in fourteen hours,' I say. 'I'll call you then.'

'OK. If you can aim for a part of the country in particular, head to the south west.'

'Will do,' I reply, closing the phone. I don't have a clue what I'm heading back to, but I know that I must be careful.

I look down and check, one last time. The coffin containing Wes Finnegan, obstinate sun-rouged cockroach with a penchant for post office murder–robberies and swimwear-wrapped Nigerian hookers, is nestled in the huge packing crate, alongside some vacuum packed rattan garden furniture. And when customs open the packing crate at the other end, and nobody appears to pick up the dear, dead relative who kicked the bucket on their holidays, the coffin will set off alarm bells. They'll check the serial number on the delivery tag and I have made sure that'll lead straight to the NCA's own Jeremiah Salix.

I drop down onto the tarmac, and head back to the terminal, hoping that some budget airline will take pity and be kind enough to offer me a quick route back home.

2.

Friday

I'm in a pub called, jauntily, The Jube. There's a Staffordshire bull terrier at my feet, a mangled tennis ball in its mouth. A pint of cool, amber ale rests in front of me. I'm allowing myself just the one, since I do feel a little swept up in the holiday spirit of my location.

I sense movement over my left shoulder, but it's only the pub manager bringing me a jacket potato choked by cheese and beans. Heaven.

'Here y'are, mate,' he says, in an accent that sounds familiar. It seems that I can't quite leave Manchester behind, and neither can this friendly barman. I thank him, as the dog glances over at him in a non-committal fashion.

'Come on, away,' says the manager. The dog looks, wet-eyed, at me.

'He's no trouble,' I say.

The manager smiles and sighs. 'He's too damn friendly for his own good.'

I tuck in heartily, watched by my new furry friend, the tennis ball still lodged tight in its jaws. As I travelled the pubs of Sheffield as a kid, playing at my Dad's feet, pub dogs were my best friends.

I sip the beer. Bliss.

The last few hours have been a blur. The return flight was cramped, sweaty, and there was an overwhelming stench of vomit wafting from the toilets at the back. These Brits abroad had clearly flown the Union Flag in lurid earnest once again.

When I got off the plane at Heathrow, finally gulping fresh air, I called Jeremiah for an update. What he told me set me off once again. I was to head to Barnstaple, a town in North Devon, in which hides, among idyllic bike trails and surf shops, an army base.

Devonshire kicks out from the left foot of England, as if the United Kingdom were dipping its toe, carefully, out into the Atlantic. It is at the south west of the country and is wild, soft and green, encircled by beaches, cliffs and blue sea. It is, I am learning, a most beautiful place.

Jeremiah then adjusted slightly, and told me to go to Woolacombe, a small seaside holiday village on the western coast of Devon, to await instruction. It is about ten miles as the crow flies from Barnstaple, and Royal Marines Base Chivenor. The coastal helicopter rescue services operate out of RMB Chivenor, answering call-outs 24/7. The base has an air strip, and at some point in the next few days, a plane will be landing there — a plane that will be carrying a cargo that is integral to the situation that Jeremiah has unveiled.

All I can do is arrive, prepare and wait. The village is full of holiday-makers and gift shops, and there is a beautiful golden beach between the village and the sea, the sand of which looks warm, clean and very inviting. I didn't realise that Britain could offer such a thing as this. Our own family holidays were never to the seaside, and I find myself more than a little seduced. It's taking some effort not to buckle, and go out to buy a bucket and spade.

Usually, I am a slave to preparation, but on this occasion I am very early. So I sit in this pub, in the middle of the afternoon, enjoying the beer and the lure of the British seaside holiday. Booze used to be an an ever-blurring cloak in which to wallow amidst uncertain thoughts. Not anymore. Life feels good.

My stay in Heaven is interrupted by a beep from my phone, which is resting on the table. The reason I picked The Jube was its advert for free wifi, and knowing how that would make contact with Jeremiah all the easier. We communicate via anonymous Twitter accounts, deleting them and starting them as we go. I check the app.

'CALL ASAP'

It's Jeremiah, and I call him immediately via Cryptocall. Like last time, he picks up near straight away, but when he does, the sound of his voice suggests that he is down a well; it's a flat, muffled echo, holding his words hostage. A stairwell maybe. There is unmistakable urgency in his voice.

'Are you in Woolacombe?' he says.

'Yes,' I reply.

'We've intercepted a communication. The plane is ahead of schedule.'

This isn't good. I'm in position in Woolacombe, not in position at RMB Chivenor, but before I can say anything, Jeremiah's next words change the game entirely.

'They are bringing it down, hard and heavy, into the sea.'

I sit bolt upright.

'Where?' I ask.

'The cliffs north of Woolacombe. Follow the coastline to a peninsular of rock about a mile away. It's called Morte Point and it's earlier on the flight path into Chivenor. You should be able to see the plane from there, and where it ends up.'

'Jesus Christ. What am I dealing with, Jeremiah?'

'You have to get there. There will be a recovery team en route, but you have to beat them to it. You *have* to get that cargo before they do. I promise you, if you knew what we are dealing with here…'

He doesn't finish.

I don't know what to do. This sounds so far-fetched, so grand, so over-blown. So much more than I bargained for. The dog looks at me quizzically, from my feet.

'It's of national importance?' I ask.

'I swear,' Jeremiah says, 'this is very big stuff. Your next move could be huge, in terms of Great Britain's safety.'

He's got me. I'm up, grabbing my trusty waterproof rucksack, and running for the door.

'Morte Point?' I say into the phone, while moving into the sunshine.

'It's about a mile and a half away, north along the coast. The plane will be with you in about twenty minutes. You can make it.'

I'm running, the phone call still open, along the middle of the road. I'm wearing board shorts, a hoodie and trail shoes. Not really equipped for an operation of any kind, but it will have to do.

'What does the cargo look like?' I ask, as I hop up onto the pavement again to run down the main street towards the shops, and bob between the members of a family plodding along with ice creams.

'We don't know. No idea,' Jeremiah replies. The tremor of his voice suggests he is fully aware of how hopeless that sounds.

'You want me attend a plane crash wreckage in order to retrieve an item which you know zero about? Have I got that right?' I don't mean to sound sarcastic, but it's almost impossible not to.

'We have an *idea* what it is, but not how it is travelling.'

'Jesus! So when I get to this destroyed plane, I need to find this mystery item before the authorities do? Is there *anything* you can tell me about it?'

His voice takes on a grave tone.

'Yes. When you find it, don't fuck with it. Under any circumstances.'

I drop into one of the small seaside shops. Chocolate, books, flip-flops and inflatables stare at me, not to mention several confused customers.

'What is the depth of the water?' I ask. 'Off Morte Point — what is the depth of the water?'

'I don't know,' replies Jeremiah. 'But I can try to find out.'

'About thirty feet, give or take,' says a quiet female voice. I turn to the source; it's the lady at the till, who looks at me with a face full of uncertainty.

I shut my phone and approach her.

'Thank you,' I say hurriedly. 'Do you have a snorkel mask?'

'Just these here,' she says, pointing at a rack of kids' swimming equipment. A Hello Kitty snorkel kit seems to be the only option. No time to be picky.

'I'll take it,' I say, reaching for the sweet counter, 'and these.' I put a handful of Snickers bars on the counter, and take a twenty from my pocket. 'I'm gonna grab two bottles of Lucozade and two of water from the fridge by the door when I go, will this cover it?'

She looks at the twenty.

'Rather,' she says.

'Thanks for the help,' I say, before scooping the items into my rucksack and heading for the door.

Back out in the sunshine, I turn right and start to run at a steady pace. I have approximately eighteen minutes to run a mile and a half across undulating rock and coastal roads. That's about four and a half miles an hour, give or take. That is extremely doable. I can make it. I keep my pack weight at around six kilograms, never more. That includes all of my worldly possessions. I certainly travel light; but I know that I can run a flat marathon with a six kilo pack in about two hours fifty minutes. So, nine miles per hour. Even over a few bumps, laden with a sodding Hello Kitty snorkel kit, I can do this.

I cross the road and head towards the sea, which I can hear over the cars, gulls and breeze. It's a beautiful place, Woolacombe. But if Jeremiah is right, in just a few moments it will be at the centre of a shitstorm, the likes of which it will never have seen before.

3.

The run feels good. It stokes memories of my training on other dusty mountain roads. If it weren't for what frankly sounds like a national incident brewing, which I'm about to unceremoniously gatecrash, I'd be enjoying myself. The breeze is pleasant, flicking invigorating sea air up my nose, and the sun isn't too harsh. No wonder people like coming here, cradled by the sea on the soft, golden sand.

I've had to veer inland slightly, as the road peels away from the immediate coast. But I can see where I am heading. Morte Point. It reaches out of the swelling ocean like a gigantic beached whale made of shattered stone, moss and grass. It is a high-ish, rocky peninsular. I can see white dots peppering the cliffs and hillsides leading to the furthermost jagged stone extremity. Sheep. Heaven knows how they exist out there.

I seem to be approaching a settlement, as I pound the tarmac up the hill. I pass an old stone church and a couple of bed and breakfast retreats. There is a quiet square, a grand oak hanging over it, with a couple of pubs and a shop. Now *this* is Great Britain. The shop sign reads 'Mortehoe Bakery'. The plane had better not come down here, on this quaint little English cranny.

I scan the square, looking for an inkling of where to go next. A side road next to one of the pubs, called The Ship Aground, has a green National Trust sign at its opening. As soon as I can make out the lettering, inscribed 'Morte Point', I'm off again. I check my watch, as I sprint past a couple leaving the pub with a couple of shandies. Do I alert them? Do I tell them that I've been warned a plane is to go down just a short distance from here?

No time. Stick to the objective. And pray that there won't be any collateral damage resulting from my silence.

The road disintegrates the further from the square I travel, becoming shingle while snaking past an ancient-looking cemetery. I don't slow down, but I would love to. I'd love to examine this unique setting and wallow in it for a while. But I know that, somewhere overhead, tonnage of steel is en route, ready to drop straight into this picture postcard setting. I have to beat it.

The shingle becomes grass, the softness most welcome, and I am out in a field, breathing hard. Sheep bleat at me. I see the highest peak of the peninsula overhead, but I don't want to go there. I want to go around it, to the other side, and get a good fix on this plane. I see that if I travel a short way up the small summit, there is a fork in the pathway, with one trail leading onwards and upwards, and the other snaking around the middle of the hill like a stone belt.

That's my route.

I feel the burn in my calves now, solid and steady. I keep my ears pricked for any sign of the inbound aircraft, but nothing yet. Keep pressing. I take the fork, and the trail levels off. I can now pick up a bit of speed, while I scour the skies.

I have to jump over a couple of boulders, but the trail is well worn and progress is steady.

And *that's* when I feel it, just as I rise around the corner.

It feels like a dip in pressure, but it's not. That's just the way my body manifests the change. It's actually a tone, pitched lower than ordinary human perception, but one that is nevertheless picked up by our sensory systems. We all have this capability, but not everyone's has been as finely tuned as mine. That's what ten years in the army will give you.

It's the rumble of something approaching from above, not yet loud enough for my ears to hear.

The plane. Jeremiah's intel, it seems, is spot on.

I keep my speed up over the next craggy rise, and I am greeted by Morte Point in all its glory. Treacherous rocks lean out into the sea from all angles of the peninsula, standing resolute against crashing white foam. I can picture there being a lot of shipwrecks here, their hulls littering the bottom of the sea floor like grand wooden elephant carcasses in a subaquatic boneyard.

I need to find a spot. A vantage point. I need to get a fix on this plane. The hum is audible now, and I'm not just feeling it in my gut. It's coming. I shimmy, crawl and scramble, across the dry stone, fixing on a small elevation close to the crashing sea itself, sitting proud over a trench swelling with gushing water, leading right out into the ocean. Perfect.

I make it, set down my backpack, and breathe.

Scanning the skies, I'm taken back to a day earlier, in Spain. How quickly things can change. The sun is beginning its slow descent, increasing the vibrancy of the sea's blue with an amplified saturation.

A huge cumulonimbus column drifts across the sun, and I am able to see better — momentarily.

There it is.

Jesus. For a start, it is fucking huge. Way bigger than I was expecting. It's a commercial jet; I was expecting a rusted Cessna, barely able to lift its landing gear, not this behemoth. That can't be full of people, it just can't. Please...

I feel massively underprepared, like a cricketer fielding in the outfield, with the ball hurtling towards me — only it's not a ball, it's a huge boulder. All I can do is watch.

Hang on — this plane is supposed to be going down, isn't it? Well, as it makes its approach heading south-easterly towards the coast through the northern sky, it looks just fine. Casual, even. It's low, on approach, but considering it is supposed to be landing less than ten miles away, that is entirely to be expected.

I turn to look back up the cliffs. Morte Point is bare. It's just cliffs, the surf, the plane and me; there is nothing and nobody else. The plane coming down is clearly a hasty addition to whatever plan is afoot. Whoever organised it hasn't even got their welcoming committee in place. It must have been urgent, a last minute change. Maybe they are bringing the plane down to sink the mysterious dangerous cargo to the bottom of the sea, away from potential harm? Maybe we have the same interests at heart?

No. Trust Jeremiah. He has not let me down before.

As I look at the plane, I am surprised to see it splitting. I can't hear anything, but it is clearly ripping apart in a burst of orange, the rear of the aircraft engulfed in flames. It's as if I am watching a horrific air disaster with the sound on mute. Then the boom of the explosion finally hits, the sound waves eventually reaching me. I feel my knees tense, my posture coiling.

The nose of the plane tips forwards, and I hear the screech of air blasting against metal, as the plane is now airborne in a way it was never supposed to be. It sounds prehistoric, a huge beast brought down from the sky, wailing as it goes. It is falling fast.

I am overtaken by the queasy thought that this plane might drop right on top of me. I might have been far too hasty and positioned myself at precisely the wrong place at the wrong time, an outcome that encapsulates the running theme of my last few years perfectly. But the plane, roaring and whistling with obscene depth and resonance, isn't going to reach me. I can see that clearly now. I reach into my pack, and grab the snorkel mask, ripping it clear of its cheery pink packaging.

I hope, beyond hope, that there is nobody on that thing. Seeing a commercial jet stricken in such a way, all I can imagine are hitherto happy families now screaming and suffering with oxygen masks dancing angrily, inches from their noses.

The nose of the plane hits water, tipping its metal body higher, the sound of the impact a titanic boom with a hot fizz of spraying seawater. My unwelcome visions burn in intensity, and, as much to shut out my horrible imagination as anything else, I throw myself at the water in a long arrowed dive, clutching the snorkel mask with both hands out in front of me. I hit the sea at the same time as the body of the plane, reaching for the sea floor, and hope that the shopkeeper's earlier assertion, that the water depth here is thirty feet, is correct. If I smash my head on a rock, this is going to have been a very short trip.

The water is cool, not cold, warmed a touch by a long day of sunshine. After the run up here, it is as refreshing as cold lemonade. Under the water, I right myself, and acclimatise. The sound underwater is amazing, with the muddied rumbling bass of a huge vessel settling after a sudden introduction to the brine, overlaid with the soft percussive whispers of surf overhead. I clamp the snorkel mask on, and clear it with a gust from my nose.

Below me, about fifteen feet down, is a thick bed of seaweed and kelp, and it is now reaching up to me with soft waving tentacles, like the inflatable men with waving arms you see on car-showroom forecourts, only these arms are waving in slow-motion and painted the drabbest of greens. I follow along the carpet of vegetation to a shelf, which descends gradually out to sea. It looks like an extremely poorly-kept golf course, with an undulating fairway that hasn't been mowed in generations.

The water visibility isn't great, and I can't see much beyond forty yards. I can hear the plane but can't see it, as the rumble settles a little, and softer splashes highlight the debris that is falling from the sky alongside its previous owner. I start swimming. Follow the rumble. I'm nervous, and the images of burning families fight their way into my brain again. I beat them away with furious propulsive kicks.

A dark shape begins to loom up ahead and slightly right of my position, down on the bottom, although in the haze its features are as yet ill-defined. The shape on the bottom alters, and extended pieces appear to poke from a central dark mass, their perspective and reach changing as I move through the water. And then my brain catches up: it is a shipwreck, with a jagged, broken mast leaning out of a decayed and smashed deck. It is quite a sight, covered in a thick green moss, its lower half embedded fully in the deep seaweed.

As I pass the downed vessel, I begin to need oxygen, so I pop up to the surface to take a deep gulp, and as I do so, I check that the plane is still ahead of me. As I break the surface, the low sun hits my eyes, even more orange now than the last time I saw it, which was only a couple of moments earlier. It will be dark soon, and this is no place to be when that happens.

Ahead of me, there is smoke, and a giant broken wing reaching skywards, its position becoming more vertical by the second. The plane is definitely sinking, straightening the wing and pulling it gradually down with the rest of the carcass.

I need to be in that plane before it sinks fully, because searching it will be so much easier that way. I press on with renewed vigour, sweeping long crawl strokes and kicking furiously. The mask is keeping to its part of the bargain, holding better than I would expect of a £2.99 kids' novelty scuba mask.

Suspended beneath the surface, looming in front of me like a huge twisted metal whale coming up for air, is the plane. It is enormous, its tail section missing, and it hangs there, presumably buoyed by air pockets in the parts of the cabin that are still pressurised. My best guess, judging from the ongoing sinking of the tail, is that those pockets are in the front cargo.

I approach, and marvel at how appropriate it is that I have been metaphorically, as well as physically, thrown in at the deep end here, and how I still don't have a clue what it is I'm looking for. The sides of the craft are scorched, burned on its sudden descent from the sky, and the charred lettering emblazoned along the plane says 'ÓdýrAir'. It's not an airline I immediately recognise, but I suspect that, as the saying goes, it ain't from round these parts. Since the rear of the plane is missing its tail, there is an opening from which bubbles erupt irregularly, as the air from the cabin slowly escapes. That's my entrance.

I make a quick trip to the surface for air, which is much hotter, acrid and more unpleasant now that I am so close to the crash site. Diving down again, I follow the scorched curvature of the plane to the opening, through which I slip gently.

As I enter the cabin of the plane, I switch to an emotionless form of mental autopilot. I used to do this often, at times of impending violence and horror, to detach myself from what I was about to witness. I can turn it on and off at will, now. If shit is heading towards the fan, my eyes glaze but my brain retains lucidity, and I subconsciously sieve out the horrors, only processing the details that are crucial to the success of the exercise. It's like a computer reading an image and processing it as binary output, just a series of positives and negatives. It keeps me calm when the world around me is crumbling in the most destructive and gruesome of ways. And I fully expect to face carnage in this cabin, with difficult choices to make.

However, I quickly find that my concern is misplaced. The cabin is empty. Two hundred and sixty blue fabric seats, with no occupants in sight. They can't have all fallen out, can they? The sea would be littered with them...

The cabin is devoid of rubbish, hand luggage, pretty much any evidence of life whatsoever. It's as clean as a submerged whistle. *What the hell is this?*

I see that the front of the cabin is not yet filled with water, so I swim down the centre aisle to check it out. I use the headrests for leverage and pull myself along swiftly, making good ground. I'm not doing badly in terms of my current oxygen store, and by the looks of things I can fill up at the end of the cabin, in any event.

But a dark shape in one of the rows catches my eye, a shadow in between seats. It sets alarm bells jangling and I pick up speed. I crane my head around the seat, and find my first evidence that there was anybody on this plane at all. A woman is slumped in the seat, her gender revealed by a black, figure-hugging trouser suit rather than her head or face — because her head is missing. It's gone, but not without argument. Ragged strips of meat and a thick white nub of spine poke from the collar of her shirt. Her head was evidently twisted clean off with a blunt force impact, presumably during the plane's impromptu tumble from the sky. I check the rest of her body, and she seems largely unharmed, save for her right knee facing the wrong way, the suit fabric around the knee having ripped. God knows how that happened. It's chilling to acknowledge that that really was the least of her problems.

I check her pockets. Nothing at all. So empty as to raise suspicion. Maybe her pockets were emptied as she got on the plane.

I turn to go, in search of the mysterious cargo and clues to its whereabouts, when I catch a glint of something shining, held in her left hand. It has been shut tight, but I must have loosened it while examining her. I open her fingers a touch, and a gold object rolls into the middle of her palm. An earring. Long and dangly, very glamorous, with a sizeable ruby encased in thick gold. It's really something, and my mind nags at the significance of it. Why is a headless woman holding an earring? It's not as though she could have known she was going to lose her head, surely? And why prioritise your earring in a crisis situation such as this? On a whim, I take it. Aside from the obvious destroyed state of it, this trinket is the first thing I've seen on the damn plane that looks out of place or off-centre, and, given that I'm supposed to be looking for something out of the ordinary, it may have some kind of significance.

I pocket the earring and leave the dead woman as I go in search of air. I need it now, and there is still some at the top end of the cabin. I swim over the seats, looking out for any more unfortunate passengers, and get to what feels like the first couple of rows. Poking my head out, I am brushed with hot sunlight blazing through the cabin windows. The plane has achieved equilibrium with its floatation, it seems. The heat is odd, though. It's too much for mere sunlight — no, surely there is a fire in the cockpit ahead, through the door? My thoughts drift to survivors, but I can't picture any, given what has clearly happened to the headless lady back there.

I don't know what to do, but in cold truth, my objective is the cargo. If there was a fully stocked hold, it would surely sink us, but that isn't happening... as yet. Maybe the contents of the hold have escaped via another hole somewhere in the plane's wounded body, and the item I seek is floating off somewhere untraceable. The ocean is an eager eater of secrets — just ask the captain of that old shipwreck back there. Any scenario that involves the loss of the cargo is unacceptable.

I approach the windows of the cabin, wading through the water and out onto the sodden carpet of the aisle, then lean across to the window to scout the surface for escaping containers or bags. There is a fair amount of debris, but nothing that immediately strikes me as something I should be looking for.

Then, my stomach does a perfect triple salchow at what I see on the rocks. Camouflage-clad marines cover Morte Point like ants, with a few fluorescent police thrown in for good measure.

Jesus, the cavalry is here. And, there, down in the water, heading out to the plane at speed, is a rigid-hulled inflatable boat (RHIB), powered by a bruising engine, racing across the surface towards me. Divers sit on the edges, ready to drop into the water.

My senses crackle. This is what Jeremiah warned me about. If they were to catch me, it would be curtains for my extra-curricular activities, and these are the very people Jeremiah warned me should not get their hands on the cargo. He said I *had* to beat them to it.

But they have resources and man power, two things I am acutely short of.

The plan will have to change, but the objective will remain. If I can get out, and avoid detection, I can watch from the beach, out of sight amongst the rocks. When they have the cargo, I'll come up with a way to intercept it, forcefully if I have to. Yes, I'll let them do the dirty work, and intervene when the time is right. That will work.

The left side of the plane is facing the shore, leaving the right looking out to sea. If I exit from the right, I won't be seen, so I dive back into the water to look for an emergency exit on the right hand side. It doesn't take me long, as one appears three rows back, as if by magic. I follow the instructions to turn the handle and pop the seal, then push outwards. Easy. As the entire door frame lifts away gently and floats softly upwards I exit, pop up for a quick breath, and then head with thunderous kicks down to the seaweed, reaching with my fingers into what feel like soft, slippery strips of leather. I grab and pull myself in, letting the fronds envelop me hungrily.

Glancing upwards, I can see the fierce blues and smouldering oranges of the dusk above, creating a grand halo around the silhouette of the jet. I lock my fingers into the seaweed, holding fast, and try to be… well, seaweed-like. The outline of the RHIB zips along at speed, before slowing alongside the plane. Four wet-suited divers throw themselves into the water, dropping and spreading in an ungainly manner, directing themselves immediately to the plane and its openings. Even before they have got themselves settled and orientated, they begin kicking for the broken tail.

This is not recon or rescue behaviour. This is an operation laden with purpose and having a clear objective. They are after something, and they are so preoccupied with it that they haven't seen me.

They seem to have been given a time limit, too, judging by their speed, and on thinking about it, you can see why. Morte Pointe is not far at all from the settlements of Mortehoe, Woolacombe, and over the other side of the hill, Ilfracombe, I believe. The sunshine has brought the holiday-makers out in force, so the populations of these places have swelled by perhaps three or four times their normal levels. A plane crashing into the sea will not have gone unnoticed.

I watch as all four divers disappear into the tin belly of the jet, bubbles gurgling out as carbon dioxide nuggets seek the surface. To my left, just visible, is the frame of the earlier shipwreck. I check above, to see that the coast is clear, and begin to pull myself along the weed bed, placing hand over hand, scaling a horizontal ladder of vegetation. I travel with speed and ease, the task easy, but I feel my own oxygen reserves will not last forever.

The shipwreck. It has a hull half sunken in the sand and weeds, but the cabin still sits proud, yet eroded. I have no idea how old it is, such is my middling grasp on history, but it must have been here for a bloody long time. The wood is discoloured, worn and thinned, and the bolts on the structure are all bloated with dull orange rust. The far end of the vessel seems to be covered in a dark dusting, giving the ship the appearance of having a five o'clock stubble. Barnacles. They are black and thick, covering the bow.

Oxygen. I need oxygen. If I go up, I'm taking my chances, and heightening the risk of my discovery. Where can I get some air? I must have about a minute left. At my best, I have a two and a half minute breath, and I'm getting a bit too close to that for comfort. I desperately don't want to go to the surface, but soon I may have no choice.

A droning causes me to look up, as a second RHIB makes its way across to the plane. I got out of there at the right time. That's now ten divers, all around the plane, if this team is equivalent to the first. The plane in the distance is still calm, hanging in space, and I can imagine the divers marauding inside, like invading scavengers in a carcass.

I hold tight to the cabin, and poke my head inside. It is darker, but the cabin is only small, and lined with windows. I need air, now.

Air can exist underwater. It's already there, *in* the water, in any event. Water is rich in oxygen, just not in a form that we, poorly-evolved humans, can process. I glance around the cabin, guessing that it must have been here for some 150 years and marvelling at both the carpentry and the sheer lack of anything I recognise as useful nautical equipment, save for the vast traditional steering wheel. Then I see some air that I *can* use.

In the recesses of the angled roof, where the corner between wall and ceiling meet at a crooked angle, is a little pocket of air. A bubble that never made it out, perfectly and amazingly harnessed by the angle of the sunken cabin roof. Incredible. I pull myself in, and over along the roof. As I approach, the bubble is neat, a last piece of air that got stuck in the mayhem and disarray of the ship's final moments, and by some quirk of fate, rested just perfectly in the corner here. It seems to be about ten inches across and a good eight inches or so deep.

I'm struck with wondering if oxygen has a sell-by-date, as I lean in to take a gulp of air from the nineteenth century. I don't think many people can say they have done this, and if I ever get to the point where I can share my exploits with someone, I think they will scarcely believe it. I slowly post my chin into the space, open my mouth and breathe a couple of slow rhythmic breaths. On the third breath I withdraw.

The oxygen was nourishing, with a taste that remains earthen and solid. Like a crutch you could lean on. It is nothing short of amazing, a pure exhilarating experience. A bubble of 150-year-old air, formed before we put the planet in an industrial chokehold. I feel as close to greatness as I've ever been.

I resume my seabed ladder crawl. Progress is steady, assured and swift. I want to get out, get my bag, which is the only evidence of my being there, and find a vantage point. As I pull myself along, I pray that none of the divers take a look down and notice a bloke in shorts, a t-shirt and a novelty scuba mask swimming away from their little search party.

The growth of the weed begins to angle upwards, towards the surface, and as we go, I turn onto my back. The sun is lower in the sky now, and there is a lot of glare here. I can afford a controlled bob between the rocks, enough only to allow my lips to break the surface. With everyone shielding their eyes from the western sun, preoccupied with the plane, I'll be amazed if anyone has noticed my quick gulp.

On my back, still gripping the seaweed beneath me for stability, I take my breath in the shallows. The waves lap around me, gently lifting and lowering me rhythmically, as if I am an infant resting on Mother Nature's chest. I'm calm. Energised. Alert.

I'm fucking *enjoying myself.*

Some people like collecting beer mats. Some like keeping tabs on birds, bugs, animals… whatever. Some like walking, running, going to the gym. We all get our kicks from *somewhere.* I'm open enough to enjoy all the above. But I'm never happier, nor more focussed, than when I am getting shit done while the chips are down. Now, floating between the shallow rocks off the Atlantic, using my wits, guts and training to elude a mysterious force, I am in my element; my absolute, unrelenting element.

It is what made me a successful soldier. It is what made me one of Her Majesty's British Army captains. I was all I could be.

As I face the sky yet again, the waves lap below my ear just for a second, and I hear voices. It is so fleeting, so brisk, that I can barely make out what they say, before my ears are safely below the surface again. But I am right in the firing line here. No question. I must be just yards from somebody who I don't *want* to be just yards from, and the only two words I picked up from the conversation were '...in time...'. At least, I think that's what was said.

I round the rocks, looking for a more secluded exit, and swim for fifty yards before I angle to shore again. I see the rocks I am heading for steeply angled beneath the surface, dictating a similarly steep exit from the sea. Not the place to launch a RHIB from. Should be safe enough.

I take it slowly, revealing myself one soaked inch at a time, and through the droplets streaming across my mask I see I am in a high-walled rocky recess, the waters swelling against the sides like a freshly-stirred tea cup. I can see nothing above the rocks, just the purple-blue high above. I look back out to sea, but such is the direction I have travelled, the rocks I have scurried behind, that I can see nothing but the blue ocean, and the sun craning down to meet the horizon in a glittering kiss.

The scene is beautiful to the eyes, but not the ears. All I can hear is the screeching of motors, and the oncoming throb of a helicopter coming from somewhere, the low thudding of its rotors resonating around the granite bowl like a subwoofer.

I have my bearings, I know where I need to be. I know just where my bag is, and how difficult it will be to retrieve it undetected. I need to see what obstacles lie between my position and my pack, so, as the swell lifts me higher up the bowl, I reach, extend, push up with my legs using whatever purchase I can get, and scramble to the crest.

I can see a total of twenty people, three of whom appear to be police. The rest are marines, equipped for a training exercise. No weaponry at all. Whoever organised this recovery mission was not expecting any resistance. The plot thickens, glooping like treacle in my mind.

I look back to where I came up for air earlier, and I see a man I haven't noticed before. I must have missed him because he was sitting down, and because he wears a slate grey suit that serves as better camouflage than any of the clothing worn by the people presumably at his command. He sits perched, a white hanky in his right hand hovering by his face, ready to mop up any hint of muck or perspiration. He has a pristine, immaculate bald head. Not a hair on it. And he looks to have left his comfort zone in an office somewhere, since he is staring out to sea with a keen agitation. I guess that he is the man I heard speaking moments before, rather than the marine standing over him, who is himself set apart from the others by a beret and a subservient posture, hands behind his back, leaning slightly to hint at attentiveness. It seems that I have found this particular scene's master and commander.

Behind the pair, just higher on the rocks, sits the outcropping that I know my pack resides upon. Can I get away with leaving it? What traces are in there, of my identity and purpose?

None, I think, aside from it being essentially a bag full of fibres, fingerprints, hair strands... a DNA treasure trove, should they know where to look, and who they are looking for.

That worries me. If they decide, for whatever reason, that the pack was left there by someone who had something to do with this curious event, they just might give it the forensic once-over.

I cannot let that happen. My mind is made up. If I want it back, I'll have to get it, but the peninsula is so open, the rock face so crawling with people, that I can't just wander over and grab it.

Shit! That's *exactly* what I *can* do.

Abruptly, yet with control, I stick my head once more beneath the surface of the recess, and gulp seawater, swallowing harshly. It is foul, but will help the sale of my story no end. I retch, the salty sweetness clawing with nauseous fingernails down my throat and poking a grim finger into my very stomach. I throw myself out of the water and up onto the bank, coughing, spluttering; in short, making a real scene. To make sure I have been noticed, I gasp and add a few extra heaves for good measure, even though the saltwater is now up from my stomach and spraying up out of my nose and mouth.

It has worked.

'Over there!' someone shouts. 'Someone's in trouble!'

'Is it a survivor?' someone shouts back.

Hook, line and bloody sinker.

I hear footsteps scraping the rocks, but I squeeze my eyes shut and breathe in and out, hard. Hands grab me, and pull me up onto a flatter plateau.

'Take it easy, mate,' says a voice. 'We've got you. We've got you.'

They put me in the recovery position, and I splutter out the last of the briny spew.

'That's it. Get it all out,' says that same someone, while thumping hard between my shoulder blades. Good man. He acted swiftly, with evident good training. Even in the circumstances I can, as an ex-military officer, appreciate, commendable behaviour on the part of another soldier.

'Thank you,' I say, between hot breaths, and begin opening my eyes. 'I was stupid, I thought I could help.'

Two men loom over me, in the familiar dark green of Her Majesty's most loyal servants.

'You gave us a proper fright!' says the man at my back. 'What happened?'

'Who is he?' another more distant voice says. 'Where did he come from?' The voice is clipped by urgency and stress, and even though I've only heard it once before, I *know* it's the main man. I look towards the voice, and see him navigating the rocks in ludicrous black leather slip-ons. White gym socks peek from beneath his trouser legs as he walks, invoking an impression of a pudgy, shorn Michael Jackson.

The other men stand to attention in greeting him.

'I heard a big smash, from round the top there,' I say, pointing up to the top of Morte Point, 'and I saw the plane. I jumped in, thinking I could help, but I'm... not great in the water.'

I look down in shame, as if I've dishonoured my entire lineage simply by being a crap swimmer.

'No harm done,' says the likeable squaddie at my side. 'Good effort, mate.'

I feel the bald man look at me, and I look back at him. He is scrutinising me with curious blue eyes, sweat dribbling down between them and pooling in a tiny hanging droplet on the end of his nose.

'I was stupid,' I say. 'I'm not really one for the big occasion. I'm sorry. I just wanted to help.'

'It's OK,' says the man, curtly. 'Take him back up to the village.'

'Thank you,' I say. 'I'm so sorry for the trouble'.

A radio crackles somewhere close by, snapping the man from his examination of me.

'Come in, alpha, come in, over,' says a scratchy voice.

'Go, go,' says the bald man, while taking the radio handset offered to him by his second-in-command. He turns to shield the conversation from me, but I'm already tuned in. 'Yes. Yes? Err... Come in? I mean. Roger? Sod it — *what the fuck is happening?*'

I almost laugh at that. As if the cloak hasn't already slipped, now the pencil-pusher is fully revealed.

The men usher me away, but I keep my focus on the conversation. The voice at the other end of the line speaks again.

'So far it's a negative, over.'

'What?' screeches the bald man, who now stares out to sea as if trying to catch a glimpse of whomever he is talking to, or whatever they are looking for. Then he hushes down to a whisper, suddenly aware of who might be listening. I feign dizziness, to slow our exit from earshot.

'Is the woman there?'

'Affirmative, but the cargo is missing. We have to engage a full search, which will take time and manpower, and won't be easy to do on a sinking plane. Over.'

I'm struggling to hear the whisper, over the rushing sea rolling foam and blood boiling in my ears.

'Jesus Christ, do you know what's on the line here? You *know* what you are looking for? It's red, small, should be attached to her head...'

'Her head is missing, sir, over.'

I can't hear anymore, but I wouldn't hear anything anyway. The bald man has been rendered speechless. And he's not the only one. Everything has changed. *Everything.*

Dear God. The earring. *I have what they are looking for.*

We keep walking, even though my mind is swimming with possibilities and racing with concern.

'My bag is just over there, could you grab it for me?' I say, trying to keep the urgency out of my own voice. I want to get away from here, right now.

'Sure mate, just a second,' says my accompanying marine, who hops the rocks nimbly to retrieve my pack. He shoulders it and brings it to me. 'I'll carry this one, while you get your breath back.'

I glance over his shoulder, down at the men by the sea. A debate is raging between the bald man and his commander. I can't quite hear what is going on, but voices are raised and tension is palpable.

'I feel better, thanks. I'll take it,' I say, trying to keep it light but plainly struggling. I need the bag. I need to get out of here *now*. At any second, they could realise that my being here is not quite as innocent and hapless as it currently seems.

And at that very moment, both the commander and the bald man turn to look at me, and I'm reacting before I even know that I have done so.

It starts with a very sharp, hard blow down onto the left knee of the marine with my bag. I don't like doing it, I don't want to do it, but the man seems honourable enough to listen to his commanding officer, and he may order my detainment. His knee buckles slightly in the wrong direction. No snap is heard. He'll be out of action for a few months, repairing those ligaments I have just jarred from the joint, but he won't be dead, which was the alternative. He screams, and drops as the knee falls from beneath him. I catch the bag as he tumbles.

'Get him!' screams the bald man.

'All hands, detain the man in shorts and red t-shirt,' bellows the commander at his side. I see heads popping up all along the rocks, like meerkats from burrows. They have a new objective, and I am it.

'Sorry,' I say. It won't mean anything now, even if the soldier hears it as he wails. But if this situation turns out to be as important as Jeremiah has made out, he may understand my actions one day.

I shoulder my pack and start running up the rocks to the trail, hopping as I go. I am so very aware that I am barefoot, but there is nothing I can do about that at the moment. The shadows arch long across the terrain, ever deeper thanks to the setting sun. The commotion behind me grows. I have to get to the trail.

I feel a sharp snag, and a hot tear in my left foot. It's an agonising rip, however small. Within a few steps, my footing is less sure, as blood is pouring onto my toes, slickening my grip. I can't stop now. I *need* the trail.

It is about fifty yards ahead, above me, and it cuts laterally across the belly of Morte Point like a slash of slate, dust and gravel. But, between me and the trail are two onrushing marines. They are not armed, so this will boil down to a quick burst of hand-to-hand.

There are two rules when it comes to taking on multiple adversaries. One, confuse them. Keep them guessing. Be unpredictable. They assume victory because of their numbers, but the solitary party has no option for this. So, two, strike to end it. Strike to injure. Strike to debilitate. Experience counts and anything goes, so when you can, act without hesitation and with prejudice, because you never know when you might get another chance.

I pick one of the men, the nearest, who is slightly to the left, and scream 'My foot! My fucking foot!' as I run towards him as fast as I can. His eyes widen and he slows his approach. His shoulders slacken a touch. He has been distracted. His colleague, with whom I have yet to make eye contact, has to divert his run slightly to address me.

We are only yards apart, but I already have the upper hand. *Confusion.* By slowing and slackening the nearest, and forcing the other to approach me at a sharper angle, they end up under each other's feet quite quickly. I keep speed, hold eye contact with the one on the left, and, darting right at the last moment, lash out hard with my right arm into the face of the soldier on the right, having estimated the angle and trajectory perfectly.

Strike to debilitate. I don't break eye contact with the man on the left at any point, but drive the heel of my right palm, at speed, straight into his friend's nose, crushing it immediately. Again, it's not a killing strike — I know all too well what it is like to be asked to follow orders without questioning their true motivation. The soldier tumbles forward, and pretty much knocks his friend over. As the remaining adversary also loses his footing, his left arm flails high as he tries to save his balance. It's a gift, and again, I act without prejudice. I take the arm, locking it at the shoulder, and force the man's head down… straight into my rising left knee.

The impact and immediate ache in my own knee lets me know I've got it right. Two broken noses. A few days out, then they'll be back. I repress a wave of satisfaction, as I make the last few steps to the trail.

It makes progress so much quicker, as I sprint along the lateral path, but the scrape of gravel behind me tells me that more boots are on the trail, and they may be quicker than me.

The trail snakes around the outcropping, and I follow it as it points me back out to sea again, this time on the northern side of the peninsula.

With their shoes, and my shredded left foot, they are surely catching up with me, and I need to swing things back in my favour. They are gaining. Fast. I can hear them scrambling after me. They'll give me a proper hammering for what I did to their mates, and quite rightly so. Army code. The sea approaches, the cliff edges near. I have risen far higher now, thanks to the incline of the trail, and we are some 100 feet up.

With the sea on my left, the track starts to make its long wind back to the hill, the cemetery and the town, but all

I can see from that direction are the red and blue lights of the emergency services, and high-visibility jackets heading towards me. No way out. At least, not with my freedom.

'Come here, you!' I can hear someone shout in the distance behind and below me, and I pause to stare at the horizon. I notice what looks to be the south coast of Wales miles in the distance, sandwiched like a layer of peanut butter between two vast slices of orange bread, such is the pallor of the sky and its reflection, and look down. The water is distant, the deepest of blues.

This peninsula is crawling with my adversaries. I would much rather take my chances down there. I have what they are looking for, and if I can put enough distance between myself and them, I can use my skills and training to make a real bid for escape.

I throw myself off the cliff.

I fall, forever. Then the water rushes up to meet me, the might of the sea's blue becoming increasingly vivid the closer I get, and I am smashed into what feels like pieces by a strangely invigorating, but altogether brutal, collision.

4.

It feels as though I've been run over by a monster truck, driven by Mike Tyson. My legs ache, having taken the force of the impact, the wind forced out of my body like toothpaste squeezed instantly from a tube.

I try to stay low, try to stop the air in my lungs from forcing me back to the surface, and for a moment I flail pathetically, ten feet under. Something keeps pulling me up, and I'm burning too much energy trying to stay low.

My pack. It's waterproof, keeping the water out, but also keeping the air in, like a flotation device. I feel almost betrayed by it, considering the lengths I went to, to get it back. But this could prove very useful. Silver linings and all that.

I slip it from my shoulders, and grip it between my knees. I slightly undo one of the clasps, and release the folded seal, just a touch, at the corner of the bag's opening to let little bubbles of air surge out. I place my mouth over the hole and take a breath.

I re-bond the seal, and clip it back up again, holding it to my chest. I no longer have a scuba mask, which seems like a huge oversight now. I can see, but not clearly, and the sub-surface world is getting darker by the second. I start kicking, using the bag for balance. The kicking smarts the legs like crazy, but I simply ignore it. If it ain't broke, no need to fret about fixing it.

I paddle east, along the coast, back inland, keeping the rocks at yards to my right. I decide to occupy my mind, and commit to the task without focussing on it. You always sustain endurance that way. Don't think. Simply *do*.

My mind drifts to the mystery item in the pocket of my shorts. That is not the kind of cargo I was expecting. It is tiny, ridiculously tiny. What on earth could be that small and yet command so much attention, carry so much weight?

The ruby. It must be the ruby. Perhaps it is extremely valuable. Perhaps it belongs to someone who will do anything to get it back. This all seems quite extreme though, ditching a plane in the sea to get your hands on a bit of jewellery. I repeat my makeshift breathing process, and glance around, taking stock of my environment, refuelling.

It seems that nobody has followed me off the precipice. Probably didn't fancy pitching themselves off a cliff in the name of somebody's lost trinket.

The sea is, thankfully, calm. This could have been a disaster otherwise.

It's at this moment that I hear the familiar rumble of the inflatable RHIB and its monstrous engine. They are looking for me. Still. I've got to hand it to either the bald guy or his commander, most likely the latter — there's persistence here. They don't know where I am but they are damn well trying to remedy that. Just as I would, if the roles were reversed.

This is survival. Am I still enjoying it? I'm not sure anymore. As the temperature of the sea drops palpably a couple of degrees with the setting sun and the cool dusk air, I hyper-urinate as I float there. It's an inbuilt heat source, albeit a fairly grim one, and I would be stupid to ignore it.

The rumble is approaching, but I can't get a fix on it. I'm certain it's close, though. The last thing I need now is to get hit by the propeller, becoming another useless head floating in the ocean like that of the poor woman I saw earlier. And if they have divers with lights, the upper hand is all theirs. I should make getting out of here a priority.

I sink a little, and get to swimming. Kicking, low and hard, and, after a final few strokes I head inland. The rumble thunders past, and I am left with a sudden quiet. One inch at a time, I breach the surface. I am up against harsher rocks with no possible means of getting out, but the sea surrounding me appears empty. It feels so much darker, again. I need to get out, now, or I might never do so. I can't hear anybody, but that doesn't mean they aren't there.

What I *can* hear, is a grunting, as if a couple of Rottweilers sit over to my right, but with vocal chords a couple of octaves lower than the usual. I'm not prone to flights of fantasy, nor hysteria, but some would find that low, twilight-masked, ownerless growling somewhat unnerving.

It can only be a seal. I hear it again, but this time with a scrape and a wet slap. That rubbery creature is on land. Or at least, something like it. I swim towards the sound, trying to weigh up in my head how to address a seal, should I need to.

As I hang in space, it comes to my attention that my left foot is really hurting now, that nick is really coming back to bite, hard. That, too, will need addressing.

There. Five yards ahead, in the dark. A chunk of rock jutting from the sea, with two levels. And on it, lying with a sense of animal entitlement, sit four seals. They all look at me; their elegant necks bent in my direction, their black eyes glinting back the measly light that is left. At the back left of the lower level is an empty space, tight to the ledge to the upper level, upon which sits seal number five, scrutinising gaze and all.

I've travelled. A lot. I undertook my training abroad, with the ambition of being the best I could possibly be, and despite all the different disciplines I have studied and perfected, nothing really has prepared me for this. Then, I was training in combat, counter-measures and tactics, and at no point did it come to my attention that I might need to strategise an approach to a band of seals.

If *I* saw someone approaching in the darkness, what would *I* want? I'd want quiet reasoning and explanation. I certainly wouldn't want screaming and hostility. So that's what I'll try.

'Hello, everyone,' I say, in a confident, low and even tone, completely belying the fact that I feel like a total dick. 'I wondered whether I could come up and join you for a moment. It's a very nice home you have here.'

Five pairs of onyx pupils look back at me, but none of the seals move forwards.

'I'm going to go a moment, and I'll be right back. I'll assume, considering that you haven't bitten my face off yet, that that will be OK.'

I drop beneath the surface, and leave them to it for a moment.

I have a crazy notion that, if I can get cover and warmth, that rock might be the perfect place to see the night through. They will comb this place piece by piece, leaving no corner un-examined... but they will never in a million years think I am among the seals.

I shut my eyes again. I don't need them at all, it's that dark. I invert my body and head down head first, arms outstretched.

My fingers touch seaweed, and that is all I need for basic food and cover. I grab as many fronds as I can between my fingers, and pull as hard as my tiring body will allow. I don't need a lot. This species of seaweed is long, and ten or twelve decent strips is what I am aiming for.

I collect my crop, while listening. It is still quiet, but I know it won't be long before divers and boats are coursing through the vicinity and, surely, the traditional emergency response parties. Police, ambulance and fire service. Whether they are in on what is really going on here is anybody's guess at this point, so I don't want to take any chances.

I head back to the surface, the long weed strands trailing behind me in the murk like a serpentine tail of vegetation. I break the surface once again, and check that the coast is clear, literally.

It is.

'I'm back, guys,' I say, turning to my company for the night, but they barely react. They literally couldn't care less. But suddenly the farthest seal on the far right begins to light up almost from within, its wet skin suddenly detailed, visible and glistening. The seal turns its head to the cliffs, and I follow its gaze. A high-powered torch is beaming down from the cliffs above. As soon as I have recognised what it is, the shaft of light has moved abruptly on to the next seal, then the next. It starts to swing again, its arc way too close for comfort, and I throw myself back beneath the surface, just as the light hits.

A couple of feet below the bridge, between air and sea, I watch the torch beam blaze an eerily beautiful trail across the exact spot that I have just been occupying. It moves with speed, and from here, could be the searching beam of a small UFO.

It really is a fucking stupid idea, trying to stay in the sea as opposed to trying to make it on land. But what are the alternatives? They're already swarming up there.

I feel a plan brewing. The geography and architecture of both my predicament and a method to come out the other side. Safely ensuring that the torch beam is well out of sight now, I kick powerfully to the surface, again noting that pain in my left foot.

At the surface again, I check for the presence of anybody that might see me, and heave the seaweed up onto the outcrop. It lands with a feathery splat, which alerts my new seal friends.

'It's alright, it's just me again,' I say, in that same even tone. They lose interest as quickly as that, and lie back to a resting state without fuss or protest. Or at least, I *think* that's what has happened. I can't really see. It is pitch black now, just a touch of a southerly moon partially obscured by the cliffs that I have only recently plunged from.

I pull myself up onto the rock, and launch into a flurry of activity. If anyone takes a glance over at these rocks again, I don't want them to get any sight of me. I need a quick turnaround here.

First, I drag my pack over to the empty corner of the shelf, then do the same with the seaweed. I smack the seaweed on the stone to blast away the excess moisture, like beating the dirt off a rug.

I sit snug up to the rocks, resting my right shoulder on the side of rocky wall to the higher shelf, and pull my pack between my legs.

Everything is there, just as I left it. I make a quick inventory. The chocolate and Lucozade from the holiday shop. My smartphone, wallet and ID documents. A roll of sandwich bags. A couple of bags of the spiciest jerky I could find. My Macbook Pro in its durable rubber case. The chargers for my electricals. All the clothes I own, which amount to my multipurpose trail trainers, another pair of shorts, a pair of jeans, a couple of t-shirts. A black micro-fleece, an old red shirt (which is as formal as I get) and some underwear. Some toiletries. A travel towel. A set of lighters. My Wenger Ranger multipurpose army knife. Duct tape. And my light rain coat. Everything a growing boy/vigilante with a penchant for travelling light might need.

Warmth. Now. I strip and use the towel to dry myself as quickly as possible, my eyes coursing the cliffs and the surrounding sea in tandem. I throw on every single piece of clothing I have, from the jeans to the fleece to the spare pairs of grits. I leave my feet bare for the time being. My rain coat is a light Superdry piece, constructed with reversible camouflage. Urban grey on one side, forest green on the other. I thought it would come in useful one day, and I've never really had the occasion before this moment. It just might save my bacon tonight.

The cold begins to grip more tightly, despite my activity. More warmth. Shelter. *Go.*

A lot can be said for building a shelter in survival situations, and not just the obvious. The mere act of building something breeds proactivity. It's a mental shot in the arm, just as much as it is anything else. My subconscious is both buoyed and occupied by undertaking such a task. If there are cracks in the psyche, at times like these, they will be prized open an inch at a time by the cold. Cold breeds discomfort, discomfort gives birth to doubt, and doubt is the first step towards death in situations like these.

I take my longer strips of seaweed, and my towel, and again I beat them on the rocks. I need to get them as dry as possible, because moisture unlocks the door to the cold, and allows it straight in. But my shelter today needs to be both warm and camouflaged, and I have a solution in mind. I leave them on the rock, and put on my coat, with the urban blue grey on the outside. In the darkness, that will withstand a quick glance, no problem.

I check my left foot, easing my first two toes apart gingerly to reveal a neat split in the webbing between them. It's a fairly nasty one it seems, but won't get near to killing me. I take the duct tape, and bind the wound as best I can. It's a rushed job, but will probably do. Duct tape fixes everything, as the saying goes. I slip my shoes back on.

This is beginning to feel like an exercise, my training flooding back to me as easily as the theme tune to a TV show you once loved but haven't seen for years. I sit again, and wedge my pack between my right hip and the rock shelf, leaving out two lighters, a bar of chocolate, Lucozade, my paper and pen, and my knife tool. I bend my legs and separate my knees, while hanging my towel between the two. In the space between my knees, I ignite the lighter and move it slowly along the underside of the towel. Being a microfibre travel towel, it begins to dry very quickly. It is a good start. Having this heat so close to me, even such a whisper of warmth as this, is another positive injection into my mindset.

I'm strong of will and confident in my training. I don't dwell on the cusps of hysteria and panic. But I do know how the mind can play tricks on even the stoutest character, and these little pick-me-ups are important. As is the piece of chocolate I place into my mouth That, out here, right now, as my pursuers scour the cliffs high above me, is sweet euphoria. It feels unfair to have it, as much as an advantage as an athlete on EPO.

I'm alive. Strong. Steeled. Limitless.

Forty minutes pass before the lighter runs out, and the towel is good and dry now. I leave it draped across my lower half, where I plan to keep it until dawn, apportioning it the duty of windbreak. With my legs covered, all human part of me is hidden from the cliffs, either by camo jacket up top or dark towel at the bottom. The towel itself, however, is a dark block of colour that just won't do. Torch light would show it up as an anomalous mass, like dead pixels in a video game, and surely instigate further investigation, which the camo will likely fail.

So I grab my strips of seaweed, and set about a ritual that I will devote myself to until daybreak. Pure sleep can wait. I might grab an hour at some point, but I need to make sure that as soon as the sun begins to rise, I rise with it.

I start by sparking the next lighter underneath the slivers of seaweed. The seaweed itself is, when not saturated with sea water, so light and opaque that it begins to crisp almost immediately, curling at the edges. It smells a little like broth as it burns, and the flickering of the lighter between my legs keeps a momentum of warmth close to my core. As the strips dry, I place them over the towel. The more I place, the more my legs look like a twisted knot of seaweed washed there by an errant wave or a stubborn tide. And my disguise is ever more complete.

Every now and then, I twist off a piece of the softly charred seaweed and chew it quietly. Seaweed, when boiled or barbecued crudely like this, can be a strong protein boost, and will keep me both hunger-less and fortified for the upcoming morning's exertions. I look up, at Morte Point, and see torches swishing this way and that through the brush, followed by audible progress reports.

They are looking for me. They will not find me. I chew harder, and mentally bed in.

5.

Saturday

I am awake long before morning, watching the reversing spectrum of the blues on the water, as light gradually floods the world once again. Without it, this is an arid world of darkness, vacuumed of life. It makes me grateful, and rattles the cage of my purpose.

The gulls wake, and I am alone on the rock. The seals have vanished, off hunting breakfast I guess. I look to the cliff, but all I can see is the green of the ferns and the grey of the bare rock. There is no visible life at all; the trails on this side are empty, even of sheep.

Let's go.

There's still only one way off this rock, so I change back into my swim shorts. I stuff my clothes back into my pack, along with the spent lighters, and stuff the strips of dried seaweed into a sandwich bag for later, in case I need an incredibly bland pick-me-up. I do one last check of the rock for any trace of my having been there, but there is none.

Satisfied, I pace to the edge of the plateau, over the water, and brace for the chill. I dive.

It is *cold*, but I am well used to it now, my body remembering what it felt like last, just hours ago. I adopt a steady crawl, taking even breaths, and trace the edge of the cliff bases in search of a beach. There will be one around here somewhere; the peninsular is just not big enough for there not to be. I think about scrambled eggs on brown granary bread, with liberal gouts of brown sauce. That would do very nicely at this point.

There, ahead. A beach. Empty in the immediate clarity of post-dawn. It is not a big beach at all, perhaps fifty metres across, but it is most welcome. My toes graze sand, and I'm greeted by a sensation of achievement. I dry and change again, buoyed. I have survived the night, where the odds were against me. I don't bother to quell the smile that is inching across my face.

I pop my phone out of my pack, and switch it on. I make my way inland, to see if I can find enough reception to get word to Jeremiah.

As I walk out of the sea and onto the sand, I observe that there appears to be a steep hillside at the back of this shallow strip of sand, with a staircase cut into it, leading up to a grand old house on top of the hill. I'm struck by the notion that this may well be a private beach, and that I have pulled myself up into someone's glorified back garden. The house is a white, wooden Victorian monument, possibly having served, at one distant time, as somebody important's summer retreat. Whoever owns it now is in residence, their presence betrayed by a soft lamp glow escaping through the ground floor windows.

I must be careful, but I'm damned if I'm not going to take advantage of these stairs. I take them two at a time, still in my bare feet, so my approach goes unheralded. It doesn't take me long to scale the winding column of steps. The light may be a permanent fixture, left on all night by routine, or the owner of the property might be an early riser. Either way, caution is the order. Unless the owner appears at the top of the steps, with a plate of scrambled eggs. If *that* happens, caution may well be abandoned.

At the top of the stairs, there is no such welcome, and I arrive on a stone patio stationed centrally in the garden of the property. I take in the layout, hoping that nobody is up, and spot a side gate. Crouching, I move past a weathered white dining set that has been nearly fossilised by years of brisk sea gales, towards the left hand side of the house.

My heart seems to short circuit as I see someone sat silent and still at the table, just a couple of yards from me, who has been hidden by a stone plant pot and the battered conifer it houses.

Staring out to sea, melancholy yet somehow proud, is a tall elderly woman. She is dressed in a long, flowing, ivory nightgown, its long hem rippling around her ankles, with a ratty maroon woollen cardigan around her shoulders. Her hair is short, her features pursed though regally poised, her eyes simmering and pensive. She looks forlorn, but still fortified with immense strength.

She isn't looking at me, and I lower my gaze, ashamed to intrude on her privacy. I want to leave her to her mournful watch.

'You're in trouble, aren't you?' Her voice is cut glass in the brisk salty air.

I look up and her eyes are fixed to mine, locking me to her gaze, that quiet sadness boring into me.

'It's either a wife you're late for getting back to, or some rumpus you are running away from.' She nods at the Point behind me in the distance, all too knowingly.

I spread my palms and speak calmly. 'I mean you no harm at all, and I apologise whole-heartedly for the intrusion.'

Her expression remains still.

'Was it worth it?' she asks, her eyes asking the question not just of me, but of whatever has put her in her current predicament. I have a sense of her loss, of an injustice that life has at some time forced her to endure. I feel shame.

'I don't know, to be honest,' I say, lowering my hands. 'But I hope so.'

'That's what they all say at the start. Just make sure it is by the time you get to the end.' Her focus drifts to the sea again, and the mournful watch resumes.

'I will do just that, I promise.' I find myself standing straighter. 'And I apologise again.'

She nods softly in the direction of the gate. I have been dismissed. It is a crazy moment, a microcosm of serenity amidst the chaos of the last twelve hours.

She is a stark reminder. The honourable remnants of Britain, the oft overlooked icons of yore, the past stoicism now overtaken by something more immediate and entitled. It is a reminder of why I do what I do. It is for people like this, who hope for a different time, but whittle away the hours until that dawn with respect and honour.

I nod thanks to the lady, not that she sees it. I will not let her down. Whatever evil I am bent to avert with my current plight, I will fight with extra vigour.

I sprint along the side of the house, through the side gate, along a passage between the house on my right and a thick privet hedge on my left, and am dispatched out into the driveway. A vintage Ford Traveller sits there on the gravel, its freshly polished wood chassis gleaming. I could almost be in the fifties, here. Perhaps that's where the lady thinks she is. Or wishes she was.

The driveway entrance is a thick knotted arch of privet and fern, manicured perfectly, and once through it I am out onto a road lined still with fat hedges. If an early car hurtles down here, there will be very little room to escape, such is the narrowness of this country road. I take my shoes from the pack, and put them on, ready for a light jog. I want to hit civilisation before the world wakes up, and get a march on a quicker route out.

A farmer's wooden access gate appears on my right, which seems the perfect way for a more direct route to Mortehoe, so I hop the wooden fence into a field of cows. The song birds are in voice, welcoming me with a staccato trill. In the distance, perhaps half a kilometre away, I can see the rooftops. I run as the crow flies precisely in that direction, keeping an eye on the floor for cow muck, nimbly hopping it as I see it. It reminds me of precise foot placement in areas strewn with land-mines, this time only with smelly shoes at stake.

I rely on the timing of my activity to be the best camouflage, but fat lot of use that was back at the beach mansion. Maybe the village is a hub of activity in the early hours, especially when wound up by the search for an intruder out on the Point.

My answer is immediate and as obvious as I could ask for.

A helicopter throbs over a distant hill, the surge of its rotors suddenly louder as it enters the valley, and I see it appear over the village. I sprint for the hedgerow which frames the field, before any airborne eyes can see me. The helicopter is the yellow rescue model, normally used in emergency situations as part of the search and rescue sea response. I know from what scant research I have managed that it is based at RMB Chivenor, which was where that crashed plane was supposed to be heading.

In the shadow of the looming hedge, I take out my jacket and slip it on, forest green to the outside, and pull the hood up tight. I follow the hedge and get closer to the village. It looks like I'm now approaching the north end of Mortehoe, and I can hear motors to the south, where the helicopter is now headed, off to the right of my field of vision. This makes sense, the south end being the principal entrance and exit to Morte Point.

They are still looking for me. They have not given up yet. But by swimming north-east and tracing the coast, I may have been fortunately ejected from the sea at the perfect spot to elude capture. I hop another access fence, and find myself in a field full of tents. A camp ground of some kind. This could work. Here, I can look just like any other early walker, an outdoorsman enjoying some active downtime. I walk with my hands in my pockets, my eyes alert as ever. A few people are up and at 'em, boiling coffee on stoves and eating cereal. They all, to a person, stare out to the south of the village, eyes fixed on the circling chopper.

I take the common path through the camp, and as I pass a group of four people, I clear my throat.

'They're up early' I say, doing my best annoying conversationalist impression. 'Can't sleep a wink with that.'

The people are a family of four, with a mum, a dad and two mid-teen boys who look for all the world as if they wish their dad hadn't made them come camping. The dad, keeping watch in the patriarchal style, gestures to the scene with a steaming mug in his hand. 'That plane crash. There mustn't be any survivors, because they would have done all that last night.'

So the plane crash itself is public knowledge. I suppose it would have been difficult to keep that quiet.

I pause, and look out at the chopper myself. It's now heading off in the direction of the Point.

'Dreadful stuff, this plane crash. What are they saying happened? Have they come up with any answers yet?'

'Nowt official yet, but the village has been crawling all night with people. I dunno why, if there's anyone to save, they'll be down off the Point. I mean they were buggering about on the Point all night and everything, but still... You missed all this? You been under a rock since yesterday?'

On one, actually. 'I am — I *was* — a heavy sleeper,' I say, as I trudge off.

The conversation has revealed some interesting pieces of information, however, namely that those pursuing me think I never left the Point, and that if they kept the village manned, they would force me to stay there. Then in the morning, they could bring in the big guns to track me down like a rat in a giant hay bale. Which is what, I guess, they are doing right now.

I follow a dirt road which has materialised from the grass, as it plots a steady course towards a block of buildings. As I get closer, and the tents become denser, I see that the buildings comprise a shower block, a sort of window-fronted office space and a corner shop with the shutters half-down. A milk float is idling there, while a man in blue overalls carries a case of milk cartons through the cracked door to the murk of the shop. The morning shipment for the campers' bowls of Cheerios and cups of tea.

Also on the back of the milk float, is a batch of bound newspapers. As I get closer, the size of the front page font reveals the headline story as the biggest piece of news this area has seen in... Well, possibly *ever*.

PLANE SINKS OFF MORTE POINT

I find the choice of words quite odd, given that the word 'sink' should surely, usually, be reserved for boats. Surely the plane *crashing* is the real news here. I pause while the delivery man takes the next milk crate in, and sneak the top copy of the newspaper out through the bindings. It's a rare chance to grab some intel, and particularly useful given that I am unsure of what the day will hold.

I need to make contact with Jeremiah at some point, but I need to pick my moment for that one. I need reception, for a start. If I start wasting phone battery now, I am on a perilous downward path to being stranded. I must place that call when the time is right. It's a difficult decision to make. Such is the nature of the terrain, and its proximity to the sea, solid phone reception is hard to find. I know that Woolacombe had none. Neither did Morte Point. I'm not expecting any until I get further inland. But I can't very well turn my phone on and wander around the countryside with my phone over my head, hoping for a bar or two.

Rolling up the newspaper, I walk through what turns out to be a farmer's yard, and am churned out onto a road again. Left is north-east, while right is south-west. The decision is easy. Left it is. I know my geography. I know that if I keep pressing in a north-easterly direction, I will keep following the coastline to Bristol. Once in Bristol, there is enough urban cover and amenities to make proper contact with Jeremiah, not to mention excellent transport links to the north and south-east.

It is a cross-country walk of about 100 miles, right through Exmoor National Park; a wilderness of rolling moors and dense woodland, punctuated by the occasional small village. I can do that in about thirty hours straight walking, or, far more realistically, two long days with a break to camp and rest. I'll need to keep hydrated, and fuelled with food if I'm to make that. But it is a realistic goal, not to mention the safest. If whatever authorities were chasing me last night expand their search, they will start with roads to the east. And that includes the very one I'm walking along now.

I break into the next field that is open and surrounded by thick, towering hedgerows, and walk at a pace, after organising my Lucozade and jerky into my pockets. I walk, munch and sip for the next hour, while thumbing through the paper, as the dawn mists are burnt from the patchwork countryside by a rapidly rising sun. It looks set to be a pleasant day, weather-wise. A lot of these fields I'm passing through seem to be in the fallow portion of the arable rotation, so the terrain is easy to navigate, quiet and thick enough with cover. It soothes me.

Reading the paper in snippets, I am amazed at what I see. This newspaper is the *South-West Gazette*, which I guess covers this corner of the country, but with this being a national incident, the coverage of the plane crash is virtually cover-to-cover, with the features and articles ranging from straight reports, editorial comments, appeals for information and stock photographs to the 'insightful' comments of a local psychic.

Shockingly, it becomes immediately apparent that the public is being misinformed as to what actually happened off Morte Point, which, I must say, doesn't entirely surprise me. That's not to say that the newspaper itself is a part of any conspiracy, but whoever is their principal source has given them a lot of falsehoods. I am shocked at how brazen the deception is.

Whoever is behind it, is very happy for the readership to believe that approximately 260 people have perished in the sea off Morte Point, and that there is no expectation that survivors will be found. The paper has some quotes from the local MP, Lloyd Weathers, who declares today a day of mourning for those lost at sea. He praises highly the efforts of the emergency services, and the assistance of the search and rescue teams from RMB Chivenor in Barnstable.

It's only when I get to the bottom of the article, and see the picture captioned 'Lloyd Weathers', that I see the duplicities fold more intricately. Lloyd Weathers, Member of Parliament, is very clearly the bald and besuited man I met on the rocks yesterday, the man who lost his rag trying to work a radio. The stock image shows him smiling and composed, and, even though the visage is far removed from the stressed ball of agitation I saw on the rocks, the likeness is unmistakeable. As positive an ID as you're likely to get.

I keep reading.

The cause of the crash is listed as unknown, but 'engine failure is presumed'. I snort, knowing that I did not witness engine failure. I saw sabotage, plain and simple. The journalists state that the plane was a commercial jet on its way to London Heathrow, but, having experienced difficulties, it was ready to attempt an emergency landing at the marine base in Barnstaple. However, it never made it that far.

I know for a fact that there were minimal casualties, but the way that references to mass loss of life are being dishonestly bandied about here is really shocking. The true facts and inconsistencies of this event are lost, in the forced morosity of a supposed tragic disaster, a morosity so strong that this area will be tainted forever. It will be often thought about, memorials will be erected, candles lit on this day, here, every year for years to come. This area and environment is being tarnished, stigmatised with grief; and all as part of a cover up.

And God knows how everyone loves to read about grief.

The public is being manipulated, and it makes my blood pressure spike. There is corruption here. An elected official is spinning lies to the public; well, this isn't the first time that that has happened, and it damn well won't be the last, but having seen that weasel flirt with a heart attack on the Point last night, only to read his two-faced quotes in the paper this morning... It gets under my skin something chronic. I want that fat bastard to pay for duping his constituents, and if he won't do it willingly, I want to make him.

Then I read a single line that I had missed on page three, which flips the game all ends up yet again.

'The authorities are looking to question a man who was seen at the scene, looting the wreckage before the emergency services could arrive. He is described as approximately six feet tall, with dark brown short hair, unshaven, carrying a black backpack. If anyone has any information on such a suspect, or has seen anyone matching this description, please call the following number immediately…'

They are framing me, dragging the public into a hunt for me, happy to skew even more facts to meet their own ends. I feel outraged. A fucking *looter*. I am used to being called all manner of things, *traitor* being the popular choice after my exit from the army. But I'm no looter, and I'm definitely no traitor.

Fresh cinders of ire waft across the landscape of my mind, and my hackles rise. They are still looking for me. And they are happy to drag the public in to help their search by lying to them. Those *fuckers*.

With renewed concern, I pick up pace. A batch of these newspapers has been delivered to that campsite, where a great number of people will have seen a man 'approximately six feet tall, with dark brown short hair, unshaven, carrying a black backpack' walk out of a neighbouring field less than two miles from the crash site. If two and two have been put together at any point, I am treading very dangerously.

My phone rings in my pocket, and it's by my ear in half a tick.

'Go,' I say.

'You've pissed off so, so many people,' Jeremiah says.

'Just doing what you told me.'

'I suppose that's true, but Christ, you have a way of going about things. Where are you now?'

83

'I can't be exact but I'm heading east, about three miles from the crash site. The heat is very heavy, I need to talk extraction.'

'Look mate, you're doing amazing, but Fallujah this ain't. If you knew what was going on behind the scenes here, you'd understand. We can't be seen to be working together in any way. I'll do what I can, but you're still too close to the epicentre.'

'Forgive me, Jeremiah, but I don't give a shit. You have to get me out of here. You want this item, I can't guarantee I can keep it from them unless you get me out of here *now*. You sent me here on this fucking escapade, you can damn well help me out of it.'

There's a silence so pregnant it could do with a raspberry leaf tea and an epidural.

'What you are doing here is beyond what we could have hoped, but we can't do anything just yet.'

'So I'm just on my own, right?'

'For now, I'm afraid, yes.'

I'd be mad, if I hadn't felt this way before. Beyond enemy lines with nowt but a slap on the back. You're on your own, son, do your best — for Queen, country and all that bollocks.

'KITDAFOS it is then.'

'What's that then?'

'Kept in the dark and fed on shit. Some things never change. Lloyd Weathers. You come across him on this one before?'

Jeremiah takes a moment before answering. 'The MP? No. You've seen him?'

'He's in charge, or at least he thinks he is.'

'That's very interesting.'

'Tell me something about him I can use, if you can't get me out of here, at least give me something about the people I'm up against.'

'All right, give me a second.'

I can hear the clicking of a keyboard, which, as the wind picks up, feels about as far away from my own setting as I can imagine.

'I've got his campaign website here, MP for North Devon, aged 56, father to two girls. No wife mentioned, the old dog. Political heroes are Margaret Thatcher, George Bush Senior, Churchill, obviously, a staunch leave campaigner by the looks of it, spearhead — self-proclaimed — of the proposed NDX Project.'

'What is that?'

'Don't know. Campaign offices are in Ilfracombe. Seems he's local.'

Very local. Ilfracombe is not far from here at all.

'You have an address for those offices?'

'Yes, 32 Ropery Road. Shit, scratch that.'

'Why?'

'I don't want you do anything stupid. The cargo. That's your only concern.'

'I thought I was on my own, Jeremiah. I'll be in touch.'

'When you're closer to Bristol, let me know, I can make a much better stab of getting you some transport somewhere like a major city. Please, don't do anything stupid.'

'Tatty bye.' I hang up.

Hold on. A sound, in the distance, carried on the light breeze and amplified by the crystal clear morning air. It is the unmistakable sound of dogs barking.

6.

I am running now, thinking of who may have given me away, and I immediately forgive them. If I thought I'd seen that swine who was looting the wreckage of an air disaster, I'd want him to meet justice too. If only they knew the truth.

Why the hell does it have to be dogs again? They still sound a way off, and if, by keeping a steady pace on this course, I can keep the volume of their howls about the same, then I know they are no closer to me.

They must have a scent on me. I have travelled six or seven miles from the campsite, so to be so close must mean they've picked up my scent. Dammit. Seawater acts well in terms of masking the smells of natural human oils, but obviously my exertions and resulting perspiration have erased its effect somewhat.

I need to throw them off.

I pass over a rise, and begin to head down into a valley, which has a wooded glade at the bottom. As I begin to head for the tree line, I notice on the horizon the cliffs of Ilfracombe, with its structures and houses peppering the hillside surrounding the valley.

I know that Ilfracombe, from the brief research I managed of the general area, is apparently, while still not huge, much bigger than Woolacombe, denser. It will create an olfactory Rubik's Cube which those dogs must solve if they are to find me.

Plus, it's where that corrupt MP Weathers is based.

I must roll with these punches, and this roll seems like a good way to ditch my pursuers, who are dogged and resourceful. They have the means, it seems, to throw whatever is necessary to capture me. Not to mention apparent government backing.

I head in the direction of the cliffs, and before long I am running out of fields as the terrain becomes hillier. As I exit the final field, I am placed on a winding road, which I cross. I have to keep my course as steady as possible, and keep these dogs with me until I find a way to elude them in the centre of town.

My watch reads 7.45am. Here in the town, things are only just getting going, but I feel like I have been at my task and on the move for ages. On the other side of the street, I scramble down a scrub embankment onto another road, which is as empty as the last. I cross again, and the land becomes flatter, more concrete.

There are houses appearing in the layout of a small estate possibly from the fifties or sixties. Perfect place to start losing the tracker dogs in a mulch of differing smells waging for their attention. I take a mouldy back alley, and then emerge into the estate. It is the Britain I remember from growing up, and has been left untouched and unaltered since then. The houses have the chipped, bobbling gravel effect up all of the walls, which ages them immediately, placing them generations before this one.

The town is on the other end of the estate, or so my instincts suggest. I adopt a jog, as opposed to a lung-busting sprint. Sprinting through here will only cause alarm, while jogging gives the impression of nothing more sinister than some dude making sure he reaches the bus stop in time. As I move through the estate, it reveals itself to be three intersecting, house-lined streets bottlenecking at a roundabout, which connects to what could be the principal road into town. I'm not expecting this sojourn into the estate to slow them down for long, but so far so good.

Now to follow the road in, at a safe distance. The trees close in again briefly, and that will give me all that I need to maintain that urgent cover necessary.

Suddenly, without any warning whatsoever, the yellow rescue helicopter bursts into the valley, over the trees before the estate; exactly where I was moments earlier. Jesus, they know I'm here. Again. I feel more of a fugitive than ever.

I sprint, as fast as I can. Fuck caution, I need to get out of sight *right now*. The chopper booms low across the estate and I can almost feel it right behind me, a giant bee on the nape of my neck as I dive into the trees.

I land hard, and try to roll through it. It's not a move blessed with finesse, but it gets the job done and sees me coming to a stop on my back in the dirt. The helicopter blasts right over my head, and I watch its flashes of yellow through gaps in the trees. What's happening here is nothing short of crazy.

And now I can hear sirens. Crazy is descending into pandemonium.

It's time to man up. *This is one of those near impossible situations you have faced in the past, Ben, and you need to adapt to prosper. Get to it.*

The siren comes closer, and I can hear the sound snaking along the roads, getting slightly louder and quieter with every turn. Then, suddenly, it screams into the road next to the trees, blazing a trail directly into the centre of town. I lie flat and wait. As the siren dissipates, I notice the dogs again, presumably marauding through the estate.

I am right in the hornets' nest. Best make it a quick visit.

I leap up and run through the trees in a crouch, keeping as low as possible. The trees open into the car park of an industrial facility, which I career through. The car park is surrounded by a wrought iron, spike-topped fence, except from on the side I have just come from, and the left hand side which is a tall brick wall. Brick wall it is.

Maintaining speed, I jump at the wall, digging my toes in and pushing up like I am stepping up its face. I grab the top of the wall with both hands, and hoist myself up. A back garden is on the other side, and, having quickly checked that there is nobody watching from the rear windows of whoever's house it is, I drop into it.

It's a small garden, about twelve foot squared, with low fences which lead to the next garden, and the next garden, and the one after that. I start hurdling the fences, crossing through each garden one at a time. This will really throw them off, while I dodge kids' toys and plant pots and — wait a second.

Perfect.

This garden, the fourth, has an old Christmas tree in it, standing in an old white pot. It doesn't look too well, but it's ideal for my needs. Without delay, and with no care for whoever might see, I bear-hug the tree, rubbing my face and hair in its branches. I turn around, and rub my back all up against it. I wipe my legs up and down it, my arms, and even rub my groin and arse against it.

Pine sap is brilliant at masking smells. It is completely natural too, so will serve as excellent cover when I re-enter the woods. That pine sap will have masked all my olfactory giveaways. The dogs will have no choice but to lose me, since effectively, I have just ended their trail.

I start to hop the fences, dip under a washing line and — *of course*. My description will be everywhere, and the dangling sleeves get me thinking. I glance across the hanging clothes, looking for something suitable, but it's all kids' babygrows, the odd strappy square of something feminine and skimpy that barely needs hanging up in the first place and there, draped across an entire plastic patio set, is a huge high-visibility boiler suit. I check it; it is crinkly and dry thanks to the sun. I consider it momentarily… talk about hiding in plain sight. But that image of a looter in shorts will be long gone.

Moments later, clad in a slightly-too-big-but-that's-ok fluorescent yellow and orange jump suit, I emerge from the alleyway, take a left turn and it becomes very apparent by the sounds and smells that I am right on the cusp of the centre of town. Reaching a road, I slow right down to a normal walk, and try to saunter along the pavements. I pay attention to every street sign, looking for the right one. The roads have cars on them now, but none seem to be paying any attention to me. I walk around the shadow of a church, while keeping an eye out either side of its towering spire for the helicopter, but I can't get a fix on it, even though I hear its steady rumble.

Suddenly, a nostalgic veil lowers over me, fuzzing the edges of the present with unwanted hazy memories. It's an intrusion, and now is not the time… But I can't help the daymares from clawing in. That feeling of being hunted, the grim reality of the consequences of capture, the frantic desire to be away. From a time in my past I keep locked away.

After the church, the buildings close in again, and I am by a row of bric-a-brac shops that offer all manner of seaside gifts and goods, from sunken ship trinkets to inflatable breasts. I could do with supplies but I can't risk recognition; even the slightest report might help put whoever is chasing me on the right path. Last thing I want is word reaching my pursuers of some smelly pine man who fits the suspect's description, seen buying a bunch of outdoor supplies.

If I need anything, tonight or this afternoon, I'll need to source it direct from Mother Nature. Survival skills back to the fore.

The road begins to incline softly, heralded by a tingle high on the back of my calves. Up ahead, the road, peppered with traffic lights, leads up to the hillside and what looks an expansive golf course. If I can get up there, I'm on my way out of here.

The chopper sounds close, getting nearer all the time, but I can't see it. I can't hear the dogs anymore, but they may just be drowned out by the soft murmur of traffic. Either that, or my plan is already working.

Rather than take a steady and predictable course, I hang the next left, which seems to lead down to the boatyards. There is also a sign for the seafront museums. There are a few groups of people in the distance, blatantly tourists with their daypacks and floppy hats, waiting in groups by the entrance to the boatyard.

I turn right again, eager to avoid any such large groups, and now I am in another back alley that smells like an unholy fusion of fish guts, rotting garbage and sailors' piss. Foul, but it will prove very good at confusing the tracker dogs even more. Following a scent trail is like listening to one conversation amongst many of varying volume. Once you have isolated the source, it can prove easy to focus on, and filter out. But if you keep pouring more noise in there, it becomes ever harder to pinpoint, and much easier to lose altogether. That effect is what I'm going for.

I can tell now, even though my hood is up, that the helicopter is somewhere behind me, but not in immediate proximity. Perhaps it has turned back to the estate, where the search party last got a decent fix on me. That would make sense if they are in radio communication with each other. It's the whereabouts of the police car that is becoming an immediate concern, as my mind starts to wander to one potential outcome — roadblocks. I think they will put the town on lockdown.

At the end of the alleyway, a junction gives me the option of left, down another alley, or right, back towards the main road I was on earlier. Keeping hidden in the side streets again appears to be the better of the two options, since the main road out of here may well be cut off by now. If that means a roadblock at the western entrance to town, they are too late, and I'm more than happy for them to waste their efforts.

Suddenly, I see the name I'm looking for. I knew it wouldn't take too long, Ilfracombe just isn't that big a place. I cross the street onto Roper Road, and immediately cast my eyes about for number 32. I hear the throb of the chopper, the urgent pulse of the sirens, and the two squeeze hot sweat beads on the nape of my neck. All I can see is The Plaice Station, a puntastically-named fish and chip shop that sits right in between 30 and 34. It's just opening up as I approach, the shutters rising, ready to feed the seaside tourists on late brunches of battered fish. I'm wondering what my plan is. If he's in, we'll have to have a tête-à-tête. But before I can mull any more, a police car screams along the end of the street, and it takes away any indecision for me.

'The grills aren't on yet,' a voice says as I enter. Heavy harsh strip lighting blinks on, illuminating white tile walls, an old wooden counter, a couple of empty grill boxes and a teenage girl.

'That's OK,' I say as I approach the counter. The girl stands non-plussed, her lifeless hair pulled into a ponytail, her features sallow with grease, hard work and limited opportunities. 'It's the campaign office I'm after.'

'Right, well, he's out,' she says, in a tone that suggests zero tolerance of nonsense.

'The office is here?' I can't help my eyebrows rising at the notion of a glamorous political campaign office also being a working chippy.

'You were expecting a bustling work force and a call centre? Budgets are budgets; we all have to work to them.'

I like her. Straight, no nonsense. In truth she could be any age between sixteen and thirty, but I erred on the younger side because of the youthful twinkle in her eye. Life hasn't stamped that out of her yet.

'No, of course. We had a meeting actually, but I'm a bit early... NDX and so on.'

She visibly gathers herself at the mention of a project that I struggled to remember. She flips up the counter top and gestures me through.

'Oh yes, I didn't know he had one today, but they've been going on all week. Come from site have you?' She nods at my outfit.

No idea how to answer. 'I'm afraid so.'

'You've had far to come?'

Shite. Stick to what you know, Ben. 'No not far. Just a little hop over from Barnstaple.'

'Excellent. I know it means a lot to Mr Weathers when a local firm wants to support him on the project. Not many do.'

'So I hear.'

'Well, if you come through, I'll get you a hot drink and make yourself comfortable. I'm Bea. I'm afraid I couldn't say when he'll be back though, with the terrible business of this plane crash.'

'Yeah, I know, desperate isn't it... I suppose Mr Weathers has to be out there doing his bit. I'm happy to wait, but we can always reschedule.'

'I can give him a call; see where he's up to?'

We enter into a small office, which is a windowless affair festooned in papers, paperwork, flyers, posters, and leaflets, all thick with a layer of grease. 'No don't bother him, he's far more things to worry about today.'

'OK, well make yourself at home if you can, and give me a shout if you need anything. Tea or coffee? Something to eat.'

I turn, to the disarray. 'A cup of tea and fish supper when you get those grills going would be marvellous.'

'You'd have to pay for the supper.'

'Wouldn't have it any other way'.

*

An hour later, and I'm full of tea, cod, chips and a bit of info. The fact that the office was a dump before I even got here means that having a good root around has been easy. I'm still no closer to working out what I've got in my pocket, but I've got a bit more of a flavour of the man who really wants it. The choppers and sirens have eased off too. It's been a good move.

Low voices in the corridor. I wasn't expecting him back so soon, but from what I've learned here, there's nothing to fear from this man; aside from him walking in here with the army. However, from the tone of the voices, I don't get the impression that's going to happen. I catch the tail end of what they are saying.

'I'll have to take it out of your packet then,' a male voice says.

'Please, Dad, come on,' replies a female. It's Bea, using a tone of voice I would never have credited her with.

'I've told you who we order from. If you want to go posh on me, you'll have to cover the extra.'

I like Weathers even less, as he enters the room. He doesn't even look at me, simply tosses down an umbrella on top of the papers on the desk. His suit is worn, his shirt buttons straining, and up close I can see he has white downy tufts around the back of his ears; I missed those on first sighting. Bea isn't with him, presumably back in the shop front. Another who deserves better.

'Sorry, my friend,' he says, dropping into the desk chair opposite mine. 'It's a hell of a day out there.'

'You didn't find him then?'

That shuts him up, and he looks at me dead on. I was unsure he would recognise me, but within a second such doubts are put to bed. Fear strangles him, his eyes widening. I keep my own posture relaxed but confident.

'You're a proper political snake aren't you? Shedding your skin whenever it suits. Labour, winning your seat at the same time Tony Blair won the biggie twenty years ago. A brief flirt to UKIP for a while when they rose in prominence, then you defected to the Tories and David Cameron. I admire a man of principles, but yours change whenever the political tide does. Anything to hold on to your crust, eh?'

'Do you have it?' If it is possible, his intensity has increased. 'Tell me it's not here.'

'Why do you want it?'

'I don't want it at all.' He looks me over.

His answer makes little sense to me. If not him, why... *ah.*

'Who are you getting it for?'

Weathers takes a second, then leans back, settling in, as if trying his own confidence on for size. 'You don't know what you're part of, do you?'

I don't answer immediately, because he's hit the truth square on and I don't like it.

'What's in it for you?' This guy will swing whichever way the wind blows best for him; he must have an angle. If he's not doing it for himself, who's he doing it for — and why? There's an acronym I kept seeing on the paperwork everywhere, from the fliers to the letters and everything in between.

'NDX?'

The corner of Weathers' mouth upturns but he corrects it quickly. 'What would persuade you to give it to me? I could call the whole search off if you hand it over.'

'And just walk away?' I smile. 'You're not a great negotiator. No wonder you have to keep switching sides.'

He doesn't like that. 'You don't have to be a brainless action man to be a survivor.'

'Not if you can tell lies like you do. The plane? The tragedy?'

'There's always a bigger picture.'

'I can see that. And I'm going to make you answer for it.'

'Brave talk for a man surrounded on all sides. I know the search is moving on, but one quick call brings them all back here.'

'You're not going to do that. You'd never tell anyone that you had me in your grasp and I somehow got away.'

That stumps him, but only for a second.

'True.' Suddenly he lashes out at himself, hitting himself in the jaw, eyes and mouth with his little bunched fists. He stops, his breath fluttering. His lips and cheeks are pink, but a little drop of blood hangs off the end of his nose.

'You followed me here and assaulted me, before I bravely fought back.'

My God, he really will do anything at all to save his own skin.

'I did a piss poor job then, didn't I?' I reach across with a straight fist, and I feel the bridge of his nose crunch between my first and second knuckle. His nose leaks scarlet immediately, right down his shirt. 'That's better.'

He tries to catch the blood in his hands, but seeing that hot spatter on his fingers causes him to faint, his head slumping onto his chest. 'Jesus.'

I need to get going. I can't learn any more here, not when Bea could come back in at any moment and see her bloodied father. I don't want to have to hurt her too — and this thing I'm carrying is clearly important, and I need to get it away from here, fast.

I pull Weathers from his chair and lay him on the floor behind his desk, before moving back through to the shop front. A small queue has formed, and Bea still seems to be the sole employee, dumping a sack of frozen chips into a sizzling fryer with one hand, while the other hand clutches serving tongs. A pencil sits tucked behind her ear.

'He asked me to tell you he's got a few phone calls to make, so please leave him to it,' I say.

'It went well then?' she asks, turning to the counter, then skilfully plucks a fish from the grill and wraps it one smooth, practiced move. I feel bad for her. She's a hard worker, a grafter, and she's trying to do it all.

'I think so,' I say, before heading past the counter to the door. 'And you can do better than this — and I don't mean the chippy.'

She looks at me, puzzled, as I leave. The afternoon sun is high, but nestled behind a bank of grey clouds. The sirens have stopped, but I can still hear the distant thud of the helicopter, somewhere. They've no idea where I am, so I make use of the advantage. I cross the street and drop down into an alleyway.

Emerging, I see that I am now on the other side of the boatyard. Across the water are those disparate groups of day-trippers, as before, and much to my concern, the tarmac I am following now seems to lead down a

concrete boat launch and directly into the sea itself. *Shit.*
On the left of the track is the water of the boatyard, and
to the right is a cliff face.

Hang on. Parked tight to the cliff face is a pickup truck,
attached to a boat-laden trailer. The boat is old, but looks
sea-worthy, with a once proud yellow trim. Perched
on the trailer, it stands tall — tall enough to give me a
chance, should I climb it, of reaching high onto the cliff,
where overhanging vegetation might give me a shot at
getting up. From there, I can follow the cliffs along the
coastline out of here. My body has already agreed, and,
after shimmying out of the boiler suit, is scaling the side
of the rusting boat trailer.

I pull myself up onto the vessel, my nose filled with
that unique fragrance of wood weathered by and infused
with years' worth of sea water, and clamber up over the
cabin roof. I hope that any bystanders will assume I'm
just making some final preparations for launch. That is
until, as I am doing now, I take a fistful of hanging ivy
which has crept over the cliff wall, and test its strength.
It should hold, but will be a close-run thing. If it snaps,
it will be a painful, noisy clatter onto the cabin roof; a
slapstick moment which will give me away and surely
provoke interest.

Balls to it. It gives me a decent chance of escape.

I take the strain, and start to step up the rock wall,
pulling up arm over arm. The vegetation gives a little, but
doesn't seem keen to snap entirely. Steady. *Steady.* Any
sudden movement may end this attempt pretty sharply.

I only have five feet to travel, but thanks to the give in
the ivy, and my carefulness, it seems to take forever. As

soon as I am able to, I throw my arm up over the cliff edge, and scrabble for something with more purchase. My palm and fingers grip something that immediately brings a tingling right through my hand, and I know right away what did it. It's a familiar childhood injury, evoking flashes of late light summer nights, dragging footballs out of hedges — the dreaded nettle sting.

It doesn't hurt as much as I remember, but give it time. I know it got me good and proper, since I grabbed it with gusto. I don't want to lose any reliability in the hand while I am precariously dangling over this boatyard, so I immediately thrust my outstretched fingers down into the ground, eking my fingers into the soil, and yank myself up.

Come on, Ben, you grizzled bastard. I do the same with my other arm, and drag myself the rest of the way to the top, grazing my knees on the cliff edge as I go.

I have made it, and I am suddenly lying on my back, breathing hard, on top of a cliff overlooking the town. On another day, it would be a lovely space to stop for a picnic. Not today, unless I want a buzz cut from those chopper blades. As I lie here, catching my breath, and my hand begins to really throb, it crosses my mind that I haven't actually checked on the crucial cargo in a while. It could be a case of '*all this for nothing*' if I have dropped it in a field or something. I run my hand down to my thigh, and pat the pocket of my shorts. I feel the solid blob of metal through the fabric. *Yep, still there.* I still haven't a clue what it is. Although Jeremiah made its importance obvious, its nature remains unclear.

I see dock leaves all over the scrub patch I sit in, the traditional folk remedy for a nettle sting. I know for a fact that their use is nothing more than a placebo, useful to placate upset children, since the dock leaf possesses precisely zero anti-nettle properties. The stings themselves are caused by the minute hairs on the nettle leaves, which are loaded with the nettle poison and swap host on contact, sticking into the skin. It's obviously a mild irritant, but an irritant nonetheless. And if you are allergic to it, well... good luck to you.

I take the duct tape from my pack and start walking uphill, following the coastal paths high over the town. I wrap my hand in tape, then rip the tape straight off, sharply. That will have pulled the stingers out, sticking them to the adhesive. In half an hour, when the swelling goes down, the hand will be back to normal, since the poison supply has been cut.

My main aim now is distance, and as much of it as I can get. From the town. From my pursuers. To Bristol. Go. Go. *Go.* I glance back at the neat little seaside town with the helicopter patrolling above, and the sirens speeding betwixt the streets. It looks like a kid's play set.

The chopper. All it would take is a quick glance toward the headland, and I may be seen. I'm sure I'm safe from sight from the ground, but from the air? No. Not yet.

I've been able to hide in plain sight at points today, blending in with people and everyday goings- on fairly easily. But I need darkness, invisibility. A couple of miles over the hills ahead are the wilds, and I need to be a ghost from now on. I'll need full improvised camouflage.

I make for the rise, and top it in moments, leaving the valley behind, and the commotion of the town ebbs ever fainter. There are thick pockets of my namesake all over this hillside, which should provide some cover, but I could really do with some water with which to mix some camouflage. I'll have to keep going.

I march for twenty minutes, and then begin to follow a track down slightly towards a small copse. Outcroppings of trees like this usually mean there is water nearby, not necessarily in the form of a stream or river, but more likely beneath the ground. Up to my right, are the higher hills and moors, and I suspect there is consistent runoff down to the copse itself. There is surely water in there.

I can no longer hear the chopper, finally, so I allow myself this break in the trees. Not a proper break, mind; I won't be getting my feet up and breaking out the rations. Once in the trees, I shrug off my pack and get down on my knees. The ground is soft and mossy and that moss is a dead giveaway that there is water not far below. I claw up clumps of the moss to reveal the deep brown earth, which is soft and moist. This is perfect. This wet dirt will serve as my pre-mixed camo paste.

There are different camouflage patterns for different environments, and here there is a decision to be made, because I really don't know what terrain lies ahead. I have encountered mainly open fields, scrub-lined trails and sparse trees. The general rule is slashes for grassy open areas and blotches for forests.

I know that the national park will be thicker, and if I get the chance, I will certainly stick to the trees and wooded areas. On that basis, I go with blotches. If I enter a coniferous landscape, then thick broad slashes become the order of the day, and I'll have to reapply in full. Adapt to survive.

I start with a base application of mud all over. Up my legs, on my head and face, on my shorts, even on my already-camouflaged jacket. I pay very close attention to my shoes, and rub mud up onto the shiny eyelets for the laces — anything that reflects light will give me away. I tuck my watch up my sleeve, and rub the mud right up my arms. I then take bigger clods of earth and pack them in irregular blotches onto me, allowing them to crumble off the second that they dry. That leaves darker patches on my skin and clothes. I repeat the routine for my backpack.

That has taken two minutes, which I am pleased with. I'll stop and do this as often as the occasion and my environment allows.

A veil drops over my mind, as if I have just walked on stage as an actor and am now portraying another character. There is a new role for me to play now, one that I must dedicate myself to; *invisibility*. Every move, every action I make, is above all things discreet. To be detected is not an option. Detection will lead to capture. And according to Jeremiah, capture will put more lives at stake; lives other than my own — and that is something that I know I can't live with.

7.

The sun is dipping again, shafts of orange breaking through the trees and illuminating the forest floor in an ethereal blaze. Greens become more green, browns more brown. It's a wonderful, magical time. And it's when animals are most likely to feed.

I have been walking all day, solidly striding at pace, sticking to trees wherever possible at the beginning, until dense forest enveloped me once and for all. I am grateful for it. As planned, I stopped approximately every two hours to reapply my camouflage, and for the first time since this infernal turn of events began, I feel truly alone, my efforts towards invisibility having been successful. I have made good ground.

I now sit downwind, crouched behind a brambled thicket. My shoes are off, resting at my side with the laces removed. I haven't looked at my split foot, because I don't want to be side-tracked. I know the pain has not increased, nor has it been a hindrance. I will leave it as is, at least until my latest task is over.

Now... *concentrate*.

My eyes are slits, almost closed, to eradicate glint and gleam. In my hand is a sling, fashioned from shoelaces and a ripped piece of fabric from the corner of my shorts. To make it, I laid the two shoelaces out lengthways, placed the five inch square of fabric in the middle, and bound it fast with tape. The hardest thing to find was the right stone, but I got there in the end. A selection of missiles now sits between my feet, and nestled in the sling is my favourite. It reminds me of old gaming dice, with lots of jagged points and edges but predominantly round. The sling is now ready in my right hand, poised.

It took me a while to locate the rabbit warren, but now that I have, I can see that there will be plenty for me to have a go at. They have been coming and going with regularity, even as I arrived in the area. They don't sit long, which is why I haven't tried my hand yet. But as they settle into the dusk, and forget that there is a presence that they can't pinpoint, they will sit for longer and graze.

One appears now at the entrance to the burrow, semi-alert yet inquisitive. I might be giving it too much credit there, actually. He might just be sniffing the shit around the burrow entrance, which was one of the ways I managed to track them down in the first place. I had noticed their little trails all around, those little more obvious gaps in the ferns with matted mud underneath, and followed them. When droppings started appearing on the tracks, I knew that I was getting close. The concentration of droppings increased, into this narrow clearing.

Once here, the warren was very easy to locate, tight to the dead roots of a long-fallen oak. All that remains is a shaded stump, under a sky filled with other trees that have filled in the gap left by their felled predecessor. The tree must have fallen long ago, judging by the dulled weathering of the exposed edges, and the dark colouration of the exposed core.

Another rabbit darts from somewhere to my right, straight down the burrow past its friend, which gives it more confidence to expose himself a little more. I can see the creature more clearly now, and it is plump and healthy. They must live a good life here, away from urban touch. I had partially resigned myself to accepting that a dinner of rabbit might be a flea-infested, bony affair, like eating a street rat with big ears. Now, I reassess that opinion. He comes out a little more, and my anticipation raises a touch. This might just be my prey. If he gives me a little more of a look, I will have to take it.

I will take no pleasure in ending the rabbit's life, but the sustenance his meat will bring is much needed. My rations are surviving thus far, but I can't thrive on chocolate, charred seaweed and dry jerky strips. Fresh meat and its nourishment will boost me through the night and on into the next day.

Yes, he's out. I can see the fullness of the rabbit now, and, for a meal, he will do nicely. I start gradually to swing my sling, at my side to begin with to establish its momentum, and to wait for the rabbit to give me the best view of its head. That's the target for the quickest kill, and will not damage the meat on the flanks.

It sniffs the air, rearing up slightly, then settles. I have remained undetected, or if it has detected me, it doesn't show. He takes one lazy hop in my direction, his nose low to the ground... to pick up the scent of his own dinner, perhaps. I raise the whirling sling over my head, look the rabbit dead in the eye, and release one end of the sling with practiced timing. That sends the stone hurtling at the target.

A dull thud tells me straightaway it was a direct hit, as he drops, jittering and prone, onto his back, his back legs jolting in a last frantic dash for a life that has already ended.

*

I have never, ever, not even once, enjoyed skinning an animal. The fact that it is a necessity has given me a relative proficiency in it, but do I take any satisfaction from it? No.

Some hunters revel in this moment, basking in the glow of their achievement, and view preparing the animal as an act of love, affection and respect. Respect for Mother Nature, and the animal that they have felled.

I always find it's hard to fulfil that aspiration while you're pulling the animal's entrails out with your bare hands. That has never struck me as the most respectful gesture, but... different strokes for different folks, I suppose.

Anyway, it's done now. I have buried the bits I don't need, since I'm sure that anybody finding an expertly-skinned rabbit pelt might realise that it signals the presence of a human — and a trained human, at that. The rabbit is roasting over a hastily-fashioned fire, on a spit made with branches. I turn it over slowly. I've kept the fire as small as I can cook with, with a pile of dirt right next to it, to choke the smoke if I sense someone in the vicinity.

As the rabbit cooks, I peel strips of flesh off with my multi-tool knife. It's good. Not bad at all. A beer to wash it down with would ice this cake quite nicely.

Buoyed by my survival successes so far, and happy that my training remains sharp as ever, I ponder my location.

I have stuck to a north-east-easterly direction, thanks to the compass point on my watch, and I guess I have walked a good thirty miles in the thirteen hours between the point at which I lost the police, about 8.30 am, and now, which must be approaching 9.30 pm. It will be dark pretty soon, but I know exactly where I am going to camp; under a conifer I spotted about 100 yards from here.

I think, thanks to the denser woodland and the fact that I have not seen a trail in hours, that I am deep in the belly of Exmoor National Park. Which is just where I am supposed to be.

However, the terrain has been more undulating than I expected, and having had to detour through Ilfracombe, I have not made as much ground as I had hoped. I have the disappointing suspicion that I may not reach Bristol tomorrow.

Despite my focus on the task at hand, I'm beginning to crave explanations again, not least of this strange omnipresence that is hunting me down. Jeremiah would know, or if he doesn't, he'd be able to make a more informed guess than I can. I take out my phone, still in its sandwich bag, and switch it on — I turned it off on the run through Ilfracombe, to save battery. After a moment, I see I have one small bar. I'm surprised, but it's enough.

I Cryptocall Jeremiah, while turning the spit. I watch the meat darken slowly as the ring tone drones in my ear. Nobody is picking up and it goes to an automated answer message. I'll be damned if I'm leaving one. I cancel the call and redial. One last go before I save battery.

After another long minute, with the static dial tone in my ear at total odds with my surroundings, the phone is suddenly answered.

'Salix,' says the voice. It's unmistakably Jeremiah, but his manner is completely new to me.

'Jeremiah, it's me.'

'Who?'

'You know the answer to that.'

'Not a clue. Don't call this number again.' And with that, he hangs up.

I'm instantly confused. We have used Cryptocall numerous times with no mistakes or crossed wires. He's usually answered immediately.

After a moment's doubt (*should I have been more explicit about who was calling him?*) I come to the uneasy conclusion that he knows who called him, but he didn't want the call. It's not a nice thing to realise, when you are on the run in an English heritage site, with an army on your trail. I'm firmly, unquestionably, on my own.

I eat the rabbit and digest the stringy meat along with recent events.

Before long my mind wanders again to the unwanted.

This situation, this primal sense of being hunted, is reminding me uncomfortably of the time I was stuck in that Afghan sewer with my closest friend in the world. Two of us were stranded down there, and only one of us came out. It's the incident that started everything.

And now, with that same awful feeling of being chased, the familiarity of the devil breathing down your neck… like any demon worth its salt, it brings the darkness with it.

I'm not prone to doubts. Not anymore. After I was dishonourably discharged from the army, my captaincy, medals and respect torn from me, and when my family had turned its back on me, my mental spiral was deadly and near-infinite and I couldn't keep the seething wolves in my darkest corners at bay.

Snap out of it, Ben. Now. Get this fire out. Busy yourself with shelter. Go.

When the fire is extinguished and dry earth scattered all over the site, and the rabbit bones and bits are safely subterranean, I take the short walk over to the conifer. In the failing light I can see its breadth and dark green fronds. I have always felt conifers looked welcoming, in an open-boughed sort of way, and a childish recess of my mind likes the idea of sleeping beneath one. I strip off a large branch, easily as big as myself, and a host of much smaller ones from irregular points in the parts of the tree I can reach.

I intend to make a warm little coniferous pocket, suitable for only one, a place for me to wedge in beneath this tree, and I hope to sleep the night through. It will be as rough, but then I remember that last night was hardly The Dorchester. This should be a doddle.

I crawl beneath the umbrella formed by the lowest fronds, about a foot from the forest floor, and pull my branches and pack in with me. I dig with my fingers a six-inch trench, which takes me about an hour. I stay focussed throughout.

Once my job is completed, I lie in the trench and cover myself with the fronds, and whip the dead leaves and dust that lie around the base up and around my sides. I use my pack as a pillow, and embrace the darkness, before I lie still and concentrate on breathing.

The depth of the forest seems to swallow me whole. I feel secure in my earthen bed, and manage to avoid any mawkish thoughts, while drifting into blackness.

8.

Sunday

Agony. Absolute rasping, frothing agony.

I feel burning, a scorching heat rippling along my left arm, like a fuse was lit somewhere on my hand and the spark is searing across the blue touch paper of my skin, right up to my shoulder.

My eyes blitz open, witnessing only blackness, and I am struck with a fierce disorientation. Where the hell am I? *What the fuck is happening?!*

I force myself to sit up, but I scrape my face raw on the branches of the conifer that I remember all too late. My face cheese-grated, I roll onto my side then onto my

114

front, shrugging off the foliage, grasping in the mud for something solid to latch onto.

My hands full of dirt, I open my eyes again. And there I see it, silent in the murk. Disappearing from beneath the canopy, out onto the woodland floor. The instantly recognisable swish of a serpent's tail, slithering from view.

A snake.

Here, in England, I have been bitten by a snake. *This can't be happening.*

The pain is agonising, ripping through me with the jagged pulse of an electrical charge. Poisonous snakes on these shores are extremely few and far between, but I must be extremely careful. It could be an escaped zoo snake, on walkies from a terrarium, and might be a horribly dangerous import. I need to identify the thing. I scramble out to make chase, my arm screaming at me as I hoist myself up.

It has not gone far, by the time I catch up with it. I can see it's not big, but then again, sometimes the nastiest things aren't. I'm not scared of snakes, but I might be now, considering the pain this thing has already inflicted upon me.

It is about a half metre in length and predominantly brown, even in the moonlight dappling through the trees. Along its back is a darker brown patchwork of criss-cross scales, right up to a thicker broader head. I *think* it's a common European adder, and relief washes across me. Adder bites are not considered to be too dangerous, that is if, the correct anti-venom is at hand…

Which, of course, it's not. *Jesus.*

Nobody knows where I am, including myself.

I let the snake skitter off into the forest, acknowledging that the deed is done now, and no ill will towards the snake itself will remove the venom that is slipping through my veins at this very second.

With great difficulty, I retrieve my pack from beneath the conifer. Everything is an effort, even the short walk back to the tree. My mind, like a computer database, is trying to pull up everything I can remember about snake bites from my training. It is so difficult to do this through this haze of maddening pain, my teeth gritting back the boil of my blood.

Why now? I had the upper hand, the ball in my court, and the momentum. *I was doing well, goddammit!*

I sit, put my head between my knees, and try to calm down. Panicking will increase blood flow, and speed the passage of the venom as it cuts a blaze through my blood stream. My left hand seems to be the source of the agony, and I examine it closely.

How did I get bitten by a snake? It wouldn't have sought me out, would not have seen me as prey. I've had a restless night, admittedly, so I can only imagine that I brushed the snake with my hand or arm while tossing and turning, and it struck on instinct.

My inspection reveals two weeping puncture marks, neatly side by side, like little crying eyes on my skin. They're at the base of my thumb, on the fleshy part of my palm.

I'm struggling to remember what I can about adders, snakes, snake bite management and what to do next. This occupies my mind while I clean the wound with some water from my pack. Useful information drips into my consciousness.

The premier cause of trouble in animal bites, regardless of whether the animal is venomous or not, is the bacteria in the animal's mouth at the time of the bite. Driving bacteria into the skin, thrusting it into flesh, can lead to an infection just as life-threatening as any toxin. I must be mindful, and keep the wound as clean as I can.

This is not the end. No, far from it. I am very lucky the snake that bit me was an adder, in so many ways. So far from civilisation, with no proper resources, a bite from a more venomous snake would doubtless kill me, but so relatively low is the toxicity of adder venom, I know that I have a good chance of survival if I give it my all.

I learned about snake bite care in Bolivia, in what feels like my previous life. I was visiting a market, seeking provisions with which to stock my boat before I hit the river once more, and as I was admiring the colours, sights and sounds of such a vibrant, other-worldly setting, I spotted a snake-charmer. I had never seen anything like that on my travels before, and found myself sparing a couple of moments.

The charmer's snake was an Eyelash Pit Viper. Like the adder, it wasn't all that big. The snake was handled by its keeper with a bizarre mix of disrespect, antagonism, love, deification and bullying. I couldn't work out if the owner wanted to marry it or smash it on the head with the mallet that he kept close by, throughout his quirky little show.

He seemed to give an in-depth talk to the onlookers, in Quechua with a smattering of Spanish, about this particular type of snake. I hadn't a clue what he was talking about, but was amazed by the way he handled the thing. It was almost as if he was daring the snake to bite him, then at the last minute calming the viper and easing it back into a relaxed state. It was at once both bizarre and mesmerising.

After his routine, the finale of which involved patting the viper on the top of the head, then offering his face to the snake by going nose-to-nose with it, I gave the man what I felt was a generous tip and asked him a couple of questions. We had an extremely broken conversation, which is now dripping back to me, leaking from wherever in my brain I had filed it away.

I asked him about venom. Miming a huge trunk and ears, I think he suggested it could kill an elephant. I asked about the fangs, and lo and behold he showed them to me. He grabbed the snake by the side of its head and split its mouth apart with his finger.

Inside were two curved fangs, and he explained in his own inimitable style that, regardless of where the bite-marks are, thanks to the curve and length of the fangs the venom will have been deposited deep into the tissue at an angle that is hard to reach. Sucking out the poison will only remove twenty to thirty per cent of the venom, if you can even *find* the venom. Cutting out the venom is not an option, because you don't know where the venom actually is, thanks to the curve of the fangs. At best you'll give yourself a nasty wound while you hack at the bite.

How do I apply what I remember to my current predicament?

A tourniquet, to restrict the flow of venom. That's a start.

No, wait. If I apply a tourniquet, the venom will be concentrated in the one extremity, increasing the likelihood that I will lose function of the limb, and possibly lose the limb entirely.

No, I must change tack. If I can get twenty to thirty per cent of this venom out of my body by sucking it, then that is twenty to thirty per cent less venom that my body has to deal with before I can get proper care — which I must acknowledge, I need. I can't jimmy anti-venom out of twigs, dirt and ingenuity. I need proper medical care to survive this.

I place my mouth directly over the two adjacent puncture marks, and suck hard. Nothing. I can feel no movement, only suction. Nothing significant. I try again. And again.

I feel a subtle bitterness on my tongue that I almost miss thanks to the throbbing in my arm. Unmistakable. I wonder if it is from the wound itself, but I am unsure. I suck at the bite again. Yes. I can taste it, a bitter harshness, it's how I always imagined the colour black would taste. It is a rancid but pure paradox of flavour. Animal kingdom meanness and evolution, right there on the tip of my tongue.

I pull away, unable to bear the taste anymore, and spit. I swill my mouth with water. I know the venom would be fine if ingested, as it is distinctly different to poison. My stomach acids would break it down, just like food. But if there is, say, a cut on my gum, or a sore somewhere in my throat that I don't know about, the venom will enter the bloodstream again.

I wash my mouth once more, to be sure.

I don't know how much of the putrid elixir I have managed to remove, but it will have to do. I need to get up, get moving, find civilisation. I must work out a plan, have an idea of who to approach when I actually reconnect with humanity. I'll need to take chances. After all, this venom is not going to leave my body by itself. It will sit in there, dwell, nestle down, and take me over. It will kill me if I do nothing.

Part of me, in a strange, sado-masochistic, begrudging way, respects the snake. The first adversary that has got to me on this strange journey. I grab my trusty duct tape, and, through blurring vision, tape up the bite, winding the binding around my hand. I check my watch, and see that it is 2.30am. I've had barely two hours of rest.

I get up. Instinct urges me to reapply my camouflage, but common sense suggests that the sooner I am seen by someone, the better. No time for that now. I need to find society and a sympathetic soul. But which way to turn? Where to head now? Which is the quickest way to find humanity, from where I stand?

If I continue to travel in the direction I have been since yesterday, I will eventually encounter signs of human life. But that may be as far as another thirty miles away, across taxing terrain which will surely weaken my body, tag-teaming with the venom to bring me down, like a trophy. I try to picture a top-down map of Exmoor National Park in my head, and work out where I am, but whenever I try to forge clarity in my mind, frantic claws rip at my nervous system, forcing me to focus on beating the pain back and so ignore the task at hand.

I can't concentrate. The pain is too great.

I start walking, hard and purposefully, keeping the venom at bay with activity. I stomp a course through the forest, the verdancy blending into a snotty, swirling, sickly mulch. I focus on my steps, my route to survival, and their rhythm. To occupy my wandering, frantic mind I try to keep my steps in time to an imaginary beat, like a primitive ritualistic dance to keep evil away. I could sure do with that now.

It is, there is no doubt, a time for mental strength and discipline. Panic is no good. I try to calm myself as I go, visualising relaxation, freshness and soothing images.

I picture a fresh white linen sheet, flung out to float down onto a king-size bed, imagining my mind in a state of mental refreshment. But as soon as the sheet lands, a giant, bloody fishhook rips up through the bed, smouldering with impossible black flames, angry embers spitting everywhere, and it retreats with fury — bloodily ripping the sheet, the bed, the whole happy image, taking them down into a hellish abyss of pure pain.

I physically shake my head to rid it of the image. I try to start again, but the same thing happens. A sheet. White, floating linen. An explosive fishhook, blood spraying, the scene destroyed. Pain again.

I start to run, as if I can leave it all behind. The landscape is transforming in front of me. Slight rises of the forest floor become jagged mountain peaks, too difficult to cross. Hanging branches become the long, swirling tentacles of land-borne octopi, huge and gnarled, reaching for me.

This is some kind of fresh hell. I try to compose myself, and bring my watch into focus. It takes a Herculean effort, and I eventually pull the face up to my own using two hands, straining as if the watch is loaded with weights. Then the numbers dance, leaping and cavorting, the second hand daring them as it turns, a game of 'What's the time, Mr Wolf?' between once-fixed numbers and a pursuing, staccato second hand.

I try to isolate the smaller hour hand. Where is it? I can't.... There. It's there.

I try to see where it is pointing, but the distance between the smaller hand and the number it points to becomes a desert of concentration, constantly interrupted by jutting, dancing intrusion. I eventually make it out. It's just gone twelve.

In the red haze of my bubbling blood, I eventually work out that I have been like this for some nine hours. Time has burned past in a feverish dream. I have no idea how far I have come, what direction I have taken, or what has happened to me.

All I can really know for sure, is that I am in a lot of trouble.

Alarm. The hair on my neck stands on end, instinct ripping me straight and upright, enlivened by my highly trained sixth sense. I drop to the deck, and scramble through the earth into the nearest patch of overgrowth.

I am not alone. There's someone else out here.

Have my pursuers finally caught up with me? Have I been stomping back towards them, and eventually presented myself to them, their prey placed in their lap with a bow on top?

I hear a crunch in the wilderness. The light snap of a soft footfall. It is not my pursuers. I just know it.

This is different. I recognise what it is like to be hunted. And that's just what is happening now.

I have a new enemy, one that seeks to take advantage of me in my moments of weakness. Perhaps my pursuers have employed a master tracker, or an elite team?

No. There is one. Only one. It's mano a mano out here. Pure combat, nature's way, martial law. Just the forest, the earth, and our separate wills to survive.

The pain in my arm recedes, overtaken by this new challenge. Finally, my mind is occupied. A part of me wishes this foe had shown up earlier.

More soft footfalls. Soft, tentative feet on a forest floor filled with much that can betray position. I turn in the direction of the footsteps, look and listen.

Nothing. It has stopped. With great care, I reach into my pocket for my multi-tool, and slide the knife out of its compartment. I grip the blade between my teeth, my eyes never wavering from the direction of the footsteps.

Silence. Time passes. The forest is eerily quiet, the wildlife paying its respects to the dance of combat that is taking place in their midst. This quiet is all-entrenching. A vacuum of impending bloodshed.

I move through the undergrowth nimbly and dextrously, my nose never far from the dirt, my eyes scanning and filtering. *Something* feels out of place, skewed and off-centre. It's strange. I feel that my brain is struggling to cope with the task, a cerebral firewall stopping me from connecting simple dots efficiently.

I keep low, and try to move with as little noise as possible, and that's when I stumble across the track.

There, in the moist dirt ahead. Freshly imprinted, the moisture still visible in the dark complexion of the mud. Two thin curved prongs. It's a hoof. And there's another. Side by side.

As if walking upright on two fucking legs.

Before I know it, the racehorses of my darkest dreams bolt from their stables and race across the rolling hills of my already-besieged mind. Images of horror and hellish beasts fill my retinas. I am in the presence of devilry. Of evil. Of the beast.

It's a tale locked in my subconscious, swapped between children in hushed tones at primary school. 'Do you know about The Devil's Footprints?', they would ask. It is a tale rooted so deeply in British myth and folklore that here and now it comes racing back to the foreground as if I have just heard about it.

In the 1850s, people awoke on a snowy morning to find curved footprints etched across the Devonshire countryside. They were unbroken, one after the other, the tracks of a hoofed creature walking upright. The tracks went on for 100 miles, across roofs, over high walls, through meadows and towns. Not a solitary step was missed. The source of the mystery was never solved.

The story left an indelible impression on me, and was the first thing that kept me awake at night. And now, in one of my darkest moments, of which there have admittedly been a few, the Devil's Footprints have reappeared.

And now, it seems, I will be the first person to see what infernal creature made them, but not only that... it wants me. It wants to bring me down. If it's a fight this creature wants, it's a fight it will get. But I can't help feeling overwhelmed and more under-prepared than ever.

My God... *It is real.* The stories, the legends, the old wives' tales... all based in truth and fact. *Jesus Christ.*

I can't believe this. Why me? Why now? After all this time, with no conclusions afforded such a myth before, why am I faced with such evil?

What do I do? What is this thing?

I need to get a fix on it. If it simply wants to pass through here, I will happily let it do so and simply take with me a story to keep my imaginary grandchildren awake at night. If I could only get a look at it, to bolster the tale...

The tracks are easy enough to follow. Hoof prints, one after the other, evenly spaced. Without warning, I feel eyes boring into me, from somewhere ahead, their sinister intentions pinning me to the spot. I have engaged the beast, without really having meant to.

Shit. You idiot, Ben.

I have provoked it. And it knows where I am. I slowly raise my eyes to look at the foliage ahead, but can't see anything amiss. I still *feel* it though. Cold, but burning. Judging and measuring. *What are you made of, Ben?*

My eyes are drawn higher, above the foliage, and all horrors reveal themselves in full. No wonder I couldn't see it down where I was looking. The beast is huge. My terror threatens to spill over, as I meet its still gaze. Its head is about nine feet above the ground, perched on broad shoulders. Its skin is clad in a dark fur, with a black, unnaturally-elongated face that will haunt me until my last breath, whenever that may be. Its nose is wet and jet black, thick nostrils gulping my scent. Its eyes are huge black billiard balls, just two deep pupils that protrude nauseously from its dreadful warped skull. Atop its head, as if growing from its very skull like weeds, is a tight, close, tangled knot of jagged horns.

It is hell personified. The devil behind the footprints.

I can't keep my terror at bay. I must transform that horror into fuel for the impending fight between man and beast. I must charge, and take the fight to my adversary. I have seen it. It is flesh and blood. Flesh can be cut and blood can be spilt. And when there's no blood left, the beast will fall. Just like any other enemy.

This abomination will be no different. It will taste steel at my hand, if it so chooses to take me on.

It shakes its head, and bellows. The trees shake and my knees quiver as it screams at me, in a voice from another world entirely.

Be strong, Ben. Show of strength. I scream back as hard as I can, long and clear.

It hurts. My chest constricts as if in a spiked vice, and my head feels as if it might explode on the spot. My brain fizzes horribly in my skull, like burning ants in a bucket. I find myself struggling to catch my breath, feel my knees buckle, and, almost immediately, sense dirt on my face.

I lie there immobile, undone pitifully by that last exertion, as I watch the devilish beast take a step towards me, knowing there's not a damn thing I can do about it.

All I can do is close my eyes, and hope that the end will be quick.

9.

The forest is whizzing by, flushing past my eyes, with a sense of detachment and futility. It is over. I fell to the beast. My dignity bled out, to be forever lost on the forest floor.

The beast has me in its whirlwind clutches, carrying me through the forest to its lair. It wants to savour me. The bastard.

It smells artificial, in the beast's grip. Unnatural, almost synthetic. I suppose that's to be expected this close to something that is so far beyond my comprehension. I try to peel my eyes from the blurred trees, but I can't. It is too difficult, the zoetrope greens too transfixing.

As if noticing my struggle, the beast speaks to me.

'We are nearly there,' it says, in a soft, almost parental voice.

'*Fuck you*,' I whisper, knowing that whatever I say will make no difference to my fate.

'You are in a bad way,' the beast says, again fooling me with how sweetly it speaks to me. I wish I could take a look at the beast, show it that it's not fooling anybody. 'We'll have you in hospital soon,' it whispers.

I find those words rattling inside me, breaking off a piece of recognition as they tumble. Hospital. No. Not now, after coming so far.

I want to tell the beast, 'No'. No! No hospitals. Just you and me. It is typical of such a beast to taunt me with salvation.

'No,' I say. 'No hospitals. Just you and me… to the bitter end.'

The beast doesn't answer. It must be mulling that over. I hope, before it decides which way to end my life, if it hasn't decided that already, that I have impressed it. That I have shown stoutness and dignity in the face of adversity. I hope so, even though none of that will mean a great deal soon, when it is feasting on my entrails.

10.

A flutter of cool breeze wakes me, whispering furtively on the hairs of my arm. My head is thumping, a smashed cranial Easter egg, left to rot after a fall. My eyes peel open, crusty sleep unbinding with effort. I feel soaked, and disgusting.

For a start, I appear to be in a bed. Alive. I have a bit of clarity back, the ability to follow a thought through. I have no recollection of how I got here, nor the events leading up to when I must have lost consciousness.

It is dark. And I remember the snake bite.

I judder to an upright position, getting more of a feel for the room. I'm in a kind of cot bed, in what looks like a darkened... laboratory? There are polished surfaces, glass tubes, computers, all glinting blue from a light source peering through a glass-panelled door in the corner. I can even see a microscope back there, on a gleaming chrome workbench. I'm in a very swish, high-end lab of some kind.

This is wrong. All wrong. I'm in the clutches of someone I shouldn't be in the clutches of, and my survival instincts grip me ferociously, thrashing me awake and alert.

This is a facility, most likely governmental, given the technological sheen I'm surrounded by. I urge the dark to cover me, before a voice cuts into it, immediately fraying my nerves.

'Welcome back,' it says, in hushed, tentative, female tones. I dart my head towards the source. She must have been here the whole time.

I can only see her outline, but it's enough for me to get a fix. I throw myself upright to address my captor, and swing my legs around on the bed. There seems to be one of them, a female, and immediately I'm primed to make her talk.

I feel woozy, but I convince myself it's an illusion. I trace the origin of the voice, or at least a point where I *think* it came from, and try to move as quickly as I can. But as I rise from the bed, my right arm is snagged down by my knees, and my knees are somehow bound by an ever-tightening elastic length. Suddenly I'm pitched forward onto my front, having managed to get myself hog-tied by *something*. Something falls onto the tiles next to me, with a clang of metal. It's not the smooth, lethal approach I was after.

'Oh dear,' says the voice. I hear her coming to me, and feel arms support me as I get my bearings. 'You've got yourself into a real mess,' she says.

I look down, and through my foggy vision I can see that I have some rubber tubing snaked around my legs, which seems to end up in the back of my right hand at one end, and run into a clear bag of fluid at the other. That clear bag was hanging from the metal stand that I pulled down with me when I fell.

An IV. I feel immeasurably stupid.

'I mean you no harm, let me help you,' my captor says, passing the tubing down over my ankles and helping me back up to the bed.

It appears, as I settle back onto the small cot bed and peruse my body, that I have been cared for. I am still dressed, which is a relief; being naked and hog-tied would have been too much embarrassment to handle. In the low light I can make out that I am utterly filthy, having caked the once-white sheets of the bed in mud, sweat and grime. They are black and stinking now, much like myself. My jacket has been removed, and my left sleeve has been rolled up. The snake bite is now covered in a surgical dressing, held in place by micropore tape and bandage, as is the cut between my toes. And in the back of my right hand, as I learned, is a canula leading to an IV drip at the foot of the bed, the stand for which my captor is now replacing. I follow the tubing up to a half-full bag of clear white fluid labelled 'saline'. On the windowsill at the foot of the bed, sit three other empty IV packets. I've obviously been a thirsty boy.

'Hello,' I say, realising that in this most feeble of positions, if she wanted me dead, she has had many opportunities prior to this point. She, whoever she is, moves around to the side of the bed so I can see her.

'Well, this is far more agreeable, you being pleasant like this,' she says.

I am confused. All I remember is a struggle, a descent and a brush with.... darkness.... and evil. I struggle for words, but I don't know what to say at all.

'I have helped walkers out in the park before, when they have got themselves into a sticky patch or two. But none of them have ever told me to fuck off before,' she says.

She reaches for a wheeled stool from beneath the nearest work bench, and scoots it to my bedside. I see a slender female form, in jeans and a dark jumper. As she sits and faces me, she presents a woman of studious fire. Wire-framed glasses magnifying huge chestnut eyes, dark hair up in a hasty pony-tail and neat features (aside from one) arranged on olive skin. A couple of simple gold rings sit side by side on the thumb and first finger of her right hand. Lithe, tall with a taut athletic frame, even when folded onto the chair. Her nose is the odd one out in this, it has been badly broken at some point, but never properly set, the tip still delicate but pointing just off-centre, and the bridge slightly depressed.

'If I said that to you, I am very sorry,' I say, trying to pull myself up. 'And I am very sorry for the mess I have made here.'

The woman smirks. 'Yes. I'm not sure how I would explain this if it wasn't the weekend. But the centre will be empty until Monday, so Sunday will now become laundry day.'

The centre?

'Where am I?' I ask, measuring her for an honest response.

'Well, I wanted to take you to the hospital, but that didn't go down too well. That only made you angrier, and you were already a bit... wound up. I saw the snake bite, recognised the symptoms, so I figured I had what I needed to patch you up here. And I'm not sure I would have made it in any case. The weekend traffic is terrible round here in summertime. You needed anti-venom. Fast. We had everything here that could help, in the short term.'

There is a hint of South-Eastern Europe about her accent, a soft lilt of something, possibly Balkan.

'I am very grateful, miss...?' I ask.

'Doctor...' she says.

'Doctor...?'

'Ridgewell. But since it's the weekend, just call me Amina.'

'Thank you for everything, Dr Ridgewell.'

'You are welcome, Mr Miller.'

Aha. She has been through my things and found my fake identity. In fact, where *are* my things? A bolt of panic fires deep within as I check the pocket of my shorts.

'All your things are safe. As is your little trinket,' says Amina, eyeing me with more than a hint of suspicion. 'It's quite a lovely little piece you have there, isn't it?'

'Where is it, Dr. Ridgewell?' I can't keep the seriousness from my voice, which I can see doesn't surprise her at all. She might know more than I do, at this point. I'm wariness personified.

'Like I said, it's all safe,' she replies with strength.

'I'll have to take your word for it,' I reply. 'What happened to me?'

'Well, if it wasn't so life-threatening, it would have been funny,' she says crossing her legs and smoothing her jeans, even though there are no creases there in the first place. 'I was in the forest on my rounds, and I heard a man — *you* — howling, like in a madness. I followed the sound and saw you, filthy, screaming at a young stag on a brow above you. Poor thing was terrified.'

'A deer?' I ask, confused. I have a memory of something...

'Yes, a young one,' she continues. She cocks her head to one side, as if trying to gauge my reactions. 'You passed out into the dirt, and the deer bolted, probably grateful for its life. I went to you, and saw fever and dehydration instantly. I found the snake bite and brought you back here.'

'And here is...?' I ask, tentatively.

'The field centre for the Exmoor National Park Authority. We manage and monitor the ecology of the park from here, with a rather average grant from the government. While we have a park that is, and for as long as they don't frack it to oblivion.'

The word *government* jangles alarm bells immediately, but the word *frack* also strikes me.

'Frack?'

'Fracking. Hydraulic fracturing. Drill a big hole in the earth, pump it full of high-pressurised water, blasting the natural gas back up out. The government is talking about giving the park over to fracking sites, which will give the gas companies a lot of pennies, but ruin the area for good.'

'Why?'

'It greatly risks poisoning the groundwater surrounding the site, which in the case of a national park, would murder the ecology.'

Weathers and NDX.

'And to top off all the excitement,' she says with dry sarcasm, 'we have one of the first cases in the country of Verticillium Dry Bubble, here in the park. I was out collecting samples when I came across your little scene.'

Catching my confusion, she clarifies.

'Verticillium Dry Bubble is a fungal disease, affecting mushroom crops. We are trying to find out how and why it got here. I'm a microbiologist working on the project. Not what I had in mind when... well, here I am.'

'Right,' I say. 'And the snake bite?'

'You should be fine now, but you still need to get to hospital for the all clear. It was a nasty one. You had fought the venom off by yourself for a long time, with little water or nourishment. You were in a state of extreme disorientation, dehydration and hallucination. It nearly killed you. We had the anti-venom here, which has done the trick, aided by a box full of saline.'

I am suddenly very grateful, and relieved, and I can feel myself relax, albeit only a little. The awful encounter with the beast, which I can only remember in fragments, was nothing more than a hallucination. My weakened mind encountered a deer, and filled in the blanks hysterically.

'Thank you very much, Amina,' I say. 'I really mean that. And I am sorry for messing up your weekend.'

'No harm done,' replies Amina.

'Who... knows I am here?' I ask, hesitantly.

That seems to alert Amina a little, and I can understand why. That's the kind of question someone asks when they don't want to be found. But she seems more than capable — hard, even. Worldly. Not to be messed with. I'll need to gauge where her loyalties lie, and her answer to my question will give me more than a fair indication.

If I'm honest, she is attractive — and I find that a bit unnerving to begin with, even before I consider that she might be an enemy. I'm no wily ladies' man, able to use his charms to bend the opposite sex to his will. It's a topic that, historically, has me all at sea.

'Nobody. The centre is empty at the weekends. Not a lot happens around here'.

I'm pleased with the answer. It is even, non-committal.

'Why does it matter who knows you are here?' asks Amina. Her face is open, her eyes wide, feigning innocence as she poses her question. She is no fool, this one.

'I'd rather... this was kept quiet,' I reply, testing the waters warily. But she could have told someone already, even if she says that she hasn't. She seems all too aware that there is a reason for my being stranded in the woods.

I was, indeed, there for a reason, and she seems keen to know what it was.

'I guessed that. Why?' She maintains that non-judgmental gaze, which, matched by a softening tone, makes me want to let my guard down. But I mustn't forget that this is a government facility, and there has been more than a whiff of crooked government to be found in this adventure so far. Taking care is a priority.

'Like I said, I'm grateful for the help,' I say, weakly shifting my legs around the side of the bed, careful this time not to repeat my earlier entanglement. It's not easy, since my lower limbs feel as reliable as soaked papier-mâché.

'You are not that talkative? Neither would I be if I had been running around all over the countryside for the last couple of days. But, I still want to know about the trinket.'

Rumbled. She knows the earring has significance, but how? Have the authorities chasing me revealed the reason for their pursuit to the public? Surely not...

'It troubles me that you are so interested,' I say, my tone guarded.

'Oh, don't get your knickers in a twist. It doesn't take a genius to work out a man like you and a thing like that are not exactly the perfect fit. Look at you. You are a rough man. The kind of man who takes it upon himself to trudge through wilderness and cake himself in mud to keep prying eyes away. You carry barely anything with you, only the basics. Your idea of a first aid kit is a roll of industrial tape. A trinket bearing an exotic jewel is not the kind of luxury item I would associate with a man like you.'

'Ouch. Thanks, I suppose.'

'I noticed it, when I dragged you onto the bed. I fished it from your pocket, so that you wouldn't damage it in the night while you were tossing and turning. As I got it out, I realised it was *already* damaged, your trinket. It is not gold. A solid gold earring doesn't crumble simply in a pocket.'

'You sound like you've been given enough crap jewellery to know a knock-off when you see one.'

'If you say so.'

'You're right. I don't know my jewellery.'

'So that makes you either very sentimental... or it is the reason you have been keeping such a low profile.' Her eyes finally show a glint of mischievous purpose. 'And I bet it is the latter.'

There's something both innocent and disarming about her. I know I can't muster the strength to sustain a glare. I really don't feel physically well enough to argue with her too vigorously. My body is craving quiet and cold water, in the immediate aftermath of fever.

'You do know that it's not a jewel it carries, don't you?' she says.

Even through the mental fog, her words pierce the veil bringing with them immediate intrigue. My reaction must have already betrayed my surprise, as her own eyebrows rise above her glasses.

'You didn't know?' she says.

I shake my head, literally not knowing what to say.

'God, I have been sat here trying to work out what to do this whole time you've been out of it. It's in a tin over there,' she says, motioning to the work benches. 'It's quite clear it's something interesting. Here, I'll show you. -'

Hold your horses, missy.

'Wait,' I say, interrupting her. 'You say nobody knows I'm here; it has to stay that way. And whatever we discuss here never happened, and you must not tell anyone. You abuse that position of trust…'

That has gained her attention, and seems to catch her imagination. She stares at me, awash with seriousness for the first time, setting her jaw and sitting straight-backed.

'Is that understood?' I say.

'Of course,' she replies without delay. 'Come on then, do you really think I became a doctor just so I could look at mushrooms all day?'

I pull myself up, but before I know it she is up and dragging me to my feet.

She walks me, one painful foot at a time, over to the work benches, where she flicks on a couple of table lamps. She places me on another wheeled stool, and scoots hers over with the precision of someone who has done so many times. The lamps' glare shines into a shallow tin that rests on the chrome bench. Inside, looking wounded, is the earring.

Amina reaches for a biro from further up the bench, and uses it as a pointer.

'See here,' she says, gesturing with the blue-inked tip at the (supposedly) gold casing. 'The casing has peeled away, almost like an onion skin.'

It's true, it has, and the edges of the jewel are revealing themselves from beneath the gold that has twisted away.

'And here, if you look closely,' she says, pointing to the jewel's exposed edges, 'are the pointed edges of the stone. But look at the soft fraying, the fibres peeling away.'

Sure enough, the corners of the stone have tiny white strands protruding scruffily from them, giving a ragged impression.

'A gemstone shouldn't do that, I take it?' I ask.

'Absolutely not,' says Amina, firmly. 'These edges are *plastic*. It's nothing more than worn plastic or rubber, these fibres fraying as they rubbed the fabric of your pocket.'

'All this for a plastic stone?' I ask.

'All what?' Amina asks. She looks directly at me again, imploring me to speak truths. 'Mr Miller, if you want my help in working out what this is, I need to know what you know. I can do nothing with bits and pieces of information. I have a *suspicion* as to what it is, but I will only share it with you if you tell me the truth.'

I am fatigued and beaten, mentally and physically. It's been a lonely few days, and I have been so far unable to fathom the quest that I have been thrust into. And now I'm at this point, such is my weariness that I actually wouldn't mind the assistance.

'I can trust you?' I ask.

'We are not going to go through that again, are we?' replies Amina. I can tell by the tone of her voice that she means it. I sigh.

'It's Ben. My name... Just call me Ben.'

'You are not Sean Miller, like your ID suggests?' she says, keeping her own interest at bay.

I glare hard at her, and quickly change the subject. 'I do a bit of work in an anti-crime capacity, with the help of the National Crime Agency.' That sounds really crap and vague, but I hope it will do.

Amina just looks at me, without smart comebacks for the first time. I continue.

'I was assigned the task of securing this earring a couple of days ago, from the wreckage of the plane that crashed off the coast.'

Amina's eyes flare recognition.

'The plane was empty when it crashed, except for a minimal crew and a dead woman who was clutching that earring. I believe it has been reported that hundreds of people died on board. It isn't true, not a word of it. There was no mass tragedy. The plane was brought down by God knows who... All I know is that a corrupt government connection is chasing me, and *this*, down. They want this, whatever it is. For what purpose, I don't know yet. And I was doing alright until the snake bit me.'

Amina regards me, and suddenly seems a little in awe at the scale of that with which she is suddenly involved.

'So... what do you think it is?' I ask, trying to snap her back into the here and now.

'I... I think those rough worn edges are the tell-tale signs of a plastic mould. I think the 'stone' as it appears to be, is not solid at all but a plastic shell. I think there is something inside.'

I had never, not once, thought of that. It hadn't even entered my mind. Jesus, how could I have missed it?

Amina seems galvanised by hearing her own theory spoken, and sets about showing me.

'The weight is all wrong. A stone of this size would be much more noticeable in weight. This is much lighter than you would expect, but no less solid. I think perhaps it is Perspex. And look, you can see the edges of the mould where the plastic has been pressed and melted shut.'

I can see straight away what she is referring to. Just next to the frayed strands I can see tiny remnants of the flat excess plastic where the two sides of the mould were pressed together.

'I think there is no doubt it is a container. I want to take off the rest of the gold housing to look for the opening,' she says, looking at me for approval. I nod slowly.

'Extra careful,' I say. Now my mind is whirring with possibilities, the aftermath of the fever becoming a footnote to the mystery of the false trinket.

She pulls over another tin, this time stocked with delicate, shining tools. She plucks out two pairs of tweezers, and with each set grips the broken metal of the casing. Very gently, she begins to slowly ease them apart.

My mind is bubbling as to what it might be.

'Look,' says Amina. 'There.'

She points with closed tweezers at the now-revealed plastic corner. Protruding from the corner is a small, clear nub. It is poking out from the plastic, with what appears to be a tiny metal screw covering its end.

'We need to get this in there, if we are to go any further,' she says.

'In where?' I ask.

'The anaerobic hood and glove box,' she says, nodding towards the far end of the bench, where a long, glass rectangle sits fitted with four, round openings, each attached to rubber gloves to allow wearers to reach inside the box. I can see that inside the box there is a microscope, the viewfinder for which is poking back through the glass in order to be used from the outside.

'It's a controlled atmosphere in there, and... If this is worth crashing a plane over, it's certainly worth taking that extra precaution.'

We wheel our stools to the anaerobic hood, and Amina pulls a tray out from beneath its reflecting frame, upon which she places the trinket and all its pieces. Along with these she also places two clear glass rectangles, of a type I have seen in countless movies, between which fluid is trapped for closer examination. She presses a couple of buttons on the unit control pad, and it whirrs into life, a light popping on and an internal fan activating.

'I think that beneath that screw cap is a modified pipette tip, or something like it,' she explains, 'and that would mean the contents of this container can be... squirted out.'

'I'm glad you are putting it in there, then.'

She replaces the tray beneath the glass box, twists a lever, and the tray appears behind the glass. Amina rolls up her sleeves and slips her delicate wrists through the openings, into the black gloves. I stand so that I can see what's going on.

'I am going to do everything very carefully, and sparingly,' she says, while her gloved hands lift the trinket up onto a higher surface, closer to our vision.

'Are you used to doing things like this?' I ask.

She puffs air out of her cheeks, blasting a lock of dark hair out of her eyes. 'Yes. This is what I do for a living. You sir, are standing in my workshop and playground. I do this every day. Am I used to aiding and abetting a plane crash looting, crime agency wilderness man carrying mysterious trinkets loaded with God-knows-what? *No.*'

'Fair enough.'

She takes a small pair of pliers in her right hand, and holds the object in her left hand. In the soft blue light, amid the hum of the box vent, she carefully twists the object's metal screw with the pliers.

'It is coming away quite easily,' she states, providing me a welcome running commentary since, I must say, I feel quite impotent sitting here, weakened, letting Amina take the lead. 'The housing must have been its primary form of protection, during its journey. Do you know anything about where it came from?'

'Aside from taking it from that woman in the plane wreckage, I can't say I know anything more than that. And the woman herself wasn't much use. She was missing her head.'

Amina pauses for a second, seemingly unsure as to whether I am messing with her or not. She carries on, no clarification necessary. The metal cap twists right off, to reveal, just as she guessed it, the tip of a pipette.

'You were right,' I tell her. 'Good call.'

I watch as she gently places the screw cap back onto the tray, and takes one of the glass slides instead. She inverts the container, and readies it between finger and thumb.

'Here goes nothing,' she says. 'Gently, gently,' she whispers, as she squeezes.

We watch intently as a solitary clear bubble appears at the end of the pipette, but it is not a bubble at all — it is a drop. Amina maintains pressure, and gives the container a tiny shake. The drop falls gloopily and reluctantly onto the glass slide.

'That will be just fine,' she whispers, almost to herself. She then takes her time in resealing the container with the cap, and placing the other glass slide atop the drop. It smears the drop out into a wider clear blob, between the two pieces of glass. She places it under the microscope.

'Do you want to go first?' she asks, showing the first hint of trepidation I have noticed.

'I'm afraid I have no idea what I am looking for,' I reply, shrugging. 'Tell me what you can see.'

She takes a deep breath, and ponders things for a moment. I feel bad for her. By helping me, and simply being inquisitive, she has been sucked into this ludicrous scenario. That phrase about curiosity and cats springs to mind...

Abruptly, she sits straighter, and aligns her eyes above the microscope's eyepieces. Her gloved hands gently manipulate the focus and magnification controls beyond the glass, and she concentrates.

I watch her, as opposed to anything else, and watch her eyes beyond her glasses as they rapidly hop from one thing to the other, all within the locality of the viewfinder. She adjusts the settings again inside the box. Then again. She eventually stops, and gazes out into her own reflection staring back at her from the glass of the box.

'Well?' I ask.

'All I can say so far is that it is not a bacterium, that's for sure. And because it isn't that, it immediately alarms me.'

I'd love to know why, but she abruptly starts moving to the other side of the room.

'I'm going to do a mass spectrometry test, that should get us identification.'

She takes a small metal slide from a drawer by the computer units, and puts it into the tray loader for the anaerobic hood, introducing it to the contents.

'I'll need another drop,' she says.

'What are you doing? And what is a mass spectrometry test?'

The new metal slide has a number of round indentations on its polished surface, and she squeezes a solitary drop from the trinket's pipette onto one of them.

'I'm adding some of our mystery chemical to this plate. It's for the MALDI-TOF machine. It's the quickest way to get a breakdown of a protein, which I can only assume this is, given what I saw in the scope, and we have one here. We do a lot of research from this facility, and it's not just to do with the National Park, so we are lucky enough to have been given some nice toys.'

'Mouldy what now?'

She ejects the plate from the anaerobic hood and snaps on some latex gloves, before moving across the room to a machine that looks like a very fancy coffee maker.

'A MALDI-TOF machine is essentially a mass spectrometer that is attached to a database. It analyses the material after it has been introduced to an enzyme matrix. These enzymes digest the protein into smaller fragments for weighing. It's really cool. The fragment sizes are run through the database and from these measurements you can work out the entire structure of the protein.'

'Umm, right.'

'So I simply add the matrix, load the plate into the machine, and we should get an answer in no time.'

'OK then.'

She takes another pre-loaded pipette and squirts the solution onto the plate, before putting the plate into the machine's opening. A computer screen next to it blinks to life, and Amina starts typing. Within mere seconds, the screen begins to change.

I give up trying to keep up. I've no idea what it is I'm looking for. I'll just leave this one to the expert, who is now studying the screen.

In hushed tones, belying far more dread than I was expecting, she speaks.

'You swear, you have no idea why this was coming into the country?'

Her seriousness has really taken me by surprise, and it scares me.

'None. I was just told to stop anyone else from getting their hands on it.'

Amina looks at me, then right through me. Her manner is transformed, that quirky bounce she exuded just moments before has been erased, evidently by what she has seen on the screen.

'Amina, what is it?' I ask.

She looks at the floor, takes off her gloves, and swivels to face me. Her hands reach for each other, and squeeze together as if seeking comfort from one another's touch.

'In short, it bears all the hallmarks of a modified isoform of botulinum toxin. It's had its amino acids... altered.'

'It's a chemical?' I reply, the penny not dropping.

'Yes, well, a protein,' Amina says, glancing back through the viewing glass of the hood at the innocuous little trinket sitting broken in the box.

'Amina, what does it do?' Chemistry was never my strong suit, so I'll really need this spelled out.

'It's a bespoke synthetic toxin, which started as botulism.'

'Botulism,' I say, the penny rattling somewhere within. 'I've heard of that.'

'It is really a beautiful system, in which the toxin is perfectly designed for its function. The toxin is a protein made up of two chains, heavy and light. The heavy chain targets the effect to nerves; it does this by binding to proteins on the surface of the nerve cells at the terminals, and once bound to the surface of the cell the toxin is taken into that cell, using the cell's normal transport system. That's endocytosis. The light chain of the toxin is an enzyme, which digests one of the proteins that cause neurotransmitters to be released from nerves, so it stops the nerve signals to your muscles which makes them contract.'

'Amina, you have lost me. What does this mean? In simple terms, what does it do?'

'Paralysis, and soon after, horrible death. It's a well-known chemical weapon, which has proven popular because it can be, by the right people, readily synthesised and weaponised.'

'Jesus Christ,' I can only whisper. And I had this thing in my pocket...

'That's not the half of it with this thing, Ben,' Amina says, now fixing me with a focussed stare. 'The amino acids have been altered, their sequence has been changed. That will have taken a great deal of calculation, time and effort. What bothers me is the motivation that might drive such a change. I know that, by doing such a thing, you could recalibrate the protein to maximise potency. It would then, on contact with human cells, focus on specific receptors and generate a more targeted effect.'

'Is there a way of working out which receptors?' I ask, hoping that I am keeping up.

'Not without extensive time and testing. But that's not what concerns me. This modification has created a new unfamiliar sequence in the toxin, unique to this particular form that we have here, in this glove box. If you don't have the code, you can't make an anti-toxin.'

'So if you are exposed to it...'

'No anti-toxin exists that can help you. An anti-toxin would have to adhere to the blueprint set out by the new structure of the toxin. And nobody knows that apart from us and whoever made it.'

Shit. I cast my mind back to when I found the thing in the first place. Did I miss the anti-toxin? Was it on the plane somewhere, travelling in a similar way?

'So, what you are saying is that this is a modified super-toxin that is extra potent, and no known antidote exists?'

'Yes,' Amina replies.

'Who would want such a thing?' I ask, but I know what a naïve question that is, naïve to the point of rendering it rhetorical. Anyone with a hint of greed would want this stuff. It's instant power in a bottle. No wonder I am being hunted down so ferociously.

'Do you know how much you have here?' Amina asks.

'Is that a real question? Because I honestly don't know.'

Amina pushes her chair back so that she slides in reverse across the lab floor.

'You have approximately one gram.'

'Is that a lot?' I say. It doesn't sound a lot.

'We've got enough here to kill about 1.4 million people, in one of the most horrible ways imaginable.'

I feel like I've been punched in the gut, my gusto pummelled away to a flat plateau of base horror. The horrors mankind is capable of...

The identity of the woman on the plane is crucial, as she seems to have been the vessel designated to get the weapon into the country. But the budget behind this, the power, influence and control required, to charter a jet and fly it to an army base in the United Kingdom, not to mention shooting the bugger down... it is staggering.

There are dark powers at work here. Emphasis on 'dark' and 'power'. Coils of injustice strangle my stomach, twisting out a vengeful toxin of my own. Who would dare to do this? And who would dare bring this to the UK?

'Can we destroy it?' I ask.

My question awakens Amina from her own reverie.

'It's a possibility, but it may prove too risky,' replies Amina.

'Why?!' I demand. 'Surely if this godawful stuff is wiped out then it can 't harm anybody else? At the very least, it will lose potential to wipe out a significant portion of the population.'

'Think about it, Ben,' Amina pleads. 'We don't know if there is any more if this stuff out there, but we have to assume there must be somewhere - and if we destroy this we have lost perhaps the only chance to synthesise our own antidote. We have an opportunity to save lives with this.'

That is an extremely good point. But what a risk it is, not destroying this heinous substance, this toxin that has found its way to these shores.

'How long will it take to create an anti-toxin?' I ask.

'A few months, at least. Maybe years. And that's if this lab was fully staffed.'

Far too long. 'There's no way we can pull that off. It won't take those hunting me long before they work out what happened to me. And they'll come knocking on this door, sooner or later.'

I think about the men chasing me, the soldiers I encountered. Do they know what they are involved with? If they did, would they continue their pursuit?

And what about that lying MP, Lloyd Weathers? Does *he* know? I'd love five minutes alone with that fat fucking worm. I'm sure I'd make him sing the truth.

It's time to boot that phone up and stick it on charge. Any information is good information at this point.

'I need to make a call,' I say. 'Can you give me a minute?'

11.

Amina has left me alone for a moment, and I think it's good timing on her part. Her demeanour, once playful and confident, seems now fragile and besieged.

My smartphone still has no reception, but I jack it into the mains anyway. She gave me a cordless phone before she went, and I dialled out, all the while fretting who might be listening in, but knowing that there is no time to waste and that caution must now be thrown windward.

The phone is answered after half a ring.

'Yes?' he answers, in a hurry. I'm glad I decided to try him again. As my only source of information at this point, I'd be in dire straits without him. It seems Jeremiah hoped I would call back, too, because even at this time of night, the speed of his response tells me that he has been nursing the phone like a wounded baby bird, waiting and hoping for any sign of life.

I called his standard mobile number this time, no encryption or caller ID protection, so I'm guessing he has seen the southern area code on his phone and had an idea who could be calling.

I say nothing, just clear my throat to let him know I'm here.

'0394 555 6099,' he says.

My brain, so used to accepting coordinates at a moment's notice, files the numbers immediately. I hang up, then dial the new number. It's a safety precaution that we have previously discussed; if we thought either party's phone device could be compromised. He's given me the number to a safe line at the NCA headquarters in Warrington. After a couple of minutes, he answers again.

'Thank God you didn't take what I said to you last night seriously. Are you OK?' he asks. There is weight to his tone, suggesting that much remains unsaid.

'I'm alright. A lot has happened.'

'You're damn right. I've had to take this phone call on a desk in a different department. There's something very fucked up going on here, and I don't know quite what's happening, at least not for sure, yet. I am told that my entire department is suddenly being subjected to some 'governmental study'. We have non-departmental people here all the time at the moment; they're crawling through *everything*, phones, logs, documents, emails. We are having to be careful, but I know for a fact these guys aren't NCA. This is an external investigation in a shitty costume.'

'I understand.'

'The timing, with you doing what you're doing down there… it's more than a bit suspicious. Now, you see why I couldn't speak freely yesterday. So… do you have the item?'

'Why, the bespoke super-botulism? Yes, I have it here.'

Silence. Just for a second. A long second which betrays Jeremiah's surprise.

'Apex. That is what it is called,' he says.

I blurt out a retort before I have even considered it.

'You realise the position that you have put me in here, don't you?' I hadn't realised that my anger towards Jeremiah had frothed so quietly, yet so fervently that I couldn't resist confronting him. My distress focused on the information, or rather the lack of information, with which he had sent me to the front line. .

'Look, I didn't know how they were transporting it, but I knew it would have to be in something you'd notice,' he says quickly. On that front we got lucky — very lucky — but it worked out in the end. And we didn't have time to go through specifics, they were crashing a fucking jet to get at it. I had to get you there, and if I'd gone into any of the half-baked bits and pieces I had over here, we'd have wasted valuable time. Point is, you've got it and they haven't. I know precisely what I was asking you to do. But, now knowing what it is, would you rather it was in someone else's possession, and not yours?'

He is right, of course, and my anger simmers down immediately. I wouldn't trust another soul on the planet with this. If anyone is going to be in possession of this vile abomination of science, given the power it bestows on the carrier, I want that person to be me — and not for any of the traditional reasons. I want no power, other than the power to keep people safe. And this stuff is the very definition of unsafe.

'Jeremiah, I'll tell you where I am up to, then we can fill in the blanks where possible — and there will be a lot of them,' I say, settling back down on the edge of the cot bed and sighing. God, I am tired. I ache in my entirety. And I try to remember everything that has happened over the last few days.

'I made it to Morte Point, just in time for the plane to ditch. I entered the wreckage, which was empty save for a skeleton crew and a solitary woman, who was carrying the earring containing the substance in question. I took the earring just before an army unit arrived, under the command of MP Lloyd Weathers. I managed to escape, but in the process they realised that I had the earring. They have followed me inland for two days, and I am now in Exmoor National Park. I have avoided capture so far. I am now in the care of Dr Amina Ridgewell at the National Park field centre, and she has assisted me in analysing the contents of the earring. She identified the chemical contents as a modified strain of botulism, enhanced for potency. On top of this, I am aware of a cover-up regarding the true circumstances of the crash. I will be leaving here soon, and will keep heading north to you, unless advised otherwise. Your turn.'

'Just give me a second,' Jeremiah replies, and I can hear the *push-push-scratch* of him jotting something down on a pad. I wait, and breathe. I hope his intel will answer the questions that bother me the most about this whole dastardly thing.

'OK,' he says, 'firstly, thank you. By getting your hands on that and keeping it out of harm's way, on behalf of the NCA, thank you.'

'You're welcome, I suppose.'

'There is indeed, it seems, a conspiracy about the plane crash and the events since. At the NCA, we first got wind of this a couple of years ago. The prevention of organised crime makes up a large part of our workload, and we try to keep abreast of all things in that area as they grow, change and evolve. Spotting these trends helps up us to predict what certain of the less carefully-organised crime groups will do next, with varying degrees of success.'

Come on, get to the nitty gritty.

'We intercepted a very obvious communication coming into the country, a classified advert on Craigslist. A common way for the criminal fraternity to communicate is through classifieds, but with the growth of Internet classifieds, such communication can now be expanded to have an international scope.'

'I *think* I follow,' I murmur.

'The ad was, on the surface, an opportunity to buy a classic Ford Mustang, a supposedly rare model. *Coming soon, baby blue Ford Mustang C6760, bespoke alterations for maximum performance, never seen before, if enough interested parties, will bring to UK.* Sounds mundane enough. But it was actually an awareness piece, intended to drum up interest in a new product, to assess demand. There is no Ford Mustang C6760, but that combination of letters and numbers is the beginning of the chemical formula for the botulism toxin, and confirmed by the mention of blue, botulism's natural colour.'

Interesting, to say the least.

'Now, what makes this different is the fact that it is coming from an entirely independent source. The production of synthetic botulism is so time-consuming and so regulated, that mere mortals can't just get their hands on it. This is why botulism for sale in a Craigslist ad was so unique, and why it caused such a stir.'

'I get it,' I say, hoping I'm not lying.

'The ad, however, was *so* obvious, that it had to have been placed to get the attention of official authorities as well as criminal bodies. And if it got our attention, who else noticed it? We answered the ad — with a dummy email, naturally, in pursuit of the lead, because obviously, someone attempting to bring a highly potent modified chemical weapon into the country falls within our area of interest. We were placed in an email group that allowed all members to see each others' addresses, which at first I felt was strange, but then realised it served to drum up competition between the buyers as they could see who else wanted it. A smart move on the part of the seller. . All these fake email accounts and monikers, more than forty of them. Who knows who all these people are, but it is scary to see so many parties interested in getting their hands on such a thing, and you can only assume that these possible buyers are a blend of criminal and governmental parties, with some straddling both.'

I find it hard not to gulp in fear. *Dear God.*

'With such parties vying for this item, this becomes a matter of not just national safety, but world safety. 'We don't know who wants this, but they've clearly got enough balls and backing to put their names in the hat for it.'

'So what brings it to the UK right now?' I ask.

'We were emailed, out of the blue, last week. To say that it was finally coming. The item, one gram of Apex, a synthetic, modified super-botulism, a sufficient amount from which to synthesise an infinite volume, and an antitoxin, would be coming to the south of the UK, and there would be an auction at a time and destination to be confirmed. Simply put, the item goes to the highest bidder.'

'And that's when you got in touch with me?'

'Not quite. When we received that email, we were called off by Westminster, on the orders of the Secretary of State for Defence herself. We didn't even know that they were aware of our involvement. *That's* when I told you to come back to the UK. I had to let it go in an official capacity, but couldn't let it go… unofficially. I felt you were the perfect man for the job.'

'But the South West, Devon, Woolacombe, Morte Point... How did you *know*?'

'We have our own intelligence sources here. Some of whom even you are better off not knowing about.

We are never, ever, fully out of the loop. We are an intelligence agency, after all.'

He is right, and I suppress a smile. Their networks, for information gathering and intel collection, are precisely why I sought to work with the NCA in the first place. That, and the fact that they have the clout to bring to justice the scumbags I bring their way.

'So, what are you thinking? What's the play?' I ask.

'First off, we can't trust anybody. No-one. Here at the NCA, the team under my direct control and command is fifteen strong, only three of them know about this. They have their own assignments, away from the main group. My superiors are also unaware. Nothing about this sits right with me, which is why I can't let it go. It might end my career, but I have to try to stop this.'

'And that's where I come in?'

'You're our man in the field.'

'What is your gut telling you?'

'I think our own government is one of the parties seeking to buy the toxin. I think it is behind one of the email accounts in the pool. And I think government staff have ordered us off the project under some bollocks pretence that they have a special unit on the matter, when in fact they are positioning themselves to take the botulism, *for* themselves. And before you suggest that they might have wanted to get their hands on it to destroy it and save the day, think about it... If that was their goal, surely they would have kept us around and worked with us? Two heads are always better than one. No. They want that shit for themselves.'

'Jesus Christ.' My image of quaint little England, the one buried in my heart that I gaze at like the faded picture in a locket, takes a huge hit. The malevolent powers swirling behind the green... it reminds me of sinister days from distant history. 'That stacks up. That MP Weathers... I had a chat with him.'

'I told you not to.'

'I'm no lap dog, Jeremiah. Not anymore. Weathers is getting it for someone else, I'm guessing it's for somebody higher up the chain than he is. Whoever that is... do you think they downed the plane?'

'Absolutely. In such a way that they would get first dibs on the spoils. But you beat them to it, my friend. Tell me... Your Dr Ridgewell, what did she say about the chemical?'

Rage and pity burn my cheeks as I smash my eyes shut. The sheer bastardy this world has to offer. The years I have spent crawling through mud and blood with bullets slicing the air above my head, all for a government that is as twisted and power-driven as any other evil I have faced. I feel my life has been a lie. What was I fighting for?

'That it is indeed very nasty, and that what I have here alone can kill 1.4 million people.' That stuns Jeremiah into a breathless silence.

They must be stopped. I must destroy the toxin. I must do it now. How does one safely do that? Amina will know, surely. But what about those bastards that want to buy it?

'And all these interested parties; they have headed to England too?' I ask.

'Yes, the auction is expected to take place somewhere in the London area within the next couple of days. They are there waiting for the date, time and place.'

'How convenient. London. The cradle of government.'

'Aye.'

'Is there anyone there we can count on? The entire government can't be bent out of shape!'

'There may be someone. Obviously, we have some people there -'

'Then that's where I'm headed. I'll call you when I get there.'

'Wait. If you head up north I can help protect you and we can figure this out -'

'No. I need to find out who's responsible, and that will only come from taking this thing to London.'

'Maybe, but you have an opportunity to end this by destroying it. You don't need to run anymore.'

'That's not good enough. If we get rid of it, there will be more. We need info; we need to find out who made it and who wants it. I'll call you when I'm in the capital.'

I hang up. And this wild ride takes a new twist.

'Amina!' I call, tossing the phone onto the bed next to me. The lab door opens almost immediately, and she walks in. She is ashen, her body language carrying the hallmarks of defeat.

'Amina, can you assist me in the safe handling of this chemical?'

'Yes,' she replies in a whisper.

'Is there a way you can help me transport it?'

'Yes,' she replies again, her eyes narrowing this time.

'Then we need to leave, together, and I need your help.'

12.

It only took about an hour's persuasion. I outlined the situation very carefully to Amina, and painted her role in obvious shades, going heavy on the part concerning all that is at stake. She understood, and with a grim frown, agreed. I think that, since she is the person who positively identified the chemical, she feels — unjustly — responsible for it. Her commitment has looked sound and solid since, but we are only an hour in.

I can't shake the fact that Amina herself is on the payroll of the very government I suspect of betraying the public. I believe she can be trusted, but...

Who really knows?

So, under my gaze, she transferred the contents of the earring to a clear vial from one of the lab cupboards, and placed it in what looked like a kitchen Tupperware container, filled with foam and closed with a clip lid. She cut a nest out of the centre of the foam inside which the vial now sits snugly. I took a quick wash in the centre's toilets, we grabbed our things, and she put the lab back the way she thought it should be. We took her car, a red Mitsubishi pickup truck with muddied flanks, and we are heading east. Amina is driving. I sit next to her, in the passenger seat, my bag in the footwell between my feet, while a saline drip hangs from the grab handle above the passenger window, a tube connecting it to the back of my hand. It's cleaning me up, rehydrating me.

The radio burbles along, a sleepy late-night DJ guiding us between heartbreakers. Intermittently, the music is interrupted by traffic updates, which I find funny — I haven't seen another car since we set off. But alas, there is no time for enjoying life's ironies.

'I'm sorry about this, Amina,' I say reluctantly. 'But we are going to have to ditch this car soon.'

'My car? Why?' she says. I notice that her accent is more prominent when she gets flustered or angry.

'When I say *ditch*, I don't mean ruin and abandon. I just mean leave somewhere, and we will carry on by other means. You can come back for it later.'

'If everything goes to plan, you mean,' she says. A touch of her fire is back, and I'm relieved to see it. I was beginning to worry she might not hack the task I've set us.

'Something like that,' I reply.

I watch her carefully, for anything that might give away a hint of duplicity. I haven't seen her touch a phone of any kind, so she doesn't seem interested in keeping anybody updated of our movements — or at least, not via such conventional means.

She seems pensive and distant, and has done since she looked into the microscope back at her lab; it's as if the sight stripped away her sense of fun and innocence. It seemed all to be a big game to her before that, a bit of a diversion. Then it all got very, crushingly, dangerously real, and she knows she is right in the middle of it now.

'Where are we headed?' she asks. 'I know we are aiming for the capital, but where exactly?'

'We need to go central. In striking distance of Westminster, I think.'

'And you are still sure you want to change vehicle?'

'Yes. Soon.'

'Then can I suggest the Night Riviera Sleeper?'

It sounds like the quaintest mode of transport ever, like a battered armchair merrily floating along on a cloud of tea cosies. Which, to be fair, would be better than this car.

'What does that entail?' I say.

'It's an overnight train that goes from Penzance, Cornwall, right through to Paddington, Central London. It lets people from the south west commute to the capital for work.'

That actually sounds perfect. Quiet, fast, direct.

'How would that work?' I ask.

'We'd have to be a bit lucky with the times, but this is Sunday night. And I know that on Sunday night, the train makes a stop at Taunton, about fifteen minutes south of here.'

A change in direction to boot. Even better. Amina is playing a blinder.

But… is it a little *too* convenient? Why would she know such a thing… unless she is walking me into a trap?

'How do you know?' I ask, trying to sound nonchalant. I watch her reaction closely.

Amina smirks. 'I told you, when I came over here, being stationed out in the sticks wasn't exactly what I envisaged. It's nice enough and everything, and I'm quite attached to my little home now. But I keep dreaming of getting a big job, in the heart of the action, and if I wanted to get there and keep my house, I'd have to commute. I learned quickly that this would be the best way to do it.'

Fair enough. I can't really argue with that, but it hinges on the believability of her entire story. I'll let it slide for now, but I'm going to keep a close eye on her.

'Can you get us there?'

The radio suddenly increases in volume, making us both jump out of our skins, as a traffic report demands to be heard. Before Amina can respond, we are drowned out.

'Not much to report in terms of traffic through the night. There are still roadworks on the A38 to Taunton and the M5 Junction 28 at Cullompton is down to one lane for scheduled repairs on electronic signs. Avon and

Somerset Constabulary have issued an alert, seeking information on a red Mitsubishi pickup truck in the Exmoor to Bristol area. Anyone with any information is to call the emergency hotline on 0800 444 9999 as soon as possible.'

They are on to us. Doubtlessly on to us. The hairs on the back of my neck stir.

A change of tactics cannot come soon enough. Amina and I exchange wordless, grim, glances, conversation has been rendered superfluous. My pursuers, as ever, are not far behind and they have recruited the general public again to search me out. At least they didn't call me a looter this time.

'We are near Bishop's Lydeard,' Amina says, breaking our silence as the radio returns to its normal hushed volume. 'Taunton is straight down here.'

'How far?'

'Ten minutes or so.'

'When we are five minutes away, let's park up somewhere quiet and abandon the car. Out of interest, how much is it worth?'

'You thinking of making me an offer?'

'I'm thinking in case I have to replace it for you.'

Amina looks at the dashboard. 'This car was my first purchase when I got the job in England. It has… sentimental value.'

'Do your own life and wellbeing carry more sentimental value than this battered old truck?'

She almost smiles. Almost.

I see a sign up ahead for Taunton, harshly illuminated by the Mitsubishi's full beams so that it is only just legible. The road is still quiet, luckily. Prying eyes can pry elsewhere.

A couple more moments drift by with that unspoken potency, activity coiling just around the corner, ready to unravel. I feel charged again by the challenge and the swinging odds. My fever is almost gone, the horrors of the adder venom an ever-distant nightmare, passing further into footnote with every steady heartbeat. Whatever I make of her and her motivations, Amina has done a good job of fixing me up. Surely, if she wanted harm to come my way, she could have got rid of me by now. *Oops, sorry, that wasn't saline in that drip, it was bleach.* Speaking of saline, that stuff is the mutt's nuts. If I was still bouncing from hangover to hangover, a ready supply of this stuff would have made a world of difference. I might not even have got so uppity about saving the country.

Never mind. Soft orange lifts from the gloom ahead, a smudged halo over a settlement beyond. That must be Taunton. Historic Taunton, which I know so little about. I remind myself to read up on this place, if its train station saves our bacon.

Our bacon. I mustn't forget that. One person can blend in, disappear, the training taking over and making the right decisions for you almost without your knowledge. But now I must think for two. And that other person, with the greatest respect to Amina, doesn't know what she's doing. She's game. I'll give her that. But she's not trained.

'You need to listen to me, and do as I say,' I say to her, with a stern edge to my voice.

'Ah. Now you are coming round are you reverting back to your true type? A sort of sexist, nineteen-sixties James Bond character?' A roundabout appears, and she guides us straight over.

'No. I... That's not what I mean. I mean, you have to let me take charge.'

'Fine,' she says. 'We'll do things your way while we are doing the silly running around, jumping and shouting. But when it comes to the toxin, *you* follow *my* lead.'

'Where that shit is concerned, please, knock yourself out. I'd only kill us anyway.'

'You nearly did.' She's right. Any more wear and tear to that earring would surely have resulted in the toxin escaping, inside my pocket. I pat that pocket, where I used to be able feel it, where I used to check for it. Nothing. I know it's in the Tupperware thing, but still...

'How far?' I ask Amina.

'About five minutes now. A mile from the station I think.'

'And you are sure we will make that train?'

'I memorised the times. It will be there in twenty minutes.'

'Then turn off this main road as quickly as you can. There,' I say pointing to a lay-by on the left. 'Head for the gate.'

Along the lay-by, for farm access, is another broad gate. Another gate, another farm, into another field. I pull the canula out of my arm with a sharp jolt and open the door as Amina brings the car to a stop.

I hop out, and approach the gate. Checking again for anonymity, I unlatch a wooden lever, swing it open with a creak and a scrunch, and usher the truck through, while pointing to a spot behind the hedges on the right. Amina follows my lead (as she said she would) and drives gingerly over to the hedge. She douses the engine, and hops out.

'Take everything,' I say when I reach her.

'About five thousand,' she replies taking her bag from the rear seats.

'What?'

'The value of the car. About five thousand.'

'This heap of shit wouldn't fetch five hundred at auction!'

'You asked for its value, to me the car is worth five thousand. And you are getting off lightly there. I didn't want to have to buy a new one. I didn't want to be on the run with a scary amount of chemical weaponry.'

Robbed at toxin-point. I have the money. But my money is finite. I did have £180,000 left from my career in the services, but that was supposed to see me through the next fifteen years. I wasn't expecting any major outlays, like trucks.

'I could always destroy the toxin right here, if you like?' she says, upping the ante.

'No, no, five thousand is fine,' I say, through gritted teeth. 'Unless I find you a suitable replacement.'

'Done,' she says. 'But I get to decide what is suitable or not.'

Consider my balls in a clamp.

'Done,' I say, weakly, and promptly stick the matter at the back of my mind. I'll worry about that later. I get the feeling she'll remind me.

A couple of minutes later, the car is empty, with flames licking the windows inside, as if clawing to get out. Since we are subject to active pursuit, and they know the make and model, I've had to adapt my plan. It will burn up nicely, throughout the course of the night. When it's done, no one will look at that heap and say, '*Oh, there's that red jeep everyone is looking for.*' I'm hoping it will just be looked at as a joyrider's leftovers, and filed accordingly. At the very least, I hope it will buy us some crucial extra hours. We slip out of the gate again, shut it tight behind us, and start walking. I take Amina's hand.

'We need to look as unsuspicious as possible. Right now we are a couple, out for a late stroll,' I say.

'Yeah, we look just super in our shorts and backpacks. A proper pair of happy campers.'

I'm not quite sure what to make of her. She is certainly a firebrand, of sorts. I think, having seen what's beneath the veneer earlier at the lab, when she identified that bloody horrible stuff, that she protects herself with bluster and a hard mental exoskeleton. She comes across as tough, but brittle. Sharp, with apparent virtue. Maybe that is why I find her true intentions hard to read, there is so much to wade through.

'We need to keep the pace up. Ten minutes and we'll be there, and we need to be on that platform, ready to hop on, tickets in hand.'

'The ticket office won't be open, we will have to buy them on the train,' she replies. 'Do you have cash handy?'

'You tell me. Do I have cash handy?' I reply.

'You have about £270 pounds in your wallet.' I'd had a feeling she had been through my things while I was out of it.

'Do I still have £270?'

'What are you asking exactly?'

'You didn't... need it for anything?'

'No, I didn't *need it for anything*.'

'Will that be enough?'

'How would I know?'

'You seem to know everything else about it.'

'That will be fine. We may even be able to get a cabin with that, to keep the toxin safely away from other travellers.'

'They have cabins?'

'So I read.'

The idea of keeping the toxin a substantial distance from anybody else is a good one, even though we both know that if it leaks, nothing will stop it from doing what it does.

However, spending a night alone in close proximity to Amina may be something else entirely. I am an insular soul at the best of times, happy when keeping my own counsel. I haven't slept anywhere near a woman in years, in fact it has been well over a decade now. Not that I am thinking in *those* terms… but I am nervous in the company of women at the best of times, let alone situations that might be subject to the instructions of my enemies…

13.

Get on board. Find an empty cabin. Get a ticket. Play the role. Keep cool.

Taunton is as dead as I've ever seen a place be. Maybe I am not looking in the right places, but at close to 11.30 pm, I am still surprised. I like the idea of places like this, where it feels as if there is an enforced period of quiet, like a curfew. It's as if the town is made to go to sleep, a clockwork calm applied to the people. I can't imagine anything ever going wrong here.

And then there's me, abandoning a car on the cusp of this enclave of rural humanity, carrying a lunchbox full of super-toxin. Wherever I go, bad things seem to follow. I feel guilty for that, not to mention for bringing our cargo into their midst. While the residents of merry little Taunton are safely tucked away in their beds, I am carrying a sample of chemical weaponry under their noses.

Narrow streets, lined with close hedges, guide us into the centre, past beautiful quaint properties that are set back from the road, with names like 'The Old Post Office' and 'Beaver's Barn', some with dimmed reading lamps in second floor windows. As we get to what feels like the middle of Taunton, an assessment I make on seeing what looks like a town hall, a convergence of roads and a heavier smattering of brick-built public buildings, I see that it is not as dead as I thought. A couple of pubs are shooing out their last drinkers, heaving them out into the street and making them somebody else's responsibility. Once despatched, the small groups congregate in pools of halogen from the street lamps, like bloated moths, and say throaty goodbyes or work out what to do next.

'Station is next left,' Amina says, breaking the silence we have come to adopt as our own. The weight of what we are doing seems to press on us in such a way that sustained conversation is impossible. On the walk we have exchanged snippets of chat, but our words soon gave way to the gravity of our task.

We step up a slight incline, to the archway of the station, and we pass under the familiar red logo of UK train stations. The station is, true to Amina's words, deserted. She knows where she is going, and marches ahead. We are on a platform before we know it, alone. Nobody else seems to be wanting the Night Riviera to Paddington.

'Have we missed it?' I ask.

Amina simply points down the tracks. I follow her finger with my eyes, and see the unmistakable shape of an approaching train, albeit shrouded in darkness. The burning eyes at the front, the whisper of a snake-like body slithering after the head. I shudder without really knowing why, and then I remember the adder. What a *fucker*...

But I'm secretly pleased. We have done well here. I watch Amina as the train comes closer, and a quiet satisfaction has animated her features. It might be happiness at pulling her weight, or delight that she is finally going to make this, a journey that she has thought so often about. Fantasising about this journey for so long appears to have eroded her conviction that it might actually happen. Yet here she is, on the platform at Taunton station, waving in that elusive train to London.

I assess the train as it approaches. Five cars. The front two cars are darker than the last three, and through the windows I can see the seats, peppered with weary faces. It is not very busy, which is again something to be grateful for. The train pulls to a stop and Amina points to the second car.

'Cabins this way,' she says. I follow her up the step onto the train, to be confronted with a ticket inspector standing right in front, expectantly, her open face waiting for one of us to furnish her with pre-paids.

'Hello,' I say, grinning like an idiot. 'Can we...'

Amina bursts into conversation, like a cup of words overflowing and spilling right down the sides, pooling at the ticket inspector's feet. 'I hope it's OK, but it is our dream to go on the sleeper. We decided last minute that we wanted a trip to London; it's an anniversary thing, and the sleeper just seems so romantic and exciting. I didn't know they did anything like this anymore, but we don't have a ticket, and... Please, please, my husband has cash, can we go to London with you?'

What a performance. She has even ramped her accent up, let it overtake her speech a little, to give her even more sweetness and innocence. She comes across as someone who, in unfamiliar territory, has made a genuine mistake and got a bit excited, but it's all in jest and *if it isn't too much troubl*e... She mentioned marriage and I look down at her left hand. She has even slipped one of her gold bands onto her ring finger, just to sell her little story.

The inspector's face seems to crumple at the corners, apology beginning to creak through.

'I'm sorry, we don't usually accept passengers without a ticket at this time of night,' she says.

'We have cash, please! And if you put us in a cabin, we would be out of the way, you wouldn't hear from us again! We'll be good as gold!' Amina gushes.

The inspector lets her kindness show, and her features relax. 'Anniversary, you say?'

'Three years,' replies Amina, quick as a flash.

'Leather,' says the inspector, misty-eyed.

'Excuse me?'

'That's the traditional gift for the third wedding anniversary. First is cotton, second is paper, third is leather.'

I barely suppress an eye roll, hoping this exchange will fizzle and we can batten down the hatches.

'Of course, leather,' Amina giggles, then turns to me. 'I forgot all about that!'

I simply smile and shrug, as if to say *'Hey, I'm just a simple husband! What do I know!?'*

'We have two cabins empty right at the front of the train. Pick one, be quiet, and don't let me down.'

Amina actually hugs the inspector, who hugs her back. They could have known each other for years, by the looks of things. 'Thank you! Thank you so much! What do we owe?'

'Away with you. Go. Now!' says the inspector, shooing us along with a flick of both hands. We smile, thank her profusely and sneak down the corridor to the left, along the second car.

I'm genuinely struck by her kindness, not to mention her apparent willingness to bend the rules if she feels like it. So the romantic, storybook impression I got of the sleeper was pretty accurate. It's a track-bound jam jar of good feelings, bygone times, smiles and secrets, swishing its way through England's quiet villages, right to the heart to of the Big Smoke.

The train begins to move, and I motion Amina to the door at the furthest end of the corridor, which opens without problem. As I swing the door open, I am met by darkness, except for the winking cats' eyes of glinting surfaces from within. Reaching around the door frame, I find a light-switch, which douses the room in cold, clinical, unfriendly tungsten light, revealing that the cabin contains a single cot bed, next to a basic wash basin, and a side table, underneath which there is a luggage store.

'The Ritz on iron wheels,' says Amina, as she shuts the door behind her.

And that is when I spring into cold, harsh action. I hate myself for doing it, but I act without hesitation or compromise. I start by wordlessly throwing Amina onto the bed, her surprise rendering her limp, with no hint of resistance.

I have listened for sirens all the way in, and heard none. It alarms me. Aside from the radio update, urging the public to watch out for Amina's vehicle, there has been no sign of pursuit. They were dogged and dedicated before, pushing me to my limits, but now... nothing.

It doesn't feel right at all.

I desperately want to take this game girl at face value, but I haven't got this far in life, survived the scrapes I have survived, by presuming everyone's innocence. If she wants to go further in this game, she will have to sing for her supper.

I run the tap, creating a full noisy stream that will serve two purposes. It will mask the sound of the horrible deed I am about to undertake, while at the same time giving me one half of a cynical weapon with which to prise out the truth of Amina's intentions.

I sit on her chest, pinning her down, and she utters something in an Eastern European language that I don't understand. Even though it is dark, I see her fear begin to shine through, and her eyes brim with tears. *No turning back now, Ben.* Even though I used to be a sucker for puppy dog eyes. I pin both her hands behind her head, and lean in close.

'I've been wondering whether I should be trusting you. Ever since I woke up, my pursuers have vanished, it's almost as if they didn't need to look for me anymore. And that's where you come in, Dr Ridgewell. A government employee, in a crooked government. What did they offer you? No, actually, what did they *promise* you?'

I put a hand over Amina's mouth to stop the frothing words of another tongue from spraying out at me.

'Did they promise you world peace? Did they promise they'd use that diabolical substance for the good of mankind? For the good of the country?'

I feel a hot pinch in the middle of the hand that is over her mouth, and I pull away subconsciously. Jesus, she is a fighter. If it weren't for the thrashing beneath my body weight, I'd sure have got it now that she has nipped a chunk from my finger.

'Fuck you and your country,' she lashes out, her accent the strongest I've heard it, vowels stretched angrily and harsher consonants rasped. I've seen this happen many times, people reverting to a previous or reset state under intense stress. It's as if the mind fights the stress by reacting with a version that is less polished but more natural. Just by the bed, on the opposite side to the sink, is a small side table furnished with a couple of face towels, two disposable toothbrushes and two plastic tumblers. I dig the fingers of my left hand into Amina's clavicle, just at the top of her chest, gripping the bone through her jumper like a handle on a climbing wall. The more I squeeze my fingers behind the bone, the more the pressure point is agonised. It cuts the thrashing down to a contorted spasm, and I have her locked in place. Reaching to the table, I take a flannel and douse it in the flowing water, drenching it thoroughly, while never loosening my grip on Amina.

'I want the truth,' I say, 'and one way or another, I am going to get it.'

She can barely move or speak, the pressure grip combined with my body weight providing all the containment necessary. She looks stuck, weak and defeated, as I put the soaking flannel over her whole face, mouth included.

'I need to know if I'm safe with you,' I say. 'I want to know if I can trust you.'

And with that, I fill one of the tumblers and pour its contents over her face, drenching the flannel again. It is a despicable act, horrible to the core, and one that is as controversial as it is useful. There is a reason why the UK and US armed forces used water-boarding during the Iraq and Afghan wars. It is feared, despicable and bloody good at getting answers.

'You can't last long, with me doing this,' I say, slowing the stream to a dribble, but then increasing the flow again. I pull the flannel away briskly, and she gasps in my face, lunging for air. 'Breathe, breathe. That is what drowning feels like.'

And I replace the flannel, and pour more water down onto her face. The words I have just uttered sicken me. I didn't need exhaustion or fever to encounter a grotesque vile beast — there has been one dwelling in my own character all this time. The guilt within me is swelling with the urgent momentum of a tornado, taking a powerful hold inside me, but I must keep going. Who knows how many lives I might save if I get this right? Britain *needs* me to be a bastard, here.

She writhes, and I wait until I can't take it anymore, before pulling the flannel away.

'Don't make me do it again,' I tell her.

She breathes, weaker again, and I can feel her body loosen beneath mine. She is beaten, the fire in her put out. I let her catch her breath, and she speaks in a tiny, cracked voice.

'Kosovo. I'm from Kosovo.'

That rings a bell, but only in terms of current affairs. I know that at the very end of the last century, Kosovo was a nation torn by violence and war.

'What difference does that make?' I ask.

'You talk about allegiance to your country; it seems to be the main thing that keeps you breathing. I have no allegiance to England at all, but I am grateful.'

I fall silent but hold her firmly. Something doesn't feel right. Her hair, now slick with water, licks over her eyes — those imploring, vast, pleading eyes.

'You are a war man. It is your character. It's so obvious. You are consumed by fulfilling orders at whatever cost, while what's left of you is twisted by the ordeal of doing exactly that. You think I don't understand what is at stake here, but I know of war. I know exactly what it is like to be in conflict. Conflict was thrust upon me. You *choose* conflict, because you know no other way.'

'I do!' I interrupt, but I can't help beginning to feel like the worst human being alive. It seems I have misjudged this situation terribly.

184

'You know nothing! You left your pretty little England to seek blood. Well, blood came to my front door and took everything I love. I came to England for escape!'

I feel my grip releasing slightly, but I still stay on top of her, however inappropriate that feels.

'I was sixteen in 1998. I was good in school, I was happy, I had good friends. I had a family, my mother, father and two brothers, aunts, uncles, a couple of grandparents. Yugoslav forces ripped us from our homes and made us refugees, while the rest of the world was trying to decide what to do with us, with each suggestion as violent as the last.

'But we were down there on the ground, moving from place to place, hoping that whatever the self-appointed police forces of the world decided to do, we wouldn't be anywhere near it. You cannot imagine what that was like. But it was our togetherness that was our downfall, and we made ourselves a target. We always had so much to lose, in our affection for each other.

'Serb militia caught us. My brothers' throats were cut in front of my parents, and my parents' throats cut in front of my grandparents, before the militia got bored and shot them just to shut them up. And I was kept as a plaything, a 16-year-old toy. I was passed from pillar to post, having watched my family bleed into the mud. So don't tell me I have any secret motives here, or desire to involve myself with corrupt government, villains and their greed. It was the greed of such men that took everything I held dear.'

I am dumbstruck. I can't even look at her. Some might argue that I have just been fed a perfectly measured depth charge of emotional blackmail. But the tears streaming onto the pillow, the shake of her voice, the vehemence of her words, all scream at me that she has just told me the truth.

And all I can do is lower myself to lie next to her, and pull her into me. She doesn't cry, or resist, or lean close. She just lets it happen. I can tell that, in so many ways, she is back there, in the horrors of the Kosovan War, in 1999, and I am just another man forcing himself upon her against her will. She is resigned to the horror of it, watching misty-eyed while acknowledging that everything is lost.

I whisper 'I am sorry.'

All I want to do is hold her; to transport her from the memories I have so terribly dragged up, from the awful act I have committed against her. I will hold her until morning if she will let me, I will hold her all the way to Paddington.

14.

Monday

I sleep the sleep of a man who knows he has done wrong. I sleep a sleep that is deep, yet forced, unbroken yet tormented, as my subconscious pretends that what I did hasn't happened at all. And if it did somehow happen, surely it is not time yet to wake and face it.

I stir, but don't open my eyes. I am almost too ashamed to do so. I don't want to see Amina looking at me, all her faith in me gone, replaced by contempt and begrudging obligation. So I lie there, barely moving, while I come round, and gear up to confront what has happened.

I know why I slept as soundly as I did. I saw the naked truth of Amina's character; I know now what has made her who she is. And she is not someone to be feared. She is someone to be trusted, respected and protected. For all that she has been through, for being the last person who would do me wrong in my sleep. And my subconscious took advantage of that, letting me use the time spent next to this emotionally wounded woman, to get some proper sleep.

It seems that even my subconscious is a proper bastard.

As my senses come back to me, one at a time, I deduce that the train is stationary, and that I am not touching anybody. Amina is out of the bed, and with that realisation I crack open my eyes.

Immediately I see that the cabin is flooded with soft daylight, and facing out of the window, her arms folded and her hair ponytailed, stands Amina.

There is defiance in her posture, as well as reflection. I can't see her face.

'I am so sorry,' I say, my words coming out in that fractured, dying-frog tone they always have for the first utterance of the day. It makes me sound somehow smug and complacent, and I feel even more like a complete shit. 'I wish for all the world that I could undo what I did.'

She turns to me, her eyes with that familiar glassy acceptance, and I know her trust in me has been utterly extinguished, along with every fragment of respect. I sit up, my body aching like a marathon runner's as the muscle fatigue of the exertions of the last few days begins to settle in.

'You are correct in everything you said about me. I am a man warped by his experiences. You are absolutely right when you say I know no different. You are right when you say I know no other way. I wish I wasn't the way I am, and I know it is my choices that led me here.'

She watches me, her hands folded, her face a mask of detached dignity. My words don't seem to enter her head, and I'm sure that even if they do, they will make no difference. But I can't help but try.

'I promise,' I say, 'that I will do anything and everything I can to protect you in whatever is to come, and I will never doubt your intentions again. I need your help, and I will never abuse your trust again. I promise you.'

I could ask for forgiveness, but I don't want it. People who earn people's trust and then torture them when their guard is down, don't generally deserve too much by way of forgiveness. I can't read her, and she seems to look clear through me. I have hurt her so deeply that I am nothing anymore, just another man who did what he liked with her. She seems to be in full business mode, and we are way past pleasantries. The playfulness, that mischief of character, is long gone, and I know it was me that flushed it out of her... by bloody water-boarding her last night.

In a dull voice, devoid of spirit, she tells me, 'We are in London. I think we need to get going.'

I want to grab her, apologise until she shows me something of the old Amina, but hate for myself gets in the way. I have always been able to make the hard decisions, but I have always felt that my judgement is shrewd enough to guide me through those decisions with a steady, just hand. How my judgement has failed me on this one...

I get out of bed and wash in the sink, using the flannel from the night before. It almost feels symbolic — as though I am foolishly trying to wash away my sins with the very tool that created them in the first place. When clean, I grab the freshest clothes from my pack and dress quickly. I decide that a business-like approach is best at this point, to bring the focus back onto our objective and to draw attention away from the elephant in the room.

'What time is it?'

'Ten past six,' she replies, as I notice that she too has changed, into a different sweater and jeans. I would ask if she's ready but I already sense that she is. I bet she can't wait to get out of this infernal cabin.

'And we are in Paddington? Did I remember that correctly?' I have remembered just fine, but I want to keep her thoughts on other things.

'Yes, that's right.' Her bags are by the door, as if a porter might come and take them away at any minute.

'Good. We did well in making it to the capital. That plane crash really feels like ages ago now,' I say, my tone almost apologetic for bothering her with such pointless small talk. 'Like I said yesterday, I think we should head to somewhere within striking distance of Westminster, since that seems to be where our enemies are. And I need to contact my friend again. Let's get a black cab and head to a hotel near there.'

She gives a single nod.

'Is the cargo still OK?' I ask.

'Yes, I've checked it twice.'

'Good. Then let's get moving.'

I open the cabin door, checking each way along the corridor. The morning light is flooding in through the open station roof, high up beyond the train car windows. I walk to the door we entered through last night, with Amina keeping pace just behind. Glancing into the next car, I see people still asleep in their seats. They must let you finish resting before turfing you off. One click of the green door release, and we are out into the brisk, oiled air of a train station at dawn.

I don't know what to expect here, and I feel as though we have just entered the lions' den. We start walking down the platform to the main body of the station, which resembles a huge, arc-shaped aerodrome, as if humans have decided to fashion it out of a discarded tin can left by giant benefactors. I see people ahead and inspectors by the main glass doors. They are already looking at us.

If they want to check our tickets, we will be in a spot. Questions will be asked, time will be taken, identities will be scrutinised. I don't fancy that. We need a diversion, and we are getting closer.

I grab Amina's hand, hoping to rely on that united front of bumbling, anniversary idiots which got us so far yesterday, but she pulls away quickly. I try again, same result.

'Don't,' she says, sharply. I look to the door, and see that the inspector has witnessed all of this, and now looks at us with eyebrows raised, ever so delicately. I shrug openly and give him that withered, reluctant smile that a man gives another man and which asks, *'What can you do?'* He smiles back a pursed grin of understanding, and waves us both through.

I almost smile for real.

'The sign says there's a taxi rank over this way,' Amina says, one step ahead of me now. I follow her lead, noticing that I have to quicken to keep pace with her. There is a determination to her, an embedded well of resolve, that shows me exactly how this woman was capable of escaping the grasp of her captors and making it across Europe to the UK, then carving out a new life for herself here. I find myself admiring her.

But before long, I am distracted by an annoying feeling of disquiet.

There is a presence here, imperceptible to anyone but myself, and as we move through the ever-growing crowds, I feel eyes upon me. I look to the newspaper stands, the people on their way to platforms and ticket offices, but nothing seems out of place. But the itch remains, coming from… *there*.

By the coffee vendors, standing over to my eleven o'clock. Two policemen, staring right at me, their eyes fixed, locked onto me from beneath the peaks of their hats. I look away again, take a few more strides, and check once more.

I am still the only thing they are interested in. *Shit*. And thanks to my ever-shifting perspective, I can see another man with them, now. Smaller, rounder, balder, vacuum-packed into a trench-coat. *No, it can't be.*

Flanked by two of the Met Police's finest, stands Lloyd Weathers, MP.

Like a small child who has been stopped outside a sweet shop with his pockets full of stolen gobstoppers, I sense that I have been caught red-handed. Weathers' eyes widen in recognition and indignation. I tense, ready to bolt.

'Amina...' I say, but as I do, Weathers looks away. His gaze drifts off down the platforms. The coppers still eye me, but the corrupt man between them looks anywhere but at me.

'What?' says Amina.

'Nothing,' I say, puzzled. I keep my head down, eyes front and follow Amina out of the wide station exit, onto the street. At the cab rank, I bundle Amina quickly into the first waiting car, while trying not to look back at Weathers. *He saw me, right? He knew it was me, surely...*

'Where to, guv?' the taxi driver asks, true to the London cabbie stereotype. I can't really see him from the back seat, apart from the long grey hair that tumbles greasily down the back of his head from beneath a flat tweed cap. Steel blue eyes lined with deep, crinkly crow's feet glance back at me from the rear-view mirror.

Amazed that I am even in the taxi, having just stared my pursuer in the eye, I stutter.

'It's our anniversary... I... we... want to do something special.'

I feel Amina looking at me warily. She has seen all sides to me, apart from this, the one that is flustered and confused. It is dawning on me that they have let me go. They know exactly where I am, they know I'm here, and by coming to this city I have played right into their hands. They have us. And if they have us, they have the toxin.

But why not take us in? Why look me in the eye, and let us go?

The driver's cockney tones pull my attention back to the taxi.

'*Something special* is kind of broad, mate. What kind of special are we talking about?'

'A hotel near Westminster,' interrupts Amina.

The driver locks the taxi into gear, the engine lurching the vehicle forward gradually to join the morning rush. 'Which one?'

Is this driver in on it? Is he going to report our whereabouts to the powers that be?

I'm paranoid. For the first time in my life that I can think of, I am paranoid. It's what put me more than half-way to killing Amina last night, and makes me want to reach over the seats now to twist this taxi driver's ear until he tells me the truth.

But I mustn't forget what brought me here. It has been, without doubt, a hell of a few days. I have been malnourished and exhausted, I'm still on the immediate comedown from a nasty snake bite, and ensuing fever. I glance down at my arm, and admire the neat dressing that covers the carefully cleaned bite marks. Guilt creeps up on me again. Amina patched me up, and what did I do to repay her?

There she is, sitting next to me, looking out of the window at the city waking up. The city that she was determined one day to visit, and prosper in. I'm sure this isn't how she imagined it.

Never mind. *Think forward, Ben. Think smarter, not harder. Considering what you've been through, no wonder your head is fucked.*

194

'Where would you recommend?' I ask.

'Well, it depends on the state of your wallet for a start. You can have a special night in the bloody Dorchester, but special can also be the Holiday Inn. Which kind of special do you want?'

'Any near Westminster?'

'Does it *have* to be Westminster? It's a big city, guv...'

'Westminster is fine. Most of what we wanted to do is round that area.'

The driver cackles the throaty, wet cough of a serial smoker, which finishes with a laugh.

'Ha, tourists. No offence. It just never ceases to amaze me that you all come here looking for a bit of a glimpse into the fabled histories of a few crusty old buildings, when there is oodles of history crawling out of every alleyway, every river bend, every rooftop. You just have to get out there.'

I don't doubt it, and I know from personal experience that there is far more to London than meets the eye. I was on the banks of the Thames when I was framed and arrested. I glance out of the window, watching a lazy drizzle blend the hues of the street into an ever-refreshing watercolour.

I remember that out there, somewhere, is Terry Masters. He can sit on his throne, for now... But before long, I will come back here. And London will give up its secret, criminal monarch. And it won't be me on the run on these streets. When I'm done with him, Masters will wish I'd killed him three years ago. I'll make him kneel in front of me, and I will make an example of him.

'How about,' begins the driver, 'I take you somewhere near Westminster with a couple of choices, and you can make your mind up from there? The bend of the river a bit further round from the Houses of Parliament has two hotels next to each other, a Holiday Inn and The Savoy. The ridiculous or the sublime. Take your pick.'

I've heard of The Savoy. 'That sounds good. Let's go with that, thanks.'

'Gotcha.'

A quiet silence beds in, Amina and I lost in our own thoughts, as the taxi driver chats amiably to himself, probably wondering why on earth the odd couple in the back of his cab are together.

If only he knew.

Actually, there's a strong possibility that he just might.

15.

The cab pulls out from a T-junction, and aligns itself with the River Thames, travelling slowly. Amina looks across me, out of the window, and I can almost feel her catch her breath. The London Eye is opposite, glistening clean, high and bright in the broadening sunlight. And below it, a short way off down the river, is the spot where I was captured. The rusted cargo vessel they found me in is long gone, presumably carted away by the authorities when they found out it had become a plaything and meeting place for those in the underbelly of their city.

After a few hundred yards of slow crawl, the taxi takes a right through a narrow street, then pulls into the thicker traffic of The Strand, a fact highlighted to me by the street sign whizzing past on the corner building. The cab comes to a stop almost immediately.

We hop out into the noisy bustle of the main road, which is in the laborious early stages of the daily commute, and I watch the driver for any suggestion that he is in cahoots with those hunting us and hunting Apex. But I doubt it matters. Weathers knows we are here, and it is up to us to sort out a strategy, to bring a bit of security and secrecy to our movements.

Seagulls caw high above, as we drag our bags from the seat. I keep my eyes firmly on Amina's bag, hoping the toxin inside is still safe and intact. It feels terrifying to transport it this way, when one jarring impact could spill the contents and decimate a significant chunk of the city's population. It is a nasty risk, bringing the toxin with us here, even though we had no choice. The stakes are so high. There is so much more human life at risk.

I pay the driver and catch Amina staring at The Savoy's grand entrance, the art deco edifice towering grandly. It is a beautiful building, a monument to Britain's historical opulence and its place in the international landscape of bygone times. A stone bastion of dignity, scale, and the promise of more. It is from an era long committed to the past, yet still proud and relevant. I immediately love it.

Nevertheless, I usher Amina over to the left of The Savoy where the Holiday Inn sits, almost deflated, in its shadow. I can feel Amina deflated with it. As we dodge beeping cars that are racing to avoid the congestion charges payable from seven o'clock each morning, I scan for anything out of the ordinary. My eyes wander, we touch the pavement, and just as everything seems to be in order, I catch him. *There*, in the reflection of the front window of an upmarket delicatessen. Having left us, the taxi driver has pulled up about 100 yards down the street and is craning back to watch us. To see which hotel we enter, I bet.

Son of a bitch.

Good job I'm a step ahead, but I need to watch that step. This town is filled with watching eyes.

We breeze into the lobby of the Holiday Inn, which is already pretty busy given the earliness of the hour, and I book a room for the night under my false identity, Sean Miller, using the ID and credit card associated with that name. Amina wanders from my side to the vending machines in the corner of the lobby, but I call her back over. She needs to stay close, and I try to tell her so with the tone of my call.

The charming receptionist hands me a key card in a little paper wallet that has a room number on it. I thank him, and press the lift call button with my finger shielded by the sleeve of my hoodie. I don't think we have much time, and when Amina rejoins me, I fill her in.

'Don't touch anything, and be ready to move,' I instruct her. She says nothing.

'It's a beautiful part of the city,' I say, still hoping to warm her a little. She surprises me with a murmured reply.

'I once read that the Thames in summer sunshine is a sight to behold. Whoever said that wasn't lying.'

I smile. After a bump and a slight jump in the pit of my stomach as we rise, the lift stops at our third floor destination, and as we step out, I tell her to 'wait by the stairs', which are right next to the lift entrances. Jogging,

I reach our room, 3029, in five seconds, and once again using my sleeved fingers, open it up and toss the key inside, before running back to Amina.

'Go, go' I say, and we start hopping down the stairs two at a time.

'What did you do?' Amina asks.

'Left a trail with a dead end.'

We reach the ground floor, and pause before re-entering the lobby.

'We need another exit. We can't go out the front,' I say. 'I saw the café over to the left of the lobby. When we go out there, go straight to it. Don't look at reception. Don't look at the front door. Just head down, into the café.'

She nods.

'Let's go,' I say, and plough through the door. Three steps across the small lobby, through the open door of the café... and *in*. And just as I hoped, at the far end, is a smokers' exit. I try to take Amina's hand yet again, and this time she lets me.

The patrons of the café are few and far between, and none look up. I can't see any staff, which works well for us, and we head out into the side street. I have already worked out as that it is the recessed main entrance to The Savoy, pulled back from the street, fronted by an impressive ornate awning over tarmac, presumably to give sufficient turning circles for the odd Rolls Royce. A hop, skip and a jump across the car port, through grand revolving doors, and we are through, into The Savoy's lobby.

The change of setting hits us immediately. The cool bite of the world outside makes way for a lavishly serene enclave, rich wooden walls above a black and white chessboard-tiled floor, the air laced delicately with notes of cinnamon and fresh linen. The taxi-driver wasn't messing around when he said it was sublime. I feel enriched and enlivened just by being here. I hope Amina does, too.

There is a convenience to us stopping here, since it allows me to keep tabs on the misguided surveillance operation which is sure to begin soon, and will focus on the Holiday Inn. At the same time, I want to make a gesture of apology to Amina, and give her a taste of the life she has dreamt about. It's the least I can do to atone for what I did, the harm that I have placed her in the way of. At least it's *something*.

We walk through the room with our jaws slack, soaking up the atmosphere. There are gold-framed pictures on the walls, and glass cases within the oak cladding contain artefacts and sculptures of many eras and styles. I wouldn't mind some extended time here, just in this lobby, to sate my curiosity.

'May I help you with your bags, madam?' a voice asks, and a porter emerges from one of the side rooms, approaching us with well-practiced grace. Amina looks at me.

'No, thank you,' I say, in a tone that offers no compromise.

'Of course, sir,' says the butler, indicating a short flight of wide stairs. 'This way.'

Once up the stairs, we are presented with a long wooden reception desk. A smiling lady is there to great us.

'Welcome to The Savoy', says the lady, teeth gleaming.

'Thank you,' I reply.

'Do you have a reservation?'

'No, I'm afraid we are here as a spur of the moment thing. I was wondering… do you have a suite available?' I know that a suite will have two rooms with an adjacent living area, and while it will set me back an arm and a leg, it will give myself and Amina the perfect place in which to prepare and plan. What is more, I'm quite sure Amina doesn't fancy sharing a room with me again.

'I can look into it, certainly. How many nights?'

'Just the one, please.'

'That's usually something we can do. Just give me a moment.' The lady begins click-clacking on a nearby computer, and I look to Amina. 'Will this be OK?' I ask.

She actually looks at me, for what feels like the first time this morning. 'Yes,' she whispers, glancing away quickly. I can tell that she's surprised. Good. And good for her.

The lady returns.

'We do indeed have a suite for tonight, no problem. The rate is £1,499 per night. Would you like to place a credit card on file?'

I almost gulp involuntarily at hearing the price, much as Bugs Bunny does in old Warner Brothers cartoons. 'No, I'm… I'm more of a cash man,' I say, shuffling my backpack as if to suggest that it is stuffed to the clasps with pressed bank notes. She smiles, as if she has seen such types of customer before. 'I have a bit of banking to do while I'm here. May I settle the balance with you when we check out tomorrow?'

'Of course. Would you like me to arrange breakfast?'

I'm familiar with this line of questioning, plus I look like I've been rolling about on a dirty beach, so to smooth things over I pull a couple of twenties from my pocket, along with a fictional Sean Miller's ID, and place them on the counter. 'That will be all, thank you,' I say.

'Of course, sir,' she says, while swapping the bank notes for a couple of key cards with a sleight of hand that would make a magician quiver. God knows the kind of clientele they're used to dealing with, but this is different gravy to most. I smile, take the cards, and grab Amina's hand. Thankfully, she lets me.

I don't think I'm doing too badly this morning.

16.

Moments later, we are padding around barefoot in a suite so lush, lavish and lovely that it would make Liberace blush. Three of last night's train cabins could fit into the decorative foyer alone. Amina had slipped her shoes off at the door, and I, eager to both appease and please, followed suit.

When the porter left, I lock the door behind us, and even prop a nearby walnut chair under the handle, just to be sure. Amina surveys the main body of the suite in quiet awe. It is an Edwardian masterpiece. I feel extremely out of place being here, in my hoodie and board shorts. Oh yeah, and carrying a box of modified super-toxin. Mustn't forget *that*.

My accomplice seems to float from room to opulent room, walking with a half-smile, taking in every polished, spotless detail. The immaculate ivory architraves, the vast beds with deep silken bedding, the fresh white roses adorning every side table. I hope she likes it.

In time, she returns to the main living space. This adjoins the two bedrooms and contains a couple of low chesterfield sofas, a red chaise longue that could be from a museum and a coffee table so slickly polished that I could play air hockey on it. I stand looking out of the window, over a shallow line of treetops, at the Thames. Once again, I am faced with the London Eye, the rushing water, and the exact spot I was arrested on. It's as if the setting has been chosen to keep me grounded.

She stands next to me, and waits.

'Please pick a room,' I say. 'We'll only be here for tonight, so please enjoy it. I don't think I could afford two nights, so I'll try to get everything done today. Please stay here until we decide otherwise. I'll leave you some cash, so please order room service, and... Whatever you want. The point is.... I know I can't make up for what I did last night, but... well, I hope this can be a start. I hope that in some way I can give you a little of that London dream you always had.'

She remains silent, so I head for the bags on the chaise longue, intending to leave her to it.

'Thank you,' she says.

I look at her, and see that she is looking at me in the eye for the first time since last night. She looks wounded, but gracious. And beautiful. Her iciness has warmed by a degree or two, and her shoulders have loosened their tension. That broken nose has become all the more endearing, yet still painful, to look at, a reminder of the vulnerability I took advantage of. I find myself wanting to go to her, to hold her, to take back what I did to her with the power of my touch.

But I'm still appalled at myself. Her words last night, the accusation that I'm nothing more than a 'war man', echo shamefully in my head. She is right. I'm the wrong instrument. It would be like trying to flip a pancake with a can-opener instead of a spatula. All I can do is bow, meekly.

'You're welcome,' I say, as I reach into my bag to pull out my phone. 'I need to go out, to find somewhere that lets me watch the Holiday Inn, see who they have sent after us.'

The suite's phone rings, an old traditional trill, splitting the atmosphere in two. Nobody, apart from the receptionist, and the porter, whom I should, perhaps, have tipped, knows that we are here. I intend to let Jeremiah know, when I have established the lay of the land here, but I haven't got round to that yet. Amina and I exchange questioning looks. It takes me a moment or two to find the phone. It's there, back in the foyer, on a stout dresser.

'Yes?' I say tentatively.

'Hello there, my friend,' a warm male voice intones. 'I know that you may be alarmed by this call, but please don't be. My name is William Grosvenor, and I am a big admirer of your work. This call isn't really the place to go into detail, but if you would be good enough to meet me downstairs, where I presently have a table in the main restaurant, for a coffee and a bite to eat, I'd love a chat with you. You have nothing to fear from me, nor does your lovely friend.'

I look at Amina as he mentions her, and as I do this she somehow understands how far from being alone in this city we are. Her eyes flash fear and she disappears into the suite.

Our bags have only been set down for two minutes before someone reared up to say hello.

'I'm buying of course,' the man calling himself Grosvenor says, 'and I assure you that I mean you no harm whatsoever. You are suddenly a very important man, in what seems an unenviable position. I believe I can help you, and if you'll give me just the time it takes to drink a coffee, I'd love to talk it through with you.'

I don't know what to say. I'm a man of action, not verbal negotiation, and I have a strong dislike of fancy coffees. What does this Grosvenor man want, and how the hell does he know we are here?

'What guarantees can you give me?' I ask.

'I can guarantee very little, in fact all I can do is promise that I have at heart only the very best interests of yourself, your friend and this country.'

'I've come across many people recently who'd say the same thing. If, for a single second, I come to doubt that you are acting from those same motives, I won't hesitate to end our conversation in a way that will be most unfavourable to *your* interests. Understood?'

'I don't doubt that for a second. Can I send anything up for your friend? On me of course?'

'That might go down well-'

'A Full English,' interjects Amina, who is now on the same phone line. She must have sneaked to one of the bedrooms and picked up an extension phone. 'With tea and brown toast.'

'Of course, my dear,' replies Grosvenor. 'English breakfast tea, or does something else take your fancy?'

'That's fine, thank you, Mr Grosvenor,' she replies.

'Please, call me William.'

I hang up. Take a deep breath, then pick up again, listening to the silence.

'Amina?' I say, hoping that she is still holding the phone in the bedroom.

'Yes?'

'I'm nipping down for a minute. If anyone other than a porter appears at the door with a Full English, don't you open it.'

'OK,' she says.

I hang up again, and head for the door. I'm glad someone else is picking up the breakfast tab. I've got a feeling our short stay at The Savoy will be a costly one, in many more ways than the merely financial.

*

The Savoy's main restaurant is what I expected and more. And just as I cross the threshold, I am accosted by a penguin-suited jobsworth who actually puts a hand on my chest and says: 'Reservation?'. My synapses fire and I fight an urge to snap his arm at the elbow joint and hand his flopping limb back to him, but before I can, a familiar voice interjects.

'Ah, my guest,' says Grosvenor, who appears at my side. He is a tall, graceful man with neat grey hair and wears a slate-coloured, three piece suit. His eyes flare light blue and his face carries the austere cheekbones, giving him an aristocratic air. He moves with purpose. I am very sure that he is ex-military, judging by the width of his shoulders and the way in which he sets them back to push his chest out. He is aged around 65, and he looks like the man every single one of my superiors hoped they would become in their later years. He shakes my hand firmly, and looks at me directly.

'I understand your mistrust, but for what it is worth, I should like to thank you for what you are doing on behalf of... well, I'd like to say the United Kingdom, but we both know that even the United Kingdom's intentions regarding this matter seem a little… muddy.'

I don't know how to answer, worried that anything I say will incriminate me, betray my identity, my activities and my history to... to whom? I don't know. I take the bull by the horns, as Grosvenor guides me to a table by the window.

'Who are you?' I ask.

'William Grosvenor. Simply put, I work for the British Government, without portfolio.'

'What does that mean?' I ask, taking a seat, while penguin-boy reappears to drape a napkin across my lap.

'I am a cabinet minister, working directly alongside the other cabinet ministers, on behalf of the PM.'

Shit me. 'I've never heard of you,' I say.

'Well, that means I'm doing my job just fine,' Grosvenor says, snapping open a thin menu. 'I'd love to find out what's good here, but an educated guess would surmise that all of it is.'

'What is *without portfolio*?'

'Those ministers in the cabinet all have titles specifying their roles. Secretary of State for Health, Work and Pensions, Communities and Local Government etc., Chancellor of the Exchequer, Lord Chancellor and so forth. And there are a couple of us, of much lower profile and out of the public eye, who are cabinet ministers without portfolio. We are appointed either by the PM, or as in my case, Her Majesty, and our role is to oversee and advise. For right or wrong, it is viewed that us non-portfolio types are worldly-wise and trustworthy, and we are appointed to assist the Government using those attributes.'

'So you are… what? The Prime Minister's agony aunt?'

'It sometimes goes a little like that, yes. Coffee, smoked mackerel, with a poached egg, please. Oh, and a round of brown toast.'

I almost think Grosvenor is directing his order at me, but penguin-boy is back again with a pad and pen. Silence falls, which I infer that I am to fill.

'I'll take the same please,' I say, 'with some bacon. A lot of bacon. And brown sauce.'

'A Savoy surf and turf. I like it,' smiles Grosvenor. 'So, not wishing to waste your time, I'll press on.'

I look him squarely in the face. He comes across as a man I can trust, but I must remain wary. I have an infernal problem with father figures and leaders, which has dumped me in the shit more times than I can remember. There is simply too much at stake here, for any of that nonsense.

'What do you know?' I ask.

'I know you've had a very eventful few days, and that there are many people interested in that which you are carrying.'

'Do you know what it is?'

'The intelligence networks call it Apex, and it is supposed to be utterly horrible.'

'Do you know who *I* am?' I ask, narrowing my eyes. I am frightened of the answer to this question. 'I have no clue at all, and no one had heard of you until just a few days ago. One thing I *do* know is that you are *not* Sean Miller.' He smiles, this time with understanding.

'You are right. I am not Sean Miller.'

'And if I had both your attributes and the same crowd after me, I wouldn't be using my real name, either.'

'How did you find out about me?'

'We knew of Apex first.'

'Who is *we*?'

'The British Government. We knew of you, when our Kirsten started referring to the man on the run with the very chemical at the centre of this whole sinister charade.'

'Kirsten?'

'Kirsten Sweetmore, our Defence Secretary.'

'So this goes that high up?'

'What you are involved with goes right up, as high as it gets. But in those lofty places, opinions are divided. The Defence Secretary has an idea regarding this Apex, whereas the PM and some others have different hopes and plans entirely.'

My anger rises. This government *knew* about this godforsaken substance coming here.

'I must tell you, my friend, that I am amazed you have come so far. The resources Kirsten has thrown at your capture, and yet here you are, a few doors down from Westminster itself.'

'I didn't bring it to you.'

'I know you didn't, but I do want to talk to you and see whether I can change your mind.'

He's just another suit looking for his own taste of power, I think.

'This situation disgusts me. *You* disgust me,' I say. 'You corrupt bastards in your upper class country club at Westminster, wanting to get your hands on this... this *abomination*... so that you can bolster your position and powers. Each one trying to outdo the other, even though the human cost of your actions will be obscene.'

Grosvenor doesn't so much as blink at this. And I'm sure a guilty man would, given the penchant of guilty men for hiding their dubious intentions.

'I understand why you would say that, but really, I aim to convince you of the opposite. The cabinet as a whole isn't aware of this situation, but those that do know are split in their opinions as to what to do here, and please believe me when I say that most of them think as you do.

The Defence Secretary has made this a personal mission of hers, to procure Apex, whatever the cost, whereas the PM, under my guidance, does not see it that way.'

'Then what are the Defence Secretary's intentions?'

'I don't think they are nearly as sinister as you fear, but they are not in line with what we consider the noble actions of a democratic government.'

Our coffees arrive, and we pause, eyes locked, while penguin-boy refreshes our cups.

'Then why don't you get rid of her, if she is acting so far outside her remit? She crashed a plane for Christ's sake, I'd say that *is* actually pretty sinister,' I say.

Grosvenor regards me evenly.

'She has a lot of support, for a start. If she were to be dismissed, a lot of angry and bitter MPs would rally to her cause. She has proved herself to be an expert at currying favour, has greased the right wheels, backed the right motions, fought the shrewdest fights, and her influence has spread to all corners and both sides of the House of Commons. It could turn mutinous.'

'And it's not like anyone's going to blow the whistle on her,' I say. 'MPs aren't exactly the first to volunteer when there's someone else's mess to clean up.'

'It would fracture the House of Commons. You'd have some supporting action, some demanding to know the PM's involvement, resignations and accountability would be called for. And where government is concerned, the media is never far away. The government is leakier than a dinghy under machine gun fire. The story reaches the press; the press spills the beans to the public. I don't think any of us want the public involved in this, do we?'

Grosvenor sips his coffee while looking at me with eyes that gently seek my understanding. And he has it. There *would* be hysteria.

'What is more,' Grosvenor continues, clinking his cup into its saucer, 'Kirsten Sweetmore would use this, undoubtedly, to her own advantage. She is a media darling, with sympathetic ears in both tabloids and broadsheets, in local press and the blogosphere. She is an expert, where the press is concerned, at giving a little to further her own interests. The media furore surrounding her dismissal would unleash another volley at the government, which, by that point, would be struggling and suffering.'

The press. The conspiracy in the south west. Is *she* behind it?

'Every media outlet I have come across is full of misinformation about the plane crash. Is this her doing?' I ask.

'Without question,' Grosvenor says, grimly.

'And there's nothing you can do about this?'

'She has the PM by the jaffers.'

'Christ,' I say, my respect for government dropping to an all-time low. If they can't do anything about their own rogue members, what on earth is the bloody point?

'Why does she want it?'

'Apex?'

'Yes.'

214

'Power. I think she does have the success of the British Government at heart, but she sees Apex as a quick fix, a tool to help her up the ladder faster than her male predecessors. She wants to wield the threat of power—'

'And she doesn't care how she does it. Lying, conspiracy, murder, organised crime?'

'Power, no matter what the cost. And in bringing that plane down, she has swindled every single entity that has come to the UK to bid for Apex, not to mention the mysterious party behind its creation.'

'Jesus. She has made the British Government... unpopular.'

'And in a world where rogue scientists create bespoke super-toxins, and criminal and terrorist elements from all over the globe are coming to the UK, that doesn't strike me as the wisest thing to do.'

'She is making a target of us. The whole country.'

'There you have it. You understand our concern. Her actions, her bringing down that plane, have set off a chain of events that is deadly to national safety.'

I'm all at sea, dizziness pitching me this way and that. In pursuit of power, Sweetmore has made Great Britain the prime enemy of every terrorist and criminal. We may have to endure revenge attacks for years.

What was she thinking? I remember what Amina said about greed, and how much blood comes with it. God, the prospect is unthinkable.

'However,' Grosvenor says, '*you* have given us a window. You see, the auction is supposed to take place tomorrow night. And the criminal fraternity that is coming to bid on this stuff, doesn't yet know that it is missing or stolen, and, judging by the emails from the seller's camp, neither do they. We don't yet know why that, however, it gives us an opportunity. There is still time to change this.'

'What would you have me do?'

'Give me the toxin. I hate this, but the auction must go ahead. We can't make Great Britain into the enemy of the world's most dangerous.'

'You can't be serious?'

'I am deadly serious. And believe me, I'm far from happy to be making that request. But think about it… what is worse? A world where the toxin has been purchased by an unknown party and disappears quietly into their corner of the globe, or one where its disappearance creates a string of parties who are furious with Great Britain, angry at being swindled. There are many more ways to hurt UK civilians than super-toxins. This really is a no win situation for the likes of you and me, but we have to decide which of the two outcomes is the lesser evil.'

'There has to be another way,' I say, but I somehow know that there isn't.

'These people are arriving in the UK, as we speak. They are coming from all over the world, representing many different groups. Some are terrorists, some are world leaders, I'm sure some of them fancy themselves as Bond-style super-villains. What are they going to do if they arrive here, only to find out that their host has already robbed them?'

It is a sound point, and a compelling argument. Grosvenor looks as distressed about it as I feel, his pursed mouth almost releasing the words reluctantly, his eyes simmering with disbelief that this course of action really is for the best.

'We can't let something as godawful as an auction for this stuff take place! We just can't!' I say.

He smiles ruefully. 'I know the gravity of this situation. I know what this stuff can do.'

'Do you?' I ask, challenging him. 'As far as I know, my partner is the only person who has seen this toxin up close. And I assure you, it is far worse than you can imagine.'

Grosvenor settles into his chair again, his previous animation soothed as he smooths his tie, but his voice communicates a weight of purpose that is even heavier than before.

'This sort of thing doesn't usually happen. Weapons of mass destruction rarely appear from unknown sources. But when they do, we take notice. As far as I am concerned, as far as the Prime Minister is concerned, this is a situation that is as dreadful as it is unbelievable.

'We *must* act to restore parity or, where Great Britain is concerned, equilibrium will be disturbed for who knows how long, and events will not work in our favour. Sweetmore seems to think Apex will unlock all sorts of power for Great Britain, and she thinks that as Defence Secretary, it is her job to secure that power. But she has forgotten the fundamental principles of defence. Defence is concerned with protection and fortification, not with securing the resources to attack. Her actions suggest that preparation for attack is her motive. Sometimes, attack can be the best form of defence. But this is not so much a plan of such attack, as...'

'As a way of putting a big fucking target on us.'

Grosvenor nods vehemently, and our plates arrive. The smell of mackerel is immediately both mouth-watering and overpowering. I'm not sure I can stomach it, so I settle for a slug of coffee.

'Forgive me,' Grosvenor says, 'but I have an audience with the PM fairly soon, so I hope you don't find my tucking in rude.'

'Have at it,' I say.

Between slivers of mackerel, Grosvenor sneaks out some small talk, in a manner that suggests his own curiosity needs satisfying.

'I assume you were a soldier. Afghanistan? Iraq?'

'Both,' I reply. 'You?'

'Kuwait, Brunei, Northern Ireland, The Falklands, The Gulf, Bosnia, Iraq again. Amongst other things.'

Jesus. This guy is military royalty, having been on the ground for pretty much anything and everything UK forces were involved in from the late 1950s onwards.

'Other things?' I ask. I like talking shop, when it's not about me. Grosvenor looks at me as if assessing whether or not to let me in, but I know I have passed that assessment when I see a flicker of a smile.

'SAS?' I venture. He nods and I smile. 'I considered that.'

'I'd have welcomed a man with your talents with open arms.'

I flush with pride. That's the nicest thing a superior has said to me in a very long time. And that's just what this man is; my superior. Anyone with his record would be. No wonder the Queen wants this guy at the PM's side in whatever capacity.

'I won't ask any further,' Grosvenor says, 'but needless to say, I feel we are on the same side. Can I persuade you to hand me the toxin, so that I can do what is necessary for the good of this country?'

Here we are. The fork in the road. The question that no man should ever have to answer. *Which evil do I pick?* Give the criminal fraternity what they want, condemning some poor sods to a horrible death at the hands of Apex, or make enemies out of all of them on behalf of the United Kingdom?

Grosvenor knows my plight. He understands the gravity of this decision.

And it is a decision I *have* to get right.

'The item in question is upstairs,' I say. 'Can I have a minute to go and get it?'

'Of course,' Grosvenor says. 'I've a coffee to finish.'

'Thank you,' I say, pushing myself up and away from the table, and head for the door.

I feel groggy, as if each sentence of our conversation has been another body blow in a long, drawn out boxing match. I lie. The toxin is right here in my pocket, in its vial. I slipped it there while Amina was enjoying her tour of the suite. *But I need time to think.*

And I need to ask Amina about Apex.

Maybe she knows of a way to neutralise the toxin, rendering it worthless before I hand it over to Grosvenor. That way, the UK still comes out of this OK and it becomes more of a quality control issue between buyer and creator. That would sit a lot better with me than handing over a tool that could be used for unstoppable mass murder.

As I cross the hall to get in the lift, my mind swimming elsewhere, I think of questions I need to ask Grosvenor when I come back, namely: *who* is selling it? How is this auction to work? Who the hell was the headless woman on the plane? And how has the seller failed to recognise that their cargo is missing?

None of this really bears thinking about, and I hop out as soon as the lift gets to our floor. I see cleaning trolleys in the hall. I have forgotten it is still so early, and the rest of the hotel is only just waking up. I enter our suite, and shout to Amina. So much to ask. I hope she knows as much about this sort of thing as she seems to.

I cross the foyer, and go into the main body of the suite, where Amina sits on a chair, as beautiful as ever.

But her cheeks are brushed with tears, and a pistol is trained point blank on the back of her head.

17.

On seeing that steel pressed up close to Amina, her eyes streaming with fear, I feel instinct ripple through me. Before I know it, I am moving low and hard for the cover of the chaise longue, which I flip over in an instant. In the course of this, I have clocked six people in the room.

There is the man holding the gun to Amina's head, dressed in a pinstripe suit and fashionably abhorrent hot-lime tie. He has a face as bland and forgettable as budget cheese, and an earpiece.

Another man covers the grand windows, turning from his view of the street to see who has just entered. He too has the curly tail of earpiece wiring wriggling down his shirt collar.

Sitting on one of the sofas, directly facing me, her legs crossed in demure confidence, is a woman in a black trouser suit flanked by two more suited, ear-pieced men. She looks to be mid-thirties, short blonde hair coiffed expertly, glittering blue eyes packed with fervour, skin of brushed porcelain. She is statuesque and has great physical presence, a fact that shines brightly even though she is sitting down. A Nordic Amazon. She carries the ghost of a very vague smile, as if she knows that she alone holds all the cards when it comes to what happens in this room.

And there, loitering in the back, is the only person in the room, aside from Amina, that I recognise. The rotundness slathered in sweat is a dead giveaway. Lloyd Weathers. He wrings his palms, as if desperate to get his hands on me.

Silence fills the room. A standoff has begun. I wish I was armed.

'Amina, are you ok?' I ask from my impromptu sofa fort.

'Yes,' she replies, low and strong, trying so hard to be brave with a tool of certain demise pointing straight at her.

I have a sneaking suspicion who the woman is, and a crawling dread that Grosvenor has suckered me in here. He fed me the lies and platitudes about Great Britain that he thought I wanted to hear, delivering them from an ex-military viewpoint that he knew I would trust. Son of a bitch set me up, surely? I don't want to believe it, but what choice is there?

Offence, Ben. *Now.*

'Kirsten Sweetmore, you should be ashamed of yourself,' I say, trying my best to sound like a weary father grounding an unruly teenager that has nudged just over her agreed boundaries. 'Where does this fit in with your oath of government?'

'You have me wrong, sweetheart,' replies a female voice, which can only belong to the woman on the couch. The Defence Secretary is answering me directly. 'It is the job of the cabinet to act in the direct interest of the people of the United Kingdom. A man gallivanting across the country, carrying a lunchbox full of botulism, is hardly in the public interest.'

'Your spin won't work in here, not like it did down in the south west,' I counter, shifting higher on my knees to peek out over the top of the chaise. As I peek, I can see the men with earpieces have handguns drawn and trained in my direction, their stances identical. Secret Service, surely.

'The people need to know precisely what the people need to know. Nothing more is necessary,' replies Kirsten, and I see that she is smiling. I look into the eyes of my adversary, who seems intent on mocking me with a fascinated, feline gaze. 'You can't get out. You can't get closer. Give us the toxin.'

'Simply put, fuck off.'

She laughs loudly at that, chucking her head back to throw her glee at the ceiling. 'I wish more people in the House of Commons spoke like that. Prime Minister's Question Time would be a lot less like the childish playground preening of a hundred rugger buggers, if there was a little more of an edge to it.'

'Weathers,' I call, and I see the corrupt MP raise his chin to look at me, hatred swirling in his eyes like wasps. 'North Devon Excavations. Destroying the countryside for fracking kickbacks. Your pension from natural gas, at the cost of the very environment you pretend to protect. But you couldn't get going without Sweetmore, could you?'

Weathers' ire cools momentarily, to supposed guilt. By following Sweetmore he has backed himself into a corner, with one incriminatory act after another. I bet he can't remember how he even got into this mess now, but his indignation returns.

'Did you want it so badly that you agreed to sell out your constituents with a fine line of bullshit, just so you could impress the Defence Secretary here? You saw an opportunity to get in the good graces of this fine public champion, get that grubby legacy you so badly wanted, so you gave her all the tools necessary to complete her dirty little side mission on your patch.'

'So you're not just a pretty face,' smirks Kirsten, cruelly revelling in the verbal disintegration of her dogsbody. She is a rum piece of work. 'But you have made life very difficult for poor Lloyd, haven't you? So much so that he had to come here cap in hand to try to make amends, watching you all the way into our grasp. It hasn't been fun, has it Lloyd?'

She turns to Weathers, still smirking. She is enjoying the act of humiliating him, and in this gesture I have the measure of this woman. Nasty, calculating and vindictive. Exactly the kind of person a substance like Apex should never be close to.

Man, government is more fucked than I thought.

Weathers flushes crimson and looks at me with that same hateful glare, the glare that says *'you did this to me'*.

'Never send a boy to do a woman's job, it seems,' says Kirsten. 'Now, where is Apex?'

'Why do you want it?'

'Why would anyone want it? Invincibility. Whoever has it cannot be fucked with. By anybody.'

'It doesn't work like that, and you know it,' I say. 'You are dragging Great Britain into some very dark places. And you shouldn't be.'

'I think that when it comes to the ultimate protection of the country and its people, those very things that some say shouldn't be done are sometimes exactly what *must* be done. Times are changing. And so should we. Finally.'

A beat of silence hits, its vacuum almost as deafening as a cacophony. Kirsten breaks it with the impatience of someone who has more pressing engagements.

'If you are deaf and dumb to any urgency, I'll have to get the lads to force the issue,' she says. 'We know nothing about you, the mysterious fly in our ointment, but we know that *this* is Dr Amina Ridgewell, Kosovan-born microbiologist. Escaped the horrors of her homeland's war to carve out a new life in Britain's generous bosom. And hasn't she done well for herself? It would be a shame if, in the end, it all counted for nothing.'

I hope Amina forgives me for what I am about to say, but I suppose my stock with her could hardly fall any lower. 'Sorry Kirsten, but the life of one person is not on the same level when talking about something that could wipe out millions. I am not going to give it to you. Over my very dead, very cold body.'

'Kill her, then,' she says, in tones as cold as ice and malevolent as hell. The room stands still. Is she serious? Even the goon pointing the gun at Amina looks at her, to check whether it's a bluff, but Kirsten's stare of pure, fiery detachment tells anyone who sees it that this is no joke, and the time for chit-chat and mucking about is over.

I look at Amina. Her eyes are wide and pleading, but her remains mouth closed and stoic. I think of how many times she has been faced with peril, how used she must be to threats, and how every time she escapes one dreadful situation, she ends up in another. She looks as though her card was marked long ago, and violent death would find her eventually, an inescapable destiny locked in place, a destiny she would have to face one day, like it or not. And it ignites a fire in me. Not today. *Not today.*

The chaise can't be too heavy, but it seems solid enough. I drop, and then lift it immediately, heaving it up and forwards, and it rises still on its side. It is heavy, but I get it up to waist height, to a height I can hide my torso behind. As soon as it is up, I charge forward at speed, as gunfire begins to erupt. Slugs thud into the wood on the other side, jolting my progress.

'Amina!' I bellow, as I stagger towards her, the chair she was seated on surely just a couple of yards ahead of me now, but she has caught my drift already. She has dived forwards, beneath the onward-marching chaise, next to my legs. 'Out into the foyer!'

I imagine how close I must be to the chair Amina was on, now, and I shove the chaise as hard as I can at the man who was holding a gun to Amina's head.

As soon as the chaise has left my fingers, I throw one hand into my pocket to pull out the vial of toxin, which has been there all along. Good job I lied to Grosvenor to buy myself time, the snake. The only place I knew it would be completely safe, was about my person, and I'm glad I followed through with that.

By the time the chaise crashes down to the floor, bouncing over the chair, and the men have retargeted me to pick an effective kill shot, I am holding the vial out to them.

'You said whoever has this, and I quote, *can't remotely be fucked with* — unquote. You don't want this to break. Believe me,' I say, waving it from side to side.

I feel six sets of eyes on me, four of which are narrowed behind pistol barrels. Lloyd has his chubby fingers stuck in his ears, while Kirsten looks positively turned on, a cheeky half-smile parting her lips. She still sits, her icy calm evident.

'Think carefully, mystery man,' she taunts me in a soft purr. 'You can't *possibly* think you can get out of here with *that*.'

'I didn't possibly think I could get Amina out of the room with a fucking chaise longue, but that worked out alright, didn't it?' I reply.

'You call that *safety*? This hotel is the epicentre of a tactical operation, of which you are the main target. Or, I should say, what you are *holding* is the main target. Two teams are downstairs, armed and ready to do whatever it is I ask of them, and considering how poorly you both are at playing along, at this point, I'd say your safety is decreasing.'

'Your actions betray your country,' I tell her, my mind already on those two tactical units.

'My actions will put my country on the map.'

'You men,' I say, looking from one to the other. 'Do you go along with this, too? You are able to make your own minds up. Can't you see what madness this is?'

'I agree with the Defence Secretary, fully,' pipes up Weathers, his fingers still poised by his ears in case it gets noisy again.

'Christ, Lloyd, you don't have to kiss her arse anymore. Do you think for one minute you'll get that fast track cabinet appointment you were hoping for? Never mind the fact that if your dear Defence Secretary's plan comes off, there might not even *be* a cabinet to try to weasel into.'

Kirsten smiles broadly, clearly relishing this. 'You are a bundle of fun,' she says. 'I get the distinct impression you are not buyable.'

'Fuck off,' I tell her. She giggles, and I see that a couple of the men look at her as she does so. They adore her, and are firmly under her spell. She is an attractive woman, for sure, but it's not just that quality that draws men to her. Her mannerisms are all of a type that makes men quiver at the knees. She literally gives men exactly what they want — while taking all that she can get. No wonder she has supporters throughout the uneasy halls of Westminster, and beyond. It's all power by seduction, and will remain so until her position contains actual, tangible power, and she consolidates her position with the continuing of the charade, her true nature coming out in closer-knit circles and quieter moments. If I kept my eyes on the gossip columns, I'm sure I'd have heard of her. Surely this type of politician is pure gold for the tabloids.

'Who are you?' she asks. 'I didn't want to be as predictable as to ask that, but you seem like such a relic from a bygone age, that I have to ask.'

'I am someone who doesn't take kindly to his country being used as a bargaining chip in a power struggle, nor to its people being lied to by the very leaders they elected to serve their interests.'

She crosses her legs and leans forward, and takes a radio unit from her jacket pocket. 'You are a fascinating specimen. Lost in time, a Palaeolithic grunt. Did Dr Ridgewell find you in a block of ice and thaw you out?'

'Something like that,' I say, while the other men smirk. 'I'm going to walk backwards out of this room now, and leave the building. If anything stops me from doing so, I'll break this vial.'

'No, you won't,' she says, holding out the radio. 'If I press the call button on here just once, the signal is given for the tactical units to converge on this suite.'

'I've faced worse odds,' I say, not sure that I have.

'Let's find out,' says Kirsten, pressing the call button. No sound comes from the handset, but I can picture boots pounding the polished floors of the lobby. I can also see it being one big ruse, a bluff to illicit panic. If that's her plan, she has messed with the wrong vigilante ex-soldier. Even if I do say so myself.

'I've got maybe thirty seconds then, haven't I?'

'Give or take.'

'Then I'd best make it count.' I turn and sprint for the foyer door, as gunfire spits behind me. The wood of the door is spraying splinters from bullet impacts before I manage to dash through, flecks flying up around my head. Once in the foyer, I see that Amina is on her knees by the door, covering her ears, almost cradling herself.

'Amina, the bedroom, now. Get in the bath,' I say, pulling her up and guiding her to the bedroom door, shoving her inside.

This is where I make my stand, and there are already six enemies in here. Thirty seconds, no, more like twenty, before I'll be overrun. I must take the six out before the rest get here. Without a weapon. Nothing like a challenge. It's now a numbers game, and the magic number is six.

As soon as Amina is safely in the bedroom, I turn back to the door I left from, hiding tight, next to the door frame. Any second now…

The first man bursts through, giving chase, and I let him pass straight to the suite door. The second comes through, as eager as the first. Good. Just wait for the third, and… there he is.

As soon as he is through, I kick the door closed as hard as I can, smashing the fourth man in the face. I reach uncompromisingly for the third man's gun, while kicking the back of his knee, buckling him down. I slip the gun from his right hand and… BOOM, BOOM. Two shots, taking down both of the men by the front door. One, two. I bring the gun back to the man buckled in front of me, hold it by his head and pull the trigger. Three. I open the entrance to the main suite again, just as the last ear-pieced goon appears to charge through, his nose bloody and off-centre. I fire point blank, and he drops like a sack of shit. Four.

I didn't want to kill these men. Not at all. I just couldn't see any other way. And now, finally, I am armed.

There is a huge dresser along the side wall of the foyer. I drag it over to and across the front door, blocking the entrance. It is heavy, but adrenaline gives me strength. I've probably got between five and ten seconds, before this place becomes a war zone. The clunky furniture won't keep them out, but it will slow them a little.

I take the bedroom door that Amina has just passed through and find her standing by the edge of the bed, confusion, hope and relief all visible in her expression. 'Follow me,' I command.

I'm in no nonsense mode now. You are either along for the ride or you ain't.

I move straight through the bedroom to the rear door, and use that to enter the living room. Weathers is standing in front of Sweetmore, and they both stare expectantly in the opposite direction, at the front exit. I walk straight towards them, and their eyes turn towards me in unison, before widening in surprised horror.

'I'm sorry to piss on your parade,' I say. 'UP.' I point the gun at them to show I mean it, but all of us are distracted by the sudden crashing that's coming from the foyer. The tactical aid units are here. They are trying to get in. She wasn't bluffing.

Weathers has moved in front of Sweetmore, in a tepid attempt at masculine protection, even though Sweetmore, now stood at her full, statuesque, six feet, has far more physical presence than Weathers ever will. I smash him hard on the top of his head with the butt of the gun, and he goes down howling. 'That's for your constituents,' I say. 'Behind me Amina, now.'

I pull Kirsten in front of me just as the living room door flies open, and I see the foyer is full of black-clad, automatic weapon-toting, assault-vest wearing bruisers looking for a target to spray with lead. The only one I offer them is the woman in charge. I notice that there are eight in total, which surely means that this is just one of the teams. The other lot must be holding the lobby.

'One step forwards and we all die,' I say, holding the gun to Kirsten's head and the vial of toxin above her left shoulder, as if I am puppeteering a little cartoon devil. 'Tell them to stand down,' I whisper to Kirsten.

'A job. I can give you a job,' she whispers back.

'I'm enjoying unemployment,' I reply, quietly.

'Money then, you'll be wanting money.'

'I've got more than I'm comfortable with already.'

'There must be something you want?'

'Accountability. For you, and that piece of shit on the floor there.'

'Why did you think I went into government? There is no accountability where government is concerned.'

'There always is. Even for you.'

'There you are, the naïve boy scout again. I'm untouchable. And you are the one holding a gun to a cabinet minister's head, in front of eight of the most loyal and well-trained operatives that the country has at its disposal.'

She has a point. This is not a great situation, and I'm acutely aware that a lot of these guys will be getting a good look at me. I raise my voice to address them.

'I am one of you. I live for the service of Her Majesty. This woman is guilty of something tantamount to treason, and she needs to face what she has done.'

No one flinches, except for Kirsten, who is actually laughing, as if I have just told her a funny anecdote over dinner. She is certainly cool under pressure, I have to give her that.

If I knew more about her, I may be able to work out a way to get to her, and use it to my advantage. I promise, if I get out of this, I will pay more attention to politics in future.

'Follow me Amina, and stay tight,' I say, while giving Kirsten a sharp push forwards. 'You are a disgrace,' I tell her.

'Make some room boys,' she says, almost jovially. 'The front door's over there.'

'Move.'

Kirsten paces slowly towards the men, and I feel Amina's hand grasp the fabric of my hoodie. She is right behind me, and I sense her close, which immediately invokes the memory of the last time I was this close to her - last night, and all I did in its darkness. I raise my voice again.

'We are going to march out of that front door. Move aside to let us pass. If you don't, I fire the gun and drop the toxin, and you'll be responsible for the death of your boss, your colleagues, and if the substance gets out, everyone in this hotel and another one and a half million people. Don't make me do that.'

I can see the men peering along their gunsights, foreheads creased with concentration on me, their target. Eyes unblinking. Postures unwavering.

I'll have to test their resolve.

We approach them, and I eye them hard. I feel like a defence lawyer, and they are the jury — if I can crack one of them, put reasonable doubt in their minds, they will lose that unity and I will get away with this. Although I'm likely to get my head blown off if they don't like what they hear.

We get closer to them.

'Men, I promise you that if you apprehend us, you will be contributing to something that will harm Great Britain in the worst of ways. Is that what you signed up for?'

Closer still, but they are granite firm.

'Amina, the bags,' I say, and I hear her grab them from the floor, where they have been flung in the confusion.

'Got them,' she replies. I raise my voice again.

'You seem to have loyalty to this woman, but to whom does this woman have loyalty? If you think it's you lot, you are dead wrong.'

Just a yard now, and I slow our progress almost to a stop.

'KITDAFOS, boys. You're eating it right now protecting her. So move, or kill us all. It's as simple as that,' I say,

234

with as much steel as I can muster. Do I really want to drop this thing? No, but I also know how stubborn I can be. If there's a chance to make a point, I've been known to go through with things, and today that might prove to be a most unfortunate characteristic.

'Let him through, gentlemen. I mean it,' says Kirsten, breaking into my racing thoughts. 'Let's watch him flounder for a bit longer.'

And with that, the men part in a regimented fashion. I'm not whether sure these are regular police tactical aid units, or those specially assigned to Ms Sweetmore. She seems to have them on a very tight leash, so tight as to have throttled their autonomy. Either that, or they have been falsely briefed about me, and told not to trust a single oily word that slips from my snake-like mouth.

A narrow channel presents itself between the ranks, and I walk Kirsten straight through it, turning when we are all safely through, to keep Kirsten and the toxin between us and them. The tension is so palpable and heavy, it can't be far from attaining physical mass.

We begin the slow walk backwards to the lift, and as we travel, the tactical soldiers follow us, matching us step for step, never more than a yard away. Their eyes are all cemented upon us with conviction, unwavering and strong. I bet they are good men, too. I never like taking on good men.

'We are nearly at the lift,' Amina whispers, and I pull Kirsten closer to us.

'Call it when you can,' I reply.

And as soon as I say that, I hear the airy ping of the lift arriving. We are already there.

We all stand together, on a precipice. It requires only a slight change in equilibrium, to drive this moment over the edge and into frantic carnage.

18.

A hum and a bump herald the opening of the lift door behind us.

Gingerly, we step backwards into the lift. 'Press for the lobby, Amina,' I instruct her, my eyes never moving from the men in front. The men are so close to the lift doors that if they encroach just a couple more feet, they will be in there with us.

'Hold it there.' They stop.

The doors begin to close, and just as I think we might have made it past the first impossible obstacle, Kirsten lunges forward.

By the time the lift doors have slid shut, it's over. Kirsten grabbed one of the gun barrels that were

237

pointed at us, and used it to pull herself out of the lift. I'd have loved to blow her brains out, but I don't want to be the guy who stole Apex *and* waxed a cabinet minister, so I shoved her hard at the men before grabbing the outstretched gun and ripping it away in the confusion, just before the door shut.

Now it's just me, Amina and the gun.

We have just switched from defence to offence. I hit the red override button, to hold us in space. That should give us a couple of moments. We need a new plan.

I check the weapon. It is one I recognise, now I see it up close. It's a Heckler and Koch MP7-SF, and it brings more revelations.

This gun is standard issue within the Ministry of Defence's own police force. The Operational Support Unit is the moniker of the general Police Support Unit that each police force has. And if this was the Metropolitan Police, which surely an incident in London like this would warrant, then this situation should be attended by a Territorial Support Group. And that, in itself, reveals that the Ministry of Defence is backing Sweetmore and her plans. *Jesus*. She has wide-reaching, dangerously corrupt aims and her own police force at hand to see them through.

But why weren't they pursuing me from day one? They must be newly recruited to her crusade. Dammit. Just another seduction of loyalty along the way.

I check the magazine. Fully loaded.

I check Amina. Fully terrified.

I check the lift. A cleaner's cart stands in the corner, accidentally abandoned in the earlier melee. I check it out, my eyes scanning the cart in the manner I would look for butter in a fridge. There are a number of items on there, all, apparently, completely normal, but I'm going to let memory and training do the work here. Keep looking and let the alarm bells go. There are all sorts of cleaning fluids to hand here, from carpet cleaner to window polish and — the ace in the pack — furniture refinisher. I grab the can, and check the ingredients. *Benzine*. I know I can use that. I keep it to one side and keep looking.

Scan. Scan. Scan. Regular toilet bleach always has something fun in it, but I need something specific to react with the benzine. I check the bottom tray of the cart, where the items take on a different theme. Away from hotel room care and over to general hotel maintenance, including chemical swimming pool treatments...

Calcium hypochlorite. Surely, in that tub of pool cleaner there. I pull it out and check. *Bingo*. I can do something special here.

'Amina, please give me a hand,' I say, and she duly joins me. The steel tub containing the pool cleaner is pretty solid, and only half full. I'll have to guess the weights roughly, but then again, that's the exciting and unpredictable part of improvising explosives. I check how much furniture refinisher I have. Not much, and to keep the volumes in a bracket that will work, I pour out a little of the pool cleaner onto the cart tray, before adding all the furniture refinisher to the tub.

'Amina, quickly, please grab the tape from my bag.' She scrabbles immediately into my backpack.

There is a wooden mop attached to the cart, so I break it across my knee, and use the smallest piece of the broken handle as a chunky makeshift stirrer for my mixture. It works a charm.

Suddenly, the lift starts moving. They have overridden the lift's internal controls. It's going to get very brutal, very fast. Amina hands me the duct tape, and I replace the lid of the steel tub, then tape it shut. I give it a solid shake for good measure, and *voila*, a HTH bomb; albeit minus a detonator. Just as well I'm not going to need one, this time.

'This is going to be a pretty nasty bang, if I've got it right,' I say, placing the tub on the cart. 'When the lift doors open, do not get out until I tell you. Stay low, and as hidden as you can. I'm so very sorry for all of this Amina, but I will do everything I can to get you out of here.'

She looks at me, dread brimming, and says, 'Thank you, Ben.'

That soft ping heralds our arrival in the lobby, and the lift lowers to a stop. I hand Apex to Amina.

'Please keep it safe. And for what it's worth, yet again,' I whisper, 'I am so sorry about last night.'

Her gaze softens, as if finally some forgiveness has been afforded — as if somehow, she can see why, in my warped sense of paranoid duty, I ended up doing what I did. I hustle my backpack on, with Amina copying. Then the doors open.

240

I peek out into the lobby, which, besides being devoid of people, is just as I left it before. It should be bustling with life at this stage in the morning, so that can only mean one thing. *They* are here.

The area has been cleared. *Good.* I whip off my hoodie and quickly arrange it on the cart, with the empty hood draped and propped atop my secret bomb on the top shelf, and the arms placed on the rails. To someone with a nervy disposition, that might just spook them into thinking someone is hiding behind it. If they see something that looks like a human shape, with a clear chance of a headshot, they might just try to make themselves a hero.

And that's what I am inviting, when I push the cart briskly out onto the marble lobby floor, scooting it into the open space. All it will take is one highly trained, on-edge chancer...

I hear the snap of the shot just before the lobby is engulfed by a booming explosion. I push Amina back into the corner of the lift, as the entire cart is replaced by an urgent fireball, billowing outwards. Glass sprays everywhere, tinkling onto the marble with all sorts of other debris.

When we were weaving our way through London's streets earlier, I didn't think that within an hour or so I would have blown up the lobby of one of London's most famous hotels.

As soon as the initial gust of flame recedes, I follow it out, weapon raised, movements swift and drilled. The tiled floor, so immaculate before, is now sprayed with intense burn marks. What a goddamn mess. I'm searching, eyes up further along the corridor to the front door, while my footsteps crunch on debris. The acrid stink of hot discharge saturates the air, as if a tourniquet constricts the atmosphere of the blasted lobby.

I spot that first glint through the swirling smoke, train my sights on it, and confirm that it is my opposition. Tactical glasses on the back of a man's head, as he faces the wrong way. I drop the barrel sharply down a degree, then right a degree, and squeeze off one shot.

The target pitches forward. The bullet will have hit low in the shoulder blade, exiting right at the top of the chest. Not a kill strike, by design. A put-down strike. I don't want to kill these guys if I can avoid it. They may not know what they have got themselves into.

The smoke lifts a little, and I see two more men, turning to see their fallen comrade. As they turn, I tag them both, aiming roughly for the same spot as the first. They both go down, although I can't confirm exactly where they have been hit, thanks to the smog. I'll worry about that later.

Thick smoke seems to descend from the ceiling and settle around me, at the end of the corridor to the front door. There's a ping and whizz of return fire, over my head, but I don't feel the whistle of a bullet so it mustn't have been that close. I hug the left-hand corridor entrance with my shoulder, keeping my eye firmly down the barrel. A couple more bullets ping off, but they seem random, without clear purpose. They are unsure of what to do, although I know there must be more armed police down there, and with the smoke receding, I should be able to see them.

The wall by my head cracks angrily, plaster and wood splitting a halo around me, and I drop to my knees. Nearly saw me off, that. *Tighten up, Ben.* The debris spray was at such an angle that the shooter can only be to my right, back by the lift. I gamble on his position in the smoke, remembering the open doorway to the restaurant, catch sight of a shape in black and fire three quick shots in rapid succession.

At least two of the shots hit home and he falls backwards immediately. I might have killed this one. That's half of the bottom team out of action, which ain't bad going. But the smoke screen is lifting, and I can see that further down the corridor, there is a lot more cover behind which to hide, and certainly a lot more chance of me getting shot going through it.

If I was going on foot, I'm sure that I'd be getting close to five stories down now, so I retreat back to the lift, where Amina is on her knees with her hands over her ears. To the right of the lift is the entrance to the stairs, which is where the team from above will surely emerge. I reach into the lift and grab Amina by the hand, dragging her towards the dining room.

'How are we doing?' she asks.

'Quiet!' I whisper.

We run into the spacious white dining room, half-eaten breakfasts still on the tables, to see the last of the diners scurrying through the rear kitchen doors. That's when a hand grabs my throat and squeezes with clawing fingers. Amina screams and it hurts like hell.

There must have been two in the dining room, hiding behind the door frame. I can almost feel my trachea being torn from its muscle housings, the tendons ripping, but I fire my left elbow back into my assailant's ribs as hard as I can, forcing him to heave the air out of his lungs in a spluttered cough.

The pressure on my neck reduces a touch, so I throw my head back at top speed, which both pulls my neck free from the grip and cracks the back of my skull off my adversary's forehead. I see stars; they pinwheel from one side to the other and I think I have split the back of my head open.

I right myself instantly when I see the second OSU team appear in the destroyed lobby. I squeeze off a few rounds down into the space, scattering them like roaches.

'Run, to the kitchen,' I gurgle, my throat struggling to recover, and Amina starts sprinting, as my immediate opponent recovers enough to throw a right hook. I grimace, instinct initiating autopilot, and before I know what I have done, I've caught the swinging wrist, twisted it and driven my right shoulder through the elbow joint, snapping it the wrong way. That's him done.

He flops backwards, and doesn't go down immediately, which prevents any of his colleagues from returning fire straight away. It gives me the second I need to dive over the nearest table just as it gets shot to pieces, spraying glass, cutlery and scrambled egg in all directions. I just hope Amina made it.

I crawl immediately back under the table I just jumped over, beneath the long white table cloth, and poke the gun barrel through the draped cloth on the other side. I see legs moving into the door way, and spray an even burst of gunfire into the group at shin height. Three more men fall, bullets smacking their legs from under them. I turn again, and crawl out, staying low, and make a break for the kitchen door, which I see Amina scamper through. I make it, just as gunfire sounds again.

I'm through into a broad kitchen space that is already empty save for Amina, who is moving between gleaming worktops through to the back.

'This way!' she shouts. 'There must be an exit.'

I waste no time in following and, as I run past the commercial ovens and hobs on the right hand wall, I twist all the hobs on, fully.

'Help me,' I shout, and Amina comes back to switch on the remaining hobs. Twelve industrial hobs in total, pouring gas into the kitchen. The tell-tale smell is almost immediate. 'Find the exit and I'll hold them off.'

Amina runs into the recesses of the kitchen again, and I turn back to the door, hoping I don't have to fire and expend the gas stores I am building up, too soon. On the closed kitchen door is a porthole window, in which a man's head wearing a black helmet appears, and I raise my weapon at him — to spook him, more than anything. He drops out of sight.

I start pacing backwards, knowing that there's no way any of them will burst in here while I've got such an obvious positional upper hand. The smell is very strong now, and not far off being uncomfortable and over-powering.

'Got it!' Amina shouts. 'Back here!'

I run to her, where she stands by a service exit, haloed by sunlight. I turn as I get closer, and fire one shot back into the kitchen, at a bank of chrome work services. The ricochet licks a spark, which ignites the entire kitchen. I am blasted the rest of the way, barrelling through the door and into the street.

I land at Amina's feet out on the pavement, spluttering and crunching hard onto the asphalt. I feel as if my eyebrows are singed and I've got that sunburnt skin buzz.

'Do you still have it?' I ask Amina, hauling myself up.

She checks her pocket, and confirms 'I do'. But I see her eyes wander down the street behind me. As I turn, I get a sense of where we are; out on The Strand, looking down towards the recessed entrance to The Savoy. And turning out onto the pavement, running determinedly, is a handful of OSU officers in hot pursuit.

'GO!' I bellow, but before I can go myself, a car screeches to a stop right next to us. I raise my gun, assuming this is the arrival of another hostile party, but the open driver's window frames a familiar face.

'*Get in*,' commands William Grosvenor.

I stand, rooted with indecision. Wasn't it he who...?

'That's an order from a superior officer,' shouts Grosvenor, making my mind up for me. I have to give this a chance. Running around London with an automatic weapon was never going to be the best means of escape.

I usher Amina in first. She seems relieved and amazed at how lucky we appear to have been. I hop in next to her, and Grosvenor guns it, the running OSU officers receding from sight.

I breathe a long sigh of relief.

19.

Two hours and eighty-five miles later, we pull into the grounds of a beautiful country estate, as the car's tyres crunch into the gravel of the driveway.

Grosvenor sped from London and didn't look back, and spent the entire journey on the phone via Bluetooth earpiece. He was business-like, unflustered and confident — even when he had a conversation with the Defence Secretary herself. I would have loved to have heard both sides of that exchange. He gave nothing away at all, parried her questions and told her, in no uncertain terms and in a voice laced with bile, to take a long, hard look at herself, while thinking of the good men she had just sacrificed in pursuit of her ugly little plan. After that conversation, he threw the phone sim card out of the window, took out a second mobile, and made more calls.

The car itself is a black Mercedes, beautiful in a functional way, with a minimalist class to its interior... It's as quick as a greased cheetah, and Grosvenor handles it deftly.

He had arranged us some accommodation, an entire, if small, hotel, which I suppose is where we have arrived. We are booked in under false names. He seems to have used some kind of protocol when booking, which opened metaphorical doors easily for him, some form of code that alerted the listener to some other, secret, directions.

Amina has sat quietly at my side throughout. Fifteen minutes into the journey, she reached for me. She grabbed onto my left wrist and held on; I guess she couldn't bring herself to hold my hand. I'd have held her, if she'd have let me, if it made her feel better. I suppose I'm the only familiar thing she has had recently, and after everything, if she needs an anchor of any kind to right her ship, I'll do anything I can to be that. I feel supremely guilty for involving her, now more than ever, but I know that I need her help with the stuff we carry.

I've a funny feeling her role isn't played out just yet.

I try to get some rest. I haven't worked out whether or not to trust Grosvenor, and if I do extend that trust, how much I should afford him. But, he undoubtedly saved our bacon back there. It helped when he tossed that sim card aside. Nobody can track a sim card that's minus a phone and lodged in a hedge somewhere, even if they are the Ministry of Defence. I think that a modicum of trust has been reciprocated, and for now it seems we are on the same page.

All I know is that we have been heading north east of London, at first following signs to Cambridge, until those signs were replaced with other places I hadn't heard of before. The last sign I saw, just a mile prior to turning into the estate, was a 'Welcome to Elveden' sign. I saw no village, just a turn off for a Centre Parcs holiday retreat.

And now we are here.

The driveway opens out, to run parallel to magnificently surgical gardens, on the edge of a rolling meadow brushed with deeper, near mystical-looking forests. *What a spot…* At the end of the garden stands a mighty period home constructed of sandstone and red brick, with an arched porch, expansive bay windows and high chimney tops. I feel a little under dressed.

Grosvenor pulls the car to a stop in front of the raised porch, where a man is already running down the steps to greet us. Grosvenor jumps out with a 'Let's go, you two' directed at the pair of us on the back seat. We do as he says, and my legs sing at me in their stiffness, reminding me that it's been a tough few days.

The man shakes Grosvenor's hand, and smiles at him with a warmth fettered by urgency. 'Always good to see you, William, however the circumstances…' he says, clipped. His accent is from about five hundred miles north of where he stands, Scottish to the very root.

'You too, John. You too. And thank you again. You manage to shift your guests?' replies Grosvenor, heading to the front door.

'The Red Mayor Inn down Elveden way was only too happy to have them,' says John, grinning.

'Well, either way, I'm sorry for the inconvenience.' Grosvenor turns to us. 'This is Dr Amina Ridgewell, and the other one is… well, damned if I know.'

I shake John's hand, as does Amina. John seems to sense Amina's unease, and he puts a hand on her shoulder, ushering her towards the house with care. 'My wife Denise is inside, she's got the kettle on. You'll be quite safe here my dear, so let's get those nerves soothed, eh?'

I pause at the top of the steps, and take a look out at the lay of the land, the terrain and the exits. I need to know I can get us out of here at speed, if necessary. I refuse to lead myself, Amina and Apex into checkmate, no matter how quaintly things seem to be working out at the present time. Grosvenor seems to catch my drift, and appears alongside me.

'We are two miles from the nearest village, a mile and half from any other buildings at all. We are off the map, and with John's help, at his bed and breakfast we are off the grid entirely. Nobody knows about this place, and very few people on the planet know of John and my connection to him.'

'Who is he?'

'He was by my side when our unit attended the siege at the Iranian Embassy,' Grosvenor says, and I can't help my eyebrows rising. 'But back then he didn't go by plain old John Smith. In short, you can trust him.'

'What does he know?' I ask.

'Nothing, but he knows enough of how these things work to know not to ask.'

'And we are safe here?'

'John and I help each other out from time to time. If I have to pick a man to trust with my life, it'll always be him. I'm going to take the car around to the stables, not that I'm expecting prying eyes here, but one can't be too careful. Go inside, get some rest. I've got a few things to follow up on, and we'll meet late afternoon. Work out what we are going to do with this thing that you have.

'I hope, by entrusting you with looking after it here, that you will take that as a gesture of good faith on my part. We are on the same side, I guarantee that. I think you are a good man in an abysmal situation, and I trust a good serviceman like yourself much more than any of those scaly bureaucrats back in the capital. You've acted in Great Britain's best interests so far, and I see no reason to question your intentions now.'

'I'll say that for you, too,' I say. 'I was worried you'd set me up back there.'

'And work with Kirsten? She's the scaliest of the lot,' he says, with a slight grin, before he hops down the steps.

I can't help but smile myself, and we enter the house.

*

I hear a door handle clunk softly, and I'm awake. My dreams were a tangle, pursuits in forests and sewers, old and new memories blending together into a sleep-fugue of near terror.

I'm in a snug double bed in an olive guest room, with the curtains drawn. Sunlight glances around the curtain edges. I must only have been asleep a couple of hours. By the time I have looked to the door, it's closed again, and Amina stands there. She has half-changed, now twinning a spare navy jumper grabbed from her office with those jeans, and her hair is wet. She looks showered, primed and action-ready.

'Couldn't sleep?' I say, croaking the words out, the last of the sleep fuzz going with them.

'Not at all,' she replies, the bed creaking while she sits on the edge of it. 'I just keep thinking of how to end this, and get out of this with our lives and careers intact. I understand that you must trust the people who have brought us here, but I need to know what's going on. You need to tell me everything you know, now.'

Her voice has become school-teacherly and firm. In the spirit that two heads are always better than one, I tell her everything, from what we know about Apex, my conversation with Grosvenor at The Savoy, about Kirsten and the scheduled auction. I go easy on the bit about the amount of international criminals who would love our heads on a spike if they only knew that we have Apex when we shouldn't. When I've finished, I sit up to face her directly.

'Any ideas? Any help is good help at this stage, at least while we fathom this one out,' I say.

'If the government is chasing you... You will never be able to outrun them, not in a million years. They will always find you.'

She speaks with the solemnity of someone with prior experience of such matters, but, either way, her mind has obviously been very active in recent hours, and she now has rather a lot to say. She continues.

'And the longer we are in this position, with these people, with this substance, the less likely it is that we are going to get away from this cleanly, if at all. In fact, I'll be amazed if things go back to any remote semblance of the way they were before.'

I'm used to change. I'm used to my world being ripped from beneath me. But it pains me to acknowledge that Amina had hoped to have left such uncertainties well behind her. She has travelled from one end of Europe to the other to avoid it. She has built what I can only imagine is a picture-book life for herself, an amazing result considering how things were shaping up originally. And now I have bulldozed it.

'I think so much depends on the next few hours, and what we discuss downstairs. I know they plan to talk to me, but I want you to have just as much involvement. This concerns you just as much as me. I trust you completely.'

'Finally,' she interrupts. I might have flushed at that, but I'm not sure.

'Well, either way… You are an expert in this field, or, if you are not, at least you are a damn sight more knowledgeable on this topic than any of us. At least as far as I know.'

She smiles appreciatively, and gives a light nod.

'I think you are integral to our progress,' I say. 'But it's also hit me that we are in someone else's wheelhouse on someone else's dime. And we must acknowledge their position. I believe that Grosvenor does indeed have the best interests of the country and the public at heart. But I just… I can't for the life of me sanction a bidding war between criminal parties for a chemical weapon, never mind one that is as bloody dreadful as this one.'

My next question is a sensitive one, and one I'm scared of the answer.

'So I can get my head around this, how would one weaponise such a thing? I mean, if I were to say to you, please go ahead and use that botulism in a way that could harm people on a grand scale — what would you *do*?'

Amina shrugs off her slight surprise at the question, and breathes out.

'It depends on the number of targets. If you have a small number of targets, mere contact is fine, preferably ingestion, to be sure. A high number of targets, well, then you'd have to get it airborne. Or into a water supply. I'd probably get a crop duster, mix it with an agent to increase volume, and spray it over a community. I feel terrible even thinking that, because those things might actually happen if this thing goes to auction.'

'Right. I hope we can come up with something that stops it from coming to that.'

Silence falls, the chasm of either indecision or magnitude squashing the need for words.

'So, what should we do?' Amina eventually asks.

'We see if there's a way that we can settle this that keeps all parties happy, even though that seems highly unlikely. And if it doesn't, I think we hit the road again.'

'OK,' Amina says, smoothing the front of her jeans that were already smooth. It's an endearing nervous habit of hers.

'Just… just don't unpack or anything,' I say. 'And I won't mess up again. You didn't bargain for this. This is your payment for trying to be a Good Samaritan. I value your safety, far above my own.'

She doesn't reply, but her brow seems to smooth. It's another indication that she is thawing towards me. But before I can say another word, I hear the low rhythmical thump of a helicopter approaching. It's unmistakable. I'm bloody sick of hearing them.

I hop up, and cross the room to the windows which are flooding it with bright daylight. Sure enough, a chopper is coming in low and hard over the trees, tracing an aggressive nose-down line, heading right for the building. I tense, but I notice that it is a lot smaller than I imagined. It is certainly *not* carrying an army, and, as it passes closer, over the garden, it looks civilian. No gunship, put it that way. It touches down on the broad gravel patch that ends the driveway, which widens to make a turning circle for the stable vehicles.

As soon as it lands, the pilot jumps out, leaving the rotors whirring. I hadn't noticed Amina join me, but I can feel her presence and warmth. Having opened the door, the pilot pulls out a steel ramp, the end of which he lowers to the stone. Within a few seconds, a man in a wheelchair is descending the ramp briskly, his jade green tie blowing up into his thick dark hair, with the whole lot buffeting wildly above his head.

'Oh, man,' I whisper.

'Who is it?' Amina asks.

'Someone I was not hoping to see face-to-face, just yet. We have met once, but I... It's Jeremiah Salix.'

20.

I gently pad downstairs, and only when I'm half way down do I realise that I've forgotten to wear my shoes. I feel a bit rude about it, but I like the soothing carpet on my battered feet. I changed clothes before coming down, so at least there's been a vague attempt at an acceptable appearance, in case anyone is keeping score. Amina follows me, her interest in developments expanding with every step.

I feel like I've got my tail between my legs, although I shouldn't. Resolve has been a cornerstone of my actions since escaping jail, and a faith that my actions, however legally complicated, are right. But now, faced with a man who is trusted completely to uphold the law, and seems so rigorous in doing so, I feel a little as though I have duped him into consorting with a criminal. It makes me very uneasy.

We find them in the hotel restaurant, settling in side by side at the central square table, both men with their backs to us, Jeremiah in the wheelchair that I know he is stuck in for the rest of his life. John is nowhere to be seen, nor is Denise, but considering John's supposed history, he must be very good at discretion.

'Hello, gents,' I say as I enter, and both men immediately turn to us.

'We were just about to call for you,' says Grosvenor. 'I'm sorry to have gone over your head on this one, but I know this is a man you trust. I thought we could use his help. Nobody knows he is here.'

'You can tell me how you know that later,' I say, crossing the room to pass around the end of the table, as Jeremiah looks up to meet my gaze. There is warmth there, certainly, his eyes deep brown and skin olive, his hair thick and wild. His tie is loose, shirt crumpled and suit worn. He looks as though he has flown directly from the NCA offices, in the clothes he wore to work.

I extend my hand to him, and he smiles with an interesting mix of curiosity and knowing, as it becomes apparent that we have built a trusting relationship without ever looking each other in the eye. He takes my outstretched hand, and I know that in this moment our relationship is forever changed. He has sighted me. He knows my face. And he could track down my identity with ease if he wanted to.

This will take some navigation.

'It's nice to finally meet you in a less dubious setting,' he says, referring to when I first made contact with him in a pitch black disabled toilet at the North West Regional Basketball Centre in Stockport.

'I'm pretty sure that dubious is the perfect way to describe the predicament we find ourselves in,' I reply. 'Can I introduce to you Dr Amina Ridgewell? She has both saved my life and assisted me on this little escapade.'

Jeremiah shakes Amina's hand, saying 'A pleasure, doctor. Thank you for everything you have done.'

'No worries, I suppose,' she replies with a smile.

'And you will know me as... Ben,' I say. It is very difficult to know how to play this, as far as salvaging any anonymity goes. I'll have to feel this out as we go. Ben is a pretty popular name, so little is exposed by revealing it.

'Have a seat,' Grosvenor suggests, and Amina and I sit opposite the two government men. 'Jeremiah, would you like to take a lead here, since this seems to be your baby, to a certain extent.'

'Of course, thank you Mr Grosvenor,' he replies, laying his palms flat on the table in front of him.

'Please, just call me William,' Grosvenor responds, waving the formalities away with a swish of his hand. The formalities suggest that this is *their* first meeting, too.

'Thank you, William. Ben, as I said it is very nice to finally meet you, and if you permit me, I will refer to both yourself and Dr Ridgewell as separate parties here — the protector, if you will, and the microbiologist — the other two parties present being myself representing the NCA in an anti-organised crime capacity, and William here representing the Prime Minister and the British Government, or at least those members of the British government that *aren't* aligned with Defence Secretary Kirsten Sweetmore.'

We all nod.

'We need to try to come up with a passable solution to this rather unenviable problem. Namely, what to do with Apex. Now I must admit it does seem strange that we should be the four entrusted to make such a decision, but when I think of our four separate roles here, it appears we are uniquely positioned and are, essentially, as good as anyone for such a task. We have the view of the government in William, the view of an anti-crime force in myself, the view of a microbiologist in Amina and the view of the substance's custodian, who has kept it safe since it came into our midst, in Ben.'

It's hard to argue with that. It's also very hard to imagine arguing with Jeremiah on anything. He exudes a competence that makes it very easy to see why he has risen swiftly through the ranks of the NCA's Organised Crime Command. I imagine him rehearsing it all the way down here. It is hard to see such a ball of potent energy confined to the limits of his chair, but he has clearly made the most of his life.

'Now, time for all the cards on the table,' says Jeremiah. 'In broad terms, what is the ideal result of this godforsaken scenario? If I can, I'll get the ball rolling by saying that there is no clear written directive or policy as to what the NCA should do in terms of a preventative strategy here. We definitely haven't trained for clandestine auctions of bespoke super-toxins. So I'm speaking from guts and instinct as much as anybody here. William, we spoke on the phone earlier about your conversation with Ben this morning, and I believe you explained the gist of the PM's way of thinking.'

'And I've relayed that to Amina,' I say.

'That's correct,' says Amina.

'I'm afraid it's not just the PM's position,' Grosvenor states, sighing, 'It's mine as well. With as much chagrin as I can muster.'

'And that option,' clarifies Jeremiah, 'is to allow the auction to go ahead, and hand over Apex to be sold to the highest criminal bidder. Now, how would that work? It seems a good time to fill in the blanks of what we know about the auction, and the intended process of its execution.'

They've obviously been busy behind the scenes, if more information has come to light. Jeremiah keeps speaking, addressing each of us in turn. He is fiery in his honesty and forthright in his delivery. The gravity of this situation is clearly not lost on him; moreover if it resonated any more with him I'm sure there'd be an echo.

'The plane was an OdyrAir 737, from Reykjavik. An Icelandic jet, chartered by a company going by the name Globex Communications, paid for from an account held at the Zurich branch of Credit Suisse. That's right, a good old fashioned bank account. Globex were incorporated in Zurich, too. There is no other reference to Globex Communications anywhere that we can find, including online.

'On examining the account, the charter jet hire is the only expenditure it has ever made, which suggests that this account, and possibly this company identity, was created for this single project. There is no paper trail detailing how the account was opened, or anything like that, but if you know the right people in the right banks, you can grease the wheels of anonymity quite easily. So, essentially, what I am saying is that the area to be scoured for the perpetrators is extremely wide. So, in the short time frame we have, dealing with the source is not going to be an option.'

'What about the woman on the plane?' I ask, trying not to recall the sight of that milky nub of bone where her head should have been.

'She was never found. The only mention of her at all is from you, Ben. Certainly, the official reports make no reference to her, but the official reports do refer to some 250 people dying when the plane went down, so I think we know how reliable such sources are.'

'But she must have some direct relationship with the powers at work here?' says Amina.

'Maybe, but perhaps she was just the mule for getting Apex into the country,' interjects Grosvenor.

'That's a possibility,' says Jeremiah, 'but, and this is just an opinion, I think she was to liaise on arrival with a team here which exists to organise and handle the auction. In fact, I'm *sure* of it.'

'More traitors,' I find myself saying, wishing I'd restricted that utterance to within the walls of my head. But I am angry. I can't help it.

'We think there is a team on standby, somewhere in the vicinity of London, that has been liaising with the Defence Secretary. We have a very talented digital cryptologist at the NCA, and I have had him working on the email accounts in the email group through which the various parties pressed their interest. Some were firewalled to hell, like the seller's for example, others were not. Most were invented for the sole purpose of communicating with the vendor, and only ever sent that one message, for confirmation. But *someone* slipped up. Our man is as close to a professional hacker as I'm allowed to employ, and he found a digital trap door through which he could sneak, via an IP address. To cut the long, technical story short, we know that one email account, which was apparently entirely anonymous, contacted the vendor to report that, after a hitch, Apex was safe in their possession after transit and would be ready for the auction on the proposed date. Now, who is this, you might ask, telling porky-pies? My man pinpointed the origin of the email as a computer at Whitehall.'

'The very offices of the Ministry of Defence,' Grosvenor clarifies.

I can't stop my eyes from blinking at how sloppy that was.

'Kirsten?' I ask.

'Who else do we know that has a vested interest in Apex, and who has the backing of the Ministry of Defence?' replies Jeremiah.

Stunned silence.

'So,' Jeremiah continues, 'it doesn't make sense to me that Kirsten was trusted to host the auction, considering that she is one of the hopeful buyers herself. I think she acted as the middle party to assist the substance's passage to the country, offering a safe airport, RMB Chivenor, for a chartered plane to land at, all in exchange for favour.'

'But she shot it down,' I say, computing the possibilities.

'She couldn't wait, it seems,' says Grosvenor. 'She couldn't leave it to chance, risk that she might not have it in the end. And if she sent the plane into the sea, she could recover the item while making it look as though it was unfortunately destroyed in an unforeseeable accident. That's when you buggered it all up for her, Ben.'

'No wonder she chased me down so hard!' I ponder. I had ruined her plan royally.

'Is there a possibility,' says Amina, 'that there are powerful parties within the MoD that want Apex, too?'

Jeremiah and Grosvenor exchange glances, betraying the fact that they have already shared the same suspicions.

'That is for another time, and another discussion,' says Grosvenor. 'With the timeframe we have, we have to work with what we know.'

'But we must assume that's a possibility,' adds Jeremiah.

'It's a damn *certainty*,' I say, again wishing my head would put a clamp on the words spewing from my heart. But I'm frothing. These people, these parties, every single one of these people, voted for and employed to look after a population — a population that tends not to question them, and puts unequivocal faith in them to do what is right. To guide the grand ship of Great Britain through stormy waters and dark, dangerous nights. All of this trust, only for them to reveal that the compass point they follow is calibrated for greed and personal gain, no matter the cost. And the cost here is so high, the safety of the population itself. Never, ever, have I felt so cynical and jaded about power, government and the relationships between the two.

This government, and these elected officials, are the ones that have sent myself and many like me around the world, on missions of bloodshed and combat. Modern day crusades to spread and enforce what *we* deem 'good' and 'democratic'. And while we were away, never questioning the reasons for our being there, those that sent us turned their attentions back to the power plays and tactical chess matches of their ivory towers. We were nothing more than pawns in a grotesque charade, a vile cut and thrust dance of power, influence and greed.

That word again. *Greed.* Amina used it only last night, when telling me how greed had ripped her family apart and got the majority of them killed. Greed is a killer, as bad as any disease or affliction. Man's infallible desire to better himself at the expense of another, for personal gain. And while the personal gains may be high, when you bring greed into a political furnace, those gains come at vast expense. The price is the very reason for government, the good of the people. Greed, when acted upon, always generates a loser. And when greed is in government, we all lose.

I can't let that happen. Not on my watch. So it surprises me all the more when I find myself saying: 'The auction has to go ahead.'

My three companions all turn to look at me, as if I've just spoken in tongues. I continue.

'Like William said. Allowing the auction to progress is the lesser of a great number of evils. If it stops Great Britain being the enemy here, then that's at least *something.*'

'Fair enough,' says Grosvenor. Amina sighs and Jeremiah shifts in his seat.

'Amina?' I ask, ushering her opinion.

'We could destroy it, and hope for the best. But I worry that that will only inflame prospective buyers further. They would want answers. And then there's the seller, who will be angry with Kirsten for messing things up, and since she represents government, that puts the country in the firing line again.'

Couldn't have put it better myself.

'So, hypothetically,' Jeremiah begins, 'we call Kirsten and tell her that the auction will take place. She gets to take credit for keeping her word…'

'And no international super-scientist will want to take revenge for her deception, because there won't appear to have been any,' I interrupt.

'Right. So, any suggestions?'

'We pick the location. One that is set for another purpose, which is surveillance.'

'Go on,' urges Grosvenor.

'This cause is all but lost, and damage limitation is the only real prospect here. But if we look deeper, and think laterally, we can get something useful out of this situation after all. Intel. Think about it. Any of the parties who want to attend the auction are obviously of criminal intent. The list of attendees will be a roll call of international criminal power players. And if we can control the event, we can get a fix on them, and learn about them. Most importantly, we have to find out who buys Apex, so we know who to keep an eye on.'

There is a moment of silence, as the reason for my sudden u-turn settles in.

'That,' Jeremiah breathes out, 'is a fantastic idea, given the options.'

'Think about what you will learn if you change the focus of the exercise,' I say.

'I'm all for that,' says Grosvenor.

'Two provisions,' I say. 'Firstly, we pick the location to suit. And I think safety is a priority. I think we need to pick somewhere that has a controllable atmosphere and environment. The people attending the event will be an unstable mix of criminal parties, all trying to get their hands on a very volatile item, and there will be winners and losers. The last thing we want is an incident and an accident occurring with Apex itself.'

'The thought had crossed my mind,' says Amina.

'So, we pick somewhere with a fully regulated environment. I don't care if Kirsten takes credit for this too. But we need somewhere that will halt the spread of the substance in the event of any accident.'

'OK, that sounds good. What springs to mind?' asks Jeremiah. 'Anybody?'

'A factory of some kind?' suggests Grosvenor.

'Too many variables,' says Amina. 'Factories contain dangerous enough chemicals at times as it is, introducing even more toxic substances to the mix is not to be advised.'

'What about,' I say, 'some kind of livestock facility, like a breeding environment that controls what the animals eat, drink and breathe?'

'That would work,' says Amina, shrugging. 'It's far less dangerous than the hit and miss nature of a larger scale factory.'

'I read about this,' I say. 'Large scale breeders control every element of their product's environment, in spaces big enough to allow livestock to move around. If we can find one that will suit, which could contain Apex in the event of an accident, and set it up for surveillance, then we are on to a winner. Kind of.'

'I think that's pretty stellar,' says Jeremiah.

'I can certainly make some calls,' says Grosvenor, with a satisfied smile.

'My second provision involves myself. I want to be there. I want to be your point man on the ground.'

Silence again, but not the good kind. I fill in the blanks as best I can.

'Like you said, Jeremiah. I have been custodian of Apex for the last three days, and everything has worked out so far. Let me guard it, right up until it is passed on to whichever son of a bitch buys it. I don't trust Kirsten. There is no way I'm going to give it to her, and hope that she's somehow going to do the right thing and take it to auction. She has burned her bridges in that regard.'

'What do we all think of that?' asks Jeremiah, casting his eyes around the room. 'Personally, I don't have a problem with it. I've got about enough pull, and favours left to call in, to get a tactical unit in the vicinity, but at a distance. Just as an absolute failsafe.'

I could be in agreement with that. Christ knows what frictions could develop, in gathering such an unscrupulous menagerie of criminal filth.

'No, that sounds OK. I like the idea of having a man on the ground,' says Grosvenor.

'I'm going with him,' says Amina.

We turn to her now, as the situation seems ever-changing. I'm not sure about this, and try to tell her so with my stare. I don't want her anywhere near the place.

'Amina could be right, there,' says Jeremiah. 'She has been as much a part of protecting Apex as you, plus she knows precisely what she is doing with the damn stuff.'

'Exactly,' confirms Amina. I could protest but I already know that, where she is concerned, my pleas will get no traction whatsoever.

'So we have a plan,' Jeremiah says. 'William, can you fill Kirsten in and get her to make the arrangements with whoever we assume is to execute the auction? I will find a suitable location and prep it for our purpose. You two, hang tight. I'll let you know when there is more to tell. But I think there is one more order of business, before we all set about making the relevant arrangements.'

I sense the elephant in the room. It's about to come crashing into our midst.

'We are placing a great deal of trust in you, Ben,' Jeremiah sighs, looking at the table top. 'I think, if you wouldn't mind, a little information about yourself wouldn't go amiss here.'

I have been waiting for this. It's only fair, I suppose. Jeremiah knows nothing about me, save that I am highly trained, motivated and loyal. I have not let him down yet, but he has trusted me based on results alone. When I have promised to deliver, I have done so, and never given him cause to doubt me. But now, face-to-face at last, it seems understandable that he should ask.

But what do I say? I'm supposed to be in prison serving a sentence for murder, even though I was framed. If I reveal too much, surely he will send me straight back there? That's exactly what I would do, in his position.

And Grosvenor? There is something very worldly and understanding about him; as if he knows that the path to the greater good is not as simple as a black and white fork in the road. Nothing is clean and easy, but still, perhaps he too might not be keen on working with me, if he were to know of my past. Particularly the part about my dishonourable discharge, no matter how much I was trying to do the right thing.

'My anonymity is very important to me. If I feel that my privacy is to be abused by any of you, I will walk out of that door now, and take Apex with me, and you can work out a solution to this all by yourselves.'

No one balks at that, so I take a deep breath.

'I'm an ex-army captain. I was dishonourably discharged a few years ago, but I'm not finished serving my country.'

There is so much more to say, and I think they know it. I'm not willing to divulge the rest, and all the grotesque ins and outs. Please, let me leave it there...

'What unit?' asks Jeremiah.

'No chance,' I say.

'Which conflicts were you involved in?' he asks again.

'I'm pinpointing nothing, but using the broadest strokes, if you think of the last ten years, you'll probably get there.'

'Iraq and Afghanistan,' says Grosvenor. I answer with a stony gaze.

'What were you discharged for?' asks Jeremiah. I transfer the stony gaze to him. 'Ben, do I need to remind you of the gravity of this situation?'

'You absolutely don't,' I reply.

'Nevertheless, I feel I should. This is of grave, national importance. I need to know that you are not the kind of man who will screw us over. The likelihood of dishonourably discharged ex-soldiers reforming to become upstanding citizens, let alone public avengers, is extremely low. I don't want to make a mistake here, and you must understand my concern.'

My anger has been stoked, but I have to accept their position. He is right. They don't know my story, my background, my history — and thank God they don't. But I know, in my heart, that I'm not one of those people, despite what the record books say.

'I am going to say no more. I think my actions so far have shown sufficient loyalty and perseverance to show that I am a man of my word,' I say, moving my gaze from Jeremiah to Grosvenor and back again. It's an appeal to them to drop it. 'It may say *dishonourably discharged* on my official record, but I assure you that it is not as simple as that. It is honour that has pushed me to this point. And if there is any more of this bullshit, questioning *me* of all people, when *you two* both work for the most crooked fucking government going, I'm going to walk out of this hotel immediately. Can we drop this and move on?'

There is a moment of silence, while the people in the room digest my words.

'OK then,' says Jeremiah, closing the file on the table and flashing a smile that eases my concerns. 'Must have been a hell of a unit you were in charge of.'

'It never quite leaves you,' Grosvenor says. 'Thank you for your continued service, Ben. The country needs more like you. Just don't let us down.'

Grosvenor actually looks proud. As though he has finally seen something that he has been looking for, for some time. Someone like him. Someone willing to go that extra mile, to do what is right. Suddenly, he is up.

'I must get back to Westminster,' he says, shrugging on his suit jacket. 'The PM will want to be appraised of the situation. You are all safe here. John won't ask any questions, and you are free to use this place for as long as you need, in privacy. When you have a site for the auction, please let me know, so I can pass it onto our wonderful, dutiful Defence Secretary.'

'I'm on it,' says Jeremiah, wheeling himself back from the table, shaking Grosvenor's hand. 'Thanks for the call, and for your assistance, William.'

'It's good to know that there are good men working hard out there, Jeremiah.' They shake.

'Ben, Amina,' Grosvenor says, while buttoning his jacket. 'Without your efforts, God knows how this could have wound up. Keep sharp tomorrow night. Keep your heads, and we all get out of this one. And as much as it hurts to admit it, this seems to be the right thing.'

He shakes Amina's hand, then mine. 'Try to keep your nose clean, Ben,' he says, in tones laced with a meaning I am unable to fully decipher. And with one last flash of a grin, he is off. Back to the belly of government, the PM's right hand man.

'If there's anything you need, just shout,' I say to Jeremiah. 'But for now, we'll give you some space.'

'That'd be great,' he replies. 'I'll let you know how I get on.'

I feel itchy, in my feet and hands. There is a long wait until tomorrow night, but I know patience is necessary. I've got to let the brains behind the operation get moving before I can, and that is a situation that I am very familiar with. I might as well embrace this. It's the calm before the storm that has been forecast.

21.

The night comes in, but only after a long, lazy dusk that seemed to stretch ever-onwards like a dog by a fireplace, the sun laying molten rays of orange on this little pocket of countryside. I have watched most of it from the back porch of the property, which has a couple of bench seats facing the sun. A hot spot from which to watch the last pages of day turn through to its epilogue.

Amina and I ate quickly in the dining room, steak and kidney pies made expertly by Denise, doused in gravy and bolstered with chips. The meal was belting, but the experience proved emotionally exhausting.

During dinner, I buckled just enough. I knew Amina's story, and I felt that she should know mine. When we were alone, she listened as I told her what *really* happened in that sewer under Lashkar Gah, when I was stuck with Stephen. I left out the more disgusting elements, since we were eating, and watched for her reaction when I told her that long before we got stuck down there, Stephen had made me promise that if he asked me to, under extreme circumstances, I would end his life.

She didn't react at all. None of the judgement and outrage that usually comes when this tale is told. I went on, how he asked me after we had been stuck for three days, infection and dehydration ravaging his body. He told me I'd promised to do it if all was lost. It took me a further three days to agree, and Amina watched with a baleful gaze as I told her that after breakfast on the seventh day, I killed him as mercifully as I could.

Her knife and fork paused as I told her that, heartbroken, I had thrown myself into the churning sewer water, letting fate decide what to do with me, hoping death would come to spare me from living with what I'd done. She reached out across the table, but her hand paused somewhere midway, the gap between us still too great. She slowly withdrew it, as I told her that the sewer spat me out two miles away in a river, and I was traded back to my superiors by a fisherman. When I told my superiors what happened, they branded me a murderer and kicked me out.

After a while, Amina spoke. 'You did what you felt was right. You did the best you could.' I could have cried, there and then.

After the meal, tiredness seemed to come and claim her. Suddenly, she was exhausted, the waves of adrenaline receding at last to reveal an abyss of depleted energy.

She excused herself, and John offered me a whisky with some cheese and biscuits for afters. I eagerly accepted, and for the last hour, it has felt like I am at a country club of the type patronised by Old Etonians. Afterwards, John replenished my glass, and told me about the spot on the porch.

Now, on the grass of the gardens, I can see that the rabbits have come out to play. They frolic confidently around the ornate stone pots and manicured hedges, without a care. I envy them shamelessly, as I remember the one I had to stone and skin just to get to this point.

I hear the door behind me on the porch click then creak, before swinging open.

'Thanks, John,' I hear Jeremiah say, and I turn to see him wheel out onto the porch. John doesn't follow.

'May I join you?'

'Of course,' I say. Within a moment Jeremiah is next to me, and I see that he is cradling a small tumbler and the familiar bottle of 12-year-old Highland Park single malt in his lap.

'John thought your glass could use refreshing,' says Jeremiah, popping off the cork.

'One thing's for definite — John is a damn good bloke,' I say as my glass is ambered.

Jeremiah pours a measure for himself, and sets the bottle down. 'Cheers,' he says, extending his glass to me. We clink and slug, the smoky warmth prickling all corners of my tongue. 'So, I have our location. A turkey farm about fifteen miles north of here. They are a specialist breeding group, who control every aspect of

277

the environment that the birds come into contact with. They can give us one of their sheds, since a batch of birds reached maturity just last week. I believe it's a very secluded spot. It should suit us down to the ground.'

'Sounds perfect. I would imagine they have been well compensated?' I say.

'Grosvenor is indeed greasing the wheels in his… his inimitable style. Plus, he has let Kirsten know.'

'It's all coming together, then.'

'Hmm. When you sneaked up on me in that disabled toilet last year, who knew that it would lead to the arrests it has, not to mention a situation like this?'

'At the time, I badly needed an ally. I needed a man with both information and drive.'

His voice carries an easy jocularity, invoking the feeling that we are old friends, reunited. The formality of speech with which he carried our discussion earlier, has gone. It was probably there because of Grosvenor — a figure like that commands proper procedure. 'You made a real bloody mess for us to wade through, you know. The pencil pushers in the offices down the hall are still at it. But I've got to hand it to you — you were more effective than any police force ever has been against Manchester's organised crime network. The fact that you are very hard to get hold of, helped. I couldn't find you if I tried.'

'But you did, didn't you?' I say, raising my eyebrows.

'I wouldn't be much of an investigator if I didn't,' he says, returning my smile. 'But it was a needle in a haystack. You gave me very little to go on.'

'That was the idea,' I say. *Progress with caution, Ben.*

'I have to say, while my superiors would slap my wrist for saying it, I don't really care. You are a man of your word, which counts for a lot more than identity and record in my book. There are very few straight shooters left. But you are one of them. The people I have to deal with every day, the agendas I have to stick to, the hoops I have to jump through, the sheer amount of arses I have to kiss... I have to say, it's refreshing.'

'I get the feeling you're a straight shooter, too.'

'I try to be. Within the rules, of course.'

There is an ease to our conversation. Despite the nature of our relationship, it has always been based on trust, and that clearly has counted for a lot, for both parties.

'I can promise you, as a man working in law enforcement, having an outside party with your... your autonomy and skill set... can be extremely helpful.'

'That's all I'd like to be,' I say.

'Which means that, whatever it is that bought you to this point, I am not interested in that. I think it's important that, in order to have each other's backs in this, we operate with a clean slate. You've never given me reason to doubt you, so I won't start now.'

'I'd like that, and will do the same.'

'OK, then,' he says, settling a bit. He seems relieved to have got that off his chest, but the relief is not his alone. I feel soothed, my anxieties about discovery and capture reduced a little.

'Where does Grosvenor fit in?' I ask.

'I contacted Grosvenor when we were called off the case in the first place. I wanted to know why that happened, and I thought, as a non-portfolio entity, he would be the most impartial. I think he had the same fears, and we have been in contact ever since. Of course, he is the friendly party I alluded to yesterday.'

'Gotcha.'

And we settle in and enjoy a brief moment. Like two pen pals who have never met, but realise that, when they do finally get together, they get on in real life as well as on the page. The sun is now just a sliver of peel on the horizon, and within seconds, the last drop of juicy glare is all squeezed out. The sky glows softly in memory.

'Confession time. When you told me your name was Ben, before, I did a little digging. I thought you might have been this guy, Ben Bracken, escaped from prison. He's got a military background, just like you. Left service about that time too. But when I looked into it, it turns out that Ben Bracken is still behind bars. The Chief Warden of HMP Manchester told me so himself. So I'm back to the drawing board in my little hunt to find out more about you.'

I coil, and then tense, ramrod straight. It takes an effort not to jolt out of my chair, and silence Jeremiah on the spot. I try not to look at him, but I can't help it. And when I do look, I see that he is sighing and raising the glass to his lips.

'It's a shame, because, from what I've read, we could really do with a guy of that calibre on the team,' he says, before sipping away the last of his whiskey.

Tawtridge, the Chief Warden, has obviously kept his word, and my insurance policy remains in place. He was utterly corrupt, and I blackmailed him, and told him that if he didn't 'forget' about my escape, I'd release what I have in my possession to bring his crooked regime down around his ankles. What I have is five of his guards' shirts, soaked in the blood of an inmate who was mysteriously killed last year. Combine that with the CCTV footage of the incident and, well, it wouldn't look good at all.

But there is no fooling Jeremiah; he looks calm and cocksure, but completely without malevolence.

'You couldn't open the door could you? I think big days deserve early nights before them,' he says.

'Sure,' I say, hopping up and obliging.

'Goodnight, Ben. I'll see you in the morning.'

'Goodnight,' I reply, weakly. I am stunned, I don't know what to say. My identity, so sacred to me, and my anonymity, so vital to the success of any goal that I may have, are both laid bare. As Jeremiah disappears inside, I take the bottle, which I assume he has left with me on purpose, and pour.

He knows exactly who I am.

Jesus. The man is an expert. He's got resources to spare, I mustn't forget. If he ever suspected I was Ben Bracken, all it would have taken to confirm that suspicion is a run through his databases to find a mugshot.

What an idiot, Ben. You pretty much told him.

His mannerisms and words though... It didn't feel at all like a warning, more like a friendly nudge. As if to say, *you are alright with me, pal.*

I want to believe that. I really do. Because I don't want to silence the first friend I've made in years.

22.

Tuesday

My eyes open and I am faced with black. My body is warm and comfortable, cocooned in linen. I can't see anything, but just as I note that, I begin to make out outlines as my eyes adjust. Then I hear a creak behind me, and I feel the weight of the grand old bed shift. Someone has climbed in with me.

I freeze. I can only imagine it being one person, but I am nevertheless very surprised. I stay still, and silent. My visitor doesn't move, just lies softly next to me. I detect a light note of pineapple-scented hair products, and assume it can only be Amina.

Why is she here? Is this some kind of seduction? Or a plea for help?

Does she find security in my presence, as I have dared to suspect?

This forces me to look at Amina in a romantic light, something I have not yet consciously done. I feel an undeniable attraction to her, but I am very worried that those desires are borne out of an overly romanticised urge to protect her. She is beautiful, funny, fiery... and tragic. Maybe that is why I like her.

She is irreparably damaged in so many ways, and those are feelings that I am very familiar with. But, like me, she fought back against the hand that was dealt her, and concocted a future of her own design. There are, indeed, similarities between us.

But is it simply because I am drawn to her, again, by that infernal sense of duty? Do I find myself propelled in her direction by nothing more than a warped desire to protect and serve, while her prettiness and bubbling personality have simply galvanised my feelings? Perhaps that's how these things always happen, with one thing leading to another. Grand trees growing from tiny seeds. Love blooming in the most unlikely of places.

She has certainly seen me at my worst, and she is still here. Perhaps she sees something in me that I don't? A good man, buried by the violence of the tasks he undertakes? I can't fight pessimism where this is concerned. I have been so burnt by love in the past, that trust in another person is not something I can configure or mould. I feel safer on my own. It's easier.

But there is something about Amina… Something I can't identify. She is strong in so many ways. Dedicated. Driven. Honest. There are so many characteristics about her that I admire.

And suddenly, her warmth pulls against me, and I feel her breath light on my neck. Her leg snakes over mine, and her palm presses on my stomach. Her touch sends a bolting tremor through my very core, something warm, giddy, galloping. Something I've not known for so long.

Have I ever thought about meeting somebody? Have I ever thought about that 'meeting somebody' progressing to the level of a relationship?

I suppose I haven't. Family is what I want, deep down. To love and to give life. I tried that once before, but… the girl, she… ended the pregnancy before I even had a chance to get excited about it. I thought my life was set, and I was ready to dive straight into it, but all my hopes were smashed on the rocks before my fall into love had ended. I will never let that happen to me again, although I know that, where such things are involved, I do have a considerable gap in my armour. Realistically, it is more like a gaping fissure; one that I keep smoothing shut.

And here is this beautiful Kosovan girl, pulling the torqued edges of my armour wide apart. Her breathing is shallow, urgent. I can feel her heart against my ribcage. Her scent is wildly hypnotising.

Be careful, Ben.

I don't know what to do, even more so now, than before. My more primal urges scream at me to roll over and kiss her, and let nature take its course. If it is meant to be, it is surely meant to be. But if that's the case, then

285

surely I can get away with doing nothing now, and it will happen if it's destined to at some point further down the road? Yes, that sounds good.

Besides, I'm far too nervous. I wouldn't have a clue what kind of move to make. But I'd love to explore that with Amina. *Love to*. She is smart, capable and knows what I am like. She knows what darkness lurks within. There can't be too many girls out there that would tolerate me and my eccentricities in the way that she has, and yet still come back for more. She could be my one in a million.

But I can't let anyone in. I just can't. There's too much at stake, and I already feel weakened by her presence. I already know that I would do anything necessary to protect her, and I don't want to compound that with any additional feelings.

I'm scared. *Face it, Ben. You are gutless*. And with that, I pretend to sleep deeply, and think firmly of all the could-have-beens.

*

When I awake naturally the next morning, I am alone, save for that soft hint of pineapple on the pillow. It's nice, even simply waking up with a whisper of someone's presence. I try not to wallow in her scent, finding the act of doing so foreign and a little disturbing, but it is unnervingly comforting.

Dread hits me like a sneaky hammer strike, right to the parts that jar, and layers itself thickly on the nervousness I already feel about the day, as the thought dawns… that I'm actually going to have to see her, and speak to her.

I swallow hard. I'd much rather do yesterday morning's gunfire-spattered breakfast call, than try to fathom quandaries as serpentine as feelings, regardless of how heavily I might have trodden on someone else's.

23.

A car arrives for us at 6.00 pm, the first sign of external life to disturb our sanctuary since the arrival of Jeremiah's helicopter, yesterday. Amina and I are already waiting on the steps, having spent the whole day in quaint denial that anything nearly-maybe-almost happened between us last night.

It has been a jam-packed day, infused with purposeful conversation and steady preparation, and as the silver BMW saloon pulls up in front of us, its solitary driver hopping out to help us with the bags, I feel like a political dignitary being ferried from a plush hotel to a conference hall.

The driver introduces himself as Sam and, seeing that there is only one bag here and I'm clearly not going to be letting it out of my sight, he opens the passenger door for us. We swap perfunctory greetings, nothing more, I assume he is already well briefed. As we settle in the car, and scrunch gravel away, I look back through the rear window at the house, and spy Jeremiah in the downstairs bay window, watching us depart.

I'm led to believe that there was an intense period of negotiation overnight, regarding our attendance at this ridiculous auction, and Jeremiah filled us in over breakfast. Kirsten Sweetmore wanted us both hung, drawn and quartered, me especially, for obstructing the actions of government and the murder of Ministry of Defence employees, and she leant hard on Grosvenor to give us up as soon as Apex is handed over. Grosvenor resisted, thankfully, while reminding her that we could just as easily destroy the infernal stuff, while Jeremiah pointed out that when we are at the auction site, it isn't Kirsten's show anymore — despite her having arranged its execution. It turns out Jeremiah was spot on when he surmised there was a team in the UK on standby, ready to run an auction when called upon, third party financed, accountable only to that very same third party. To curry favour, it seems Kirsten has told them that I am somehow on her side, a trusted sub-black ops man, keeping the damned substance safe following the 'accidental' plane crash. She really will stop at nothing to get what she wants.

'Why are you taking your bag with you?' Amina asks, slicing through my thoughts.

'Habit,' I say. 'I just feel better that way.'

'Oh,' she replies. 'Should I have done the same?'

'You're fine,' I say. 'It'll all be over soon.'

'OK.'

My mind diverts back to the people we discussed today, to all those mysterious parties destined to attend tonight's little get-together. How little is known of their true identities, but how awful some of the suspected parties are. It will be a time for a cool head, and a steady grip.

I get the feeling that, with a delicate concoction of corrupt government figures, terrorist representatives and absurdly rich criminals, tonight's recipe will be spicy to say the least, if not downright flammable. One bad move could initiate World War Three, either at the auction site or out in the real world, should certain parties rub each other up the wrong way.

'Won't be long now,' says Sam. 'About twenty minutes or so.' He speaks cheerily, as if he's about to drop us off at the theatre for an early evening showing of 'The Mousetrap'.

Five years ago, it would have appalled me to enter a situation like this, devoid of back-up, but unfortunately, those are the rules we have been given. I know that Jeremiah has arranged for a tactical unit nearby, but that is extremely last resort and hush hush. They are only there to watch, anyway, and to take notes. Jeremiah's negotiations with Kirsten have revealed that the powers that be won't sanction the auction unless it is completely covert, and minimal. No extra faces permitted.

It is a buyers only event, and attendance is strictly by invitation only. And the invitation provides, in a move that I find oddly charming and old fashioned, a password. Each attending party has been given one that is unique, to be submitted on the door, and each admits one person only. The secret protector and the microbiologist have been assigned one each, valid and applicable only to ourselves. It feels vaguely ridiculous, but I understand it. It keeps numbers, and potential friction, to a minimum. If every buyer is accompanied by five goons, the likelihood of all hell breaking loose is amplified.

I glance towards Amina, who stares out of the window. She is a picture of focus, and such is her desire to see things through that we have almost had to invent a role for her in this. The mercenaries actually conceded it would be a good point to have a microbiologist present, in the event of accidents. I get the picture that this is one of the few things they have overlooked. It crossed my mind that perhaps that was the occupation of the woman on the plane. So maybe Amina is filling in for her, in a professional capacity, and judging by her determined stare, it is a duty she is taking very seriously.

The time passes quickly, and as it does, I distil what is to happen in the coming hour into a form that is as concise as I can make it. But as simple as it is — namely get in, hand over Apex, and get out while catching glimpse of who bought it — I can't find even the tiniest comfort in it. I'm not happy with what I have to do. I hold something of such innate danger and value, that placing it into the wrong hands seems directly opposed to everything I stand for. And this place we are taking it to will be jammed to the rafters with the wrong hands. No one is a safe bet, there is no horse for me to back. I suppose that in such circles, hoping for a super-rich shining light to buy Apex for good was always going to be a bit of a stretch. But I have Apex, now, in my possession.

I know I am not necessarily the most conventional force for good, but surely my intentions will be better than those of anybody else there? I can't hand this over, can I? Grosvenor's argument was so tight, Jeremiah's reasoning so astute, that it certainly does seem the lesser of a great many evils…

Just do it, Ben. As Jeremiah put it earlier, 'Just go, hand it over, and come back here so we can try that nice pub in the village and get fat and rat-arsed on the local food and grog'. I'd love to take him up on the second part of that offer, but I'm struggling with the first.

'How are you feeling?' I ask Amina.

'Fine. I finally get to use my qualifications for something a bit more interesting than mushroom bugs,' she says.

'Keep smiling,' I say. 'Follow my lead and it will be over soon. And I won't let you out of my sight.'

'With your habit of getting into trouble, that's what worries me,' she replies, with a smile. The old Amina is nearly back. I fight the urge to reach out to her, knowing that to do so would further complicate what is already complicated.

'Two minutes,' says Sam, and I look ahead down the road we travel. It is quiet, and leafy, with high trees on either side of the road that have been buffeted into a distinctive tunnel shape high over the concrete, presumably thanks to the routine of heavy goods vehicles passing through. Must be the frequent transport of stock and supplies to and from the factory site.

We round a bend, and the farm opens out ahead of us, beyond a thick green gate that stands shut. Two armed guards patrol it. I think of Jeremiah's men, and where they must be. They are reporting back to Jeremiah from a distance, since there is a ban on radios and cellphones inside, and the CCTV has been switched off. The intel operation has been reduced to little more than a spotting exercise, with Jeremiah's team secreted in the woodland to the north of the site. It's my intel and Amina's that they are relying on primarily — and Sam's, I guess.

We pull up at the gates, behind a couple of other cars, each of which looks like a nondescript airport rental — ostentation has now clearly given way to secrecy. I see guards clad in grey overalls checking out the cars and the occupants, before ushering them through one at a time.

Within a moment, we are approached. I spot a shouldered automatic weapon before anything else. A youngish, terse man, broad and solid with a no nonsense expression, gestures for Sam to lower the window, which he does. This is our first sight of the clandestine team behind the auction.

'I have two for you here,' says Sam, calm and poised. He must be a field operative. Amina and I lean forward for examination.

'Ladies first,' says the man in a tone that is deep, but not rude. Another man of experience, it seems.

'Piccolo,' she says, and the man's eyes divert to me.

'Pegasus,' I say, trying to measure the man who looks back at me.

'Have fun,' replies the man. 'Park in the parking bays on the right with the others. Only Piccolo and Pegasus to approach the building.'

And with that, he is off behind us, to inspect another car that has arrived.

We move through the gates, and turn right as instructed, where a makeshift car park has been laid out with cones. Each car has someone at the wheel, some smoking cigarettes, reading or snoozing. Other drivers, whose charges must all be on their way inside. At the edge of the car park, I see suits walking towards what looks like a path to the front door. The path itself is short, but well manned. Four armed security guards patrol the thirty-foot walkway.

'Stay alert, Sam,' I say, as I open the door and hop out with my bag. Amina follows hastily.

'Of course. Take care in there,' he replies.

We immediately start the walk to the front door, and are ushered forwards by the men lining the route, all of them clad and equipped exactly as the man at the gate.

'This way, please,' one says.

I take in the farm, which seems to be a series of interconnecting metal sheds, all feeding into a central smaller office hub. It looks clean, well maintained and efficiently scientific. Vents line the roofs, and fans. This is the perfect place for such an event.

As we reach the door, two more darkly clad guards bar the way, one with a clipboard. 'Names?' the clipboard wielder says.

'Piccolo,' says Amina.

'Pegasus,' I say.

'Do you have the item, Pegasus?' clipboard man asks.

'Yes.'

'We can take it from here,' he says, reaching out for my bag.

'No chance,' I say, holding firm. 'You know the terms.'

The man smiles, and loosens. 'I was told you were a stickler. Go inside but you guys go left. Through the double doors... there is an office where The Chief is getting set up. He'll take care of you.'

We go in. It all feels rather jovial, as though we are at a movie premier. No one seems to appreciate that there are potentially millions of lives at stake. As we walk, I see that two armed guards have quietly become our big, burly, no-nonsense shadows. Special treatment, just for us.

We turn left, and through the double doors, to a shallow flight of stairs. We take them, our silent watchmen in tow, and are faced with another door, which leads into a wide office.

The window blinds are all shut, and the office is lit purely by the ceiling strip lights. The two security staff that followed us move to the left of the room, and I can now see that they are uniformed in a manner identical to their colleagues and regard me with passive features. Over to the right is a man adjusting a shirt and tie. He is red faced, with highlighted blonde hair and a trim physique. As he looks up, there is the suggestion of plastic surgery to his face. Certain parts don't move as naturally as they should.

'The Chief?' I say. 'It's Pegasus and Piccolo.' On hearing that, he smiles, revealing a too-perfect set of pearly whites, and comes over with arms wide.

'You're here!' he says in a jovial sing-song cadence. He walks over and hugs Amina warmly, as if they have known each other for years. Amina glances quizzically at me over his clamping shoulder, and all I can do is shrug back. I too am then given the full treatment. 'Thank you so much for coming!'

'Anytime,' I reply, very unsure of how to go. I feel he is as likely to burst into a rendition of 'The Hills Are Alive' as much anything else. I catch sight of the two men stationed near the windows, who watch with fingers hovering near triggers. 'I have the item here.'

'Perfect!' he says. 'Right on time. Our guests are almost all here, readying themselves for the main event. So exciting!'

What had I expected? Not this. Not some kind of stage-managed performance conducted by a sub-Broadway dropout. And the security is so tight. We are pinned here. While I assess the environment, The Chief puts an arm around Amina, and guides her away towards the far end of the room.

'Now Piccolo, I wondered if, for the purposes of showmanship, and since you are here, you would verify the item in front of everybody. The buyers, I mean. I've been reliably informed that the equipment is set up out on the stage, for you to examine the item in question. It is for show more than anything. I thought it would give the auction a special start, really drum up some excitement. What do you think?'

He speaks like a convivial firing squad, barraging the listener with enthusiasm and froth. Amina seems unsure, as am I, and I think our faces show it. I don't think that is a good idea.

'It will only be for a moment. You don't even have to look at it! You just come over, say what you see, confirm what we all have been told about the item, and you're done.'

We swap a glance, and I'm unaware I've conveyed anything to her when she says quietly 'I suppose I could do that'.

'Splendid!' says The Chief.

'I'll be close by,' I say, which seems to bristle the security, given away by the squeak of boot leather and the rustle of their uniforms.

'Well, of course you will!' replies The Chief, brushing the tension under the carpet. 'We are nearly ready, and when we are, we will go out onto the platform outside the office. Our bidders are all below us, nattering away.'

'Where?' I ask.

'Just down there,' he says, while crossing to the closed blinds on the left hand side of the room. 'Have a little peek.'

I approach cautiously, the guards shadowing me yet again — something tells me they may have heard about me — and part the blinds with a couple of fingers.

Spread out, ten feet below, is a large empty barn, clinical and clean. Lights have been pulled high, right up to the ceiling, the walls are lined with feeding trays, and dismantled cage sections have been pulled to the corners. And on the floor of the barn stand thirty or so people, with a couple of grey-clad guards for good measure. They are milling about, chatting to each other, and some even hold glasses of wine or munch on little snacks. There must have been a buffet laid out for them in an adjacent room.

These are the buyers, the people interested in acquiring Apex, and my anticipation grows. I spot Kirsten immediately; her shock of peroxide hair is a beacon. She holds a glass of red wine, and looks to be laughing too vociferously with… with a man I recognise so quickly that it takes my breath away. He is packed tightly into his suit, his thinning hair reflecting the glare from above, his mouth smiling thinly beneath a slender, long nose. He is the Russian Prime Minister, Valentin Lechkov.

I am stunned.

If I was ever in any doubt about just how big the big hitters involved with this auction are, those doubts have been put to rest. The possibilities of this man's presence alone blow the magnitude of the circumstances to places unimaginable. Yet there they are. The British Government's Defence Secretary and the Russian Prime Minister, laughing along at some in-joke while munching on canapés, about to bid against each other in an auction to acquire a hellish super-botulism.

I would fall down, if I wasn't already looking to the next people. I'm alive more than ever to the dangers we are all in. There are people here I don't recognise, sure, but there are faces that spark immediate recognition and amp my terror and awe levels up significantly.

There is the retired US Army Chief of Staff, Blake Bresciano, whom I recognise from his occasional visits to

Camp Bastion in Afghanistan. What on earth is he doing here? He's supposed to be out of action, retired.

And over there is a guy I read about in *The Times*. They call him the Instagram Poker Millionaire. I can't remember his name, but I certainly remember the face, from all those smug Instagram shots replicated in the papers. Him rolling on the floor with half-naked women and gold bars, writhing in swimming pools filled with champagne and porn stars. He made a fortune on the American poker circuits, they wrote. I guess now, in his parlance, he is upping the ante.

The back door to the barn opens, and I see another man enter, holding an orange juice. He wears a well-tailored grey suit and a white turban, his long grey beard reaching to his mid-chest. I know him straight away, from intel documents I studied on the ground in Afghanistan. Jesus *Christ*.

A long time ago, I was part of a specifically designed team destined for a brief sojourn to northern Pakistan, to try to take out a supposed Taliban stronghold, in the hunt for a man called Mohammed Al Jahlel. We knew him better as Osama Bin Laden's number three. His left hand man. We stormed the stronghold, and found no trace, merely ghosts of an operation not long since abandoned. The trail died with our failure. It was the disappointing culmination of a three-year operation, and as far as I know, nobody has seen him since. Or rather, nobody had, until he just walked through that door, trying to get his hands on chemical weapons.

I'm more dumbfounded with every passing recognition, and scared by the ones I don't immediately know. The prim, exceptionally tall blonde man who seems very reluctant to socialise, who is so pale he is bordering on albino, wearing red sunglasses even though there is no natural sunlight in the barn. To my amazement there is a sort of 'granny' figure, chatting amiably with a flamboyantly-dressed man. She wears a cardigan over a pastel dress, her hair grey yet set joyously in a post-war whisk. God knows who *she* is.

'OK, time to get things started. It's 6.30,' The Chief says, and before I know it, he is walking to the door at the end of the office. 'Are you both ready?'

Amina responds with a 'yes' and I nod, while taking the modified Tupperware out of my bag. I take it to The Chief, and slowly hand it to him, imagining what future horrors I have set in motion by doing so. He thanks me with a curt nod, and throws the door open, onto a high walkway stationed above the barn. A guard waits there, and The Chief walks out onto his stage, turning to address his subjects. Amina and I wait in the doorway, listening, while the two armed guards stand just behind us, poised as ever.

'Good evening everybody, and welcome. Thank you so much for coming. I hope you are all refreshed and moderately comfortable. I am hosting this auction on behalf of a seller who wishes, understandably, to remain anonymous.'

The room is hushed, and as I peak around the door frame, I see faces locked onto the man on the catwalk. The Chief continues, wringing out every last drop of theatre.

'In this room are some of the most important figures in the world today. Make no mistake, the cream rises. It is in this room right now. And, I'm pleased to announce that our seller has a product here that is utterly befitting of such high calibre customers. A product befitting only the most impressive of buyers. I give you... Apex.'

The Chief opens the small box, and holds the vial aloft, the clear glass glinting in his rising hand. A smattering of applause breaks out. My word, the world's worst can be civil.

'I'd like to introduce our specialist microbiologist, Piccolo. Anonymity dictates her name, but you will be in no doubt of her qualifications and suitability when you hear her speak and see her in action.'

The Chief turns to the side, and waves Amina over.

'Good luck,' I whisper, as she moves onto the catwalk to join the speaker. She moves quickly and doesn't address the crowd, who applaud again. I take a look at the masses. One person definitely isn't clapping — Kirsten. It looks like she might be sick with rage.

'If you would, Piccolo, please use the glovebox and microscope to tell us what we have here,' says The Chief, as a wheeled glovebox unit is pushed by a guard towards the middle of the catwalk. No expense has been spared on the fine details here, it seems.

Before my eyes can make their way back to the stage, my breath pauses in my throat.

It can't be. *It just can't.*

That man, there, on the right hand side, in the leather bomber jacket. It's the scowl that tugs at me first, and then I see the earring. Everything from the heavy tan, leathered skin, thinly coiffed hair, right down to the espadrilles he saunters in. This must be a cruel joke?

But it is not.

I can't believe it.

Without a doubt, that is Terry 'The Turn-Up' Masters, London crime lord, who views himself as the real royalty of the Big Smoke. The man who shot my leg out from beneath me, who set his dogs on me and framed me for murdering his son. Who put me in the jail I had to escape from.

The nights I have spent thinking about this man, and how to bring him to justice. The fixation I have on bringing him to account. The ire I feel brimming just as I look at him.

His power must be significant, if he is at an auction like this. You need serious capital to get into this room, but here he is, looking right at home. He looks as though he is just biding time before he nips off down the pub, and, such is the nature of his habits, I know that will probably happen. But hopefully not with a vial of super-botulism nestled in his jacket pocket.

What money will be required to win this auction today? One party down there has the financial clout of the entire Russian nation, banking system and all. Surely Terry Masters can't hope to match *that*?

But then he looks at me. Square, plum centre, dead on. His eyes give away nothing at first, no indication that he has recognised me at all — but I notice his complexion change, a ruddiness breaking out on his forehead. His jaw shifts and clenches as though he is chewing a stone. His eyes fill with a hatred that's clearly untameable.

I stare back at him, unsure of what to do. It's yet another standoff.

Abruptly, he takes a step back. Then another, and his eyes finally leave me, and then he's walking to the rear exit. He must know that my being here is bad for business.

No. Don't go. Stay, *fucker*.

I want to chase him, rip him to sinew, but I can't. The bigger picture is just too... *big*. Like a fisherman losing the ultimate catch, I've got to let him go.

'The excitement must be too much for some,' The Chief says to a few laughs, bringing my focus back to the auction, and Amina.

In my preoccupation, I have missed the fact that Amina has gone to work in the glovebox, repeating her lab routine from a couple of days earlier. She looks trapped, out there on this makeshift stage, all these criminals watching her, under the instruction of Christ knows who. I have to get her out of here.

'Piccolo, please tell us what you are doing,' says The Chief.

'I'm about to look at Apex under a microscope,' Amina replies, rather stating the obvious.

'How much of the chemical is there, in the vial?'

'Approximately one gram.'

'Is that a lot?' There is more than a whiff of rhetoric to The Chief's voice, suggesting that, for him, this is all part of the spiel.

For the last minute or so I have been slowly inching my belt undone and out from the holes in my trousers, slowly winding it around my right hand. By hook or by crook, I'm coming up with *something*. My heart is screaming at me.

'That is ample to synthesise as much as you could possibly need, as well as an antidote.' She lowers her eyes to the microscope.

'That's right. Of course. There is no known antidote to this, is there?'

'No. This is a completely unique toxin.'

'Bespoke, would you say?'

'Yes. One of a kind,' she says, but her eyes rise, momentarily, from the viewfinder. *Come on, Amina.* She pauses, briefly, her gaze drifting to somewhere else. *Please, Amina, go with it.*

She looks back into the scope.

'What do you see?' asks The Chief.

Amina doesn't look up, but at the floor between her feet. 'A modified isoform of clostridium botulinum, which has had its amino acids shuffled in a unique style.'

I begin to act, while listening to the rest via the tannoy system.

'And what is the result of said shuffling?' I can hear The Chief say.

I turn at speed, knowing that I'm going to have to act quickly, quietly and really bloody dirtily. My sudden movement has caught the two guards cold, but they have inched so close to me, that they can't raise their rifles quick enough. With my twirling left leg, I knock the door shut mid pirouette, dousing the room in darkness. I hear

Amina answering, muffled now through the shut door, as I go to work.

'It increases the potency of the toxin exponentially. It will now attack specific nervous receptors for maximum efficiency. It will not waste time on other less important receptors; rather it will go straight for the ones that matter.'

I throw myself at the guy on the right, my right fist swinging for his face. My belt is wrapped fully around my fist now, and I clutch the buckle in my palm, with the metal tongue poking between the knuckles of my first and second fingers.

'And this means?' The Chief says outside.

'This chemical is a quick, unstoppable killing machine,' Amina answers, as I punch the man square in his right eye, driving the metal tongue straight into his eye socket. The second man is on me in a flash, pulling me off, and I strike him in the neck three times, savagely and in the same place each time. It's awful, as I feel the tear of flesh, and hot splash of blood on my hands and arm, while Amina continues with her part. 'I would imagine that death will result within two hours of contact, as opposed to several. Said death will be aggressive and irrevocable, and with no known antidote, there is nothing to stop it.'

The man with the neck wound flops off me, and onto his back, gurgling. I know just where the carotid is, and his is no longer in good working order. I hear the soft, wet thrum of blood pouring into the carpet.

'Would you say that this gives immediate global power to whoever may own it?' The Chief asks.

I unravel the belt.

'Yes. Without doubt,' Amina answers.

I tie the belt around the neck of the man with the injured eye, and tighten it, my knees pressed firmly into his back, literally yanking the life from him.

'Thank you for your time, Piccolo,' I hear the Chief say.

It has been so well handled, so expertly timed, that one can only assume that this isn't The Chief's first rodeo. This team, here in Great Britain, that was ready to execute this auction at a moment's notice, is a very interesting bunch. I'd love to have had a chance to question the guy I'm strangling, but you can't have everything. The man slumps lifelessly, his last breath spent, and I lie him on top of his comrade who won't have long left either — a spent and savaged update of Tweedle-Dee and Tweedle-Dum.

The door opens, and Amina enters, her face still troubled but suddenly awash with surprise.

'I think we've done our part. Let's get out of here,' I say, knowing full well there is something she would want to say to me, had she not just found me disposing of the two guards. Her body language suggests indecision, and she looks at me with an intensity I have seen many times in our short relationship.

'I'm sorry you ended up on the spot, but it's not like we could discuss it,' I say, ushering her to the door at the back of the office.

'Which part?' she asks, as she comes over, wide-eyed. 'What did you do...?' She can't see the full extent of their fate, and I block her view of it. She must be able to smell the bloodshed in the air, because a hand rises to cover her mouth.

'Nothing they didn't deserve,' I reply.

'The vial. Were you going to *tell* me at any point?' she asks, her voice quivering while she attempts to compose herself.

'I'm not sure,' I say, sighing. We don't have much time. The Chief is already pressing on with what sounds like the rules of the auction, then, when the bidding starts, the auction could end at any time. If you can believe it, I was trying to protect you via blissful ignorance. Come on. It won't be long before these two are discovered, and our absence is noted.'

I grab one of the rifles, now discarded on the floor, and take her through the rear office doors, which open out onto another catwalk over a different barn. On entry, I see that it is clearly a mirror image of the other side, only this one is empty of criminal sycophants. Instead, there are hundreds of young turkeys, gobbling at us frantically. The walls and windows must be reinforced, since I had no hint that they were here. The smell is that damp, grim mix of bird shit and more bird shit.

We take the catwalk, and cross above the barn floor. There is a ladder at the end, leading up to the rafters, which we begin to climb... and then, the door to the office swings open behind us with a squeaky whoosh. I turn back, and three guards enter, eyes and rifle barrels scouring the room in tandem. They spot us instantly; we are, after all, halfway up a ladder in the middle of the room. They must have heard the scuffle and investigated.

'Oh God!' Amina says, as she hurries after me.

'Go, now, GO!' I reply, reaching the top, where a series of cramped maintenance walkways span across the ceiling. There are rows and rows of very dimly-lit bulbs right across the roof. The farm owners really do control every detail, simulating daylight in this case.

Further down the catwalk, I see an access point. That must be the roof; perfect. I look back down from whence we came, and see the men reaching the bottom of the ladder. I aim the rifle down at them, and they back off at once.

'The roof — go now,' I command, and she catches my drift immediately, haring for the roof access ladder. The roof is where I was aiming for anyway. I am readying myself mentally, but I'm virtually there. I know what must be done, and I am ready for it. There is no turning back when my mind is made up. Some things *must* be done, for the greater good.

The men keep a distance, knowing that with my elevated position and high-powered rifle, I could make mincemeat of them if they push it. Sunlight suddenly rains in on us, making the turkeys gobble maniacally in unison, as I turn and see that Amina is climbing through the roof hatch. This is the first real daylight any of the turkeys will have seen. God, I feel sorry for them.

I make my move, running for the ladder up to the sky, and the men take their opportunity too, climbing up in pursuit. At the ladder I climb end on end as fast as I can, my arms pumping, and before I know it I am there in the sunlight, dragging myself into the evening air. A shot rings out, the tinny ping of a ricochet coming from where my feet were just a split second ago.

I poke the rifle back through the hatch, and aim for the walkway support struts. I fire a controlled burst, which shatters the joint into pieces. I swing to the only other binding I can see, and do the same again. The clanging of feet on the walkway gets louder below me, as the men arrive at the foot of the ladder; but the catwalk gives way, their weight tipping the damaged support brackets beyond breaking point, and the whole structure dismembers, clanking, bouncing and tumbling into the throng of turkeys below, rag-dolled men and all.

Amina closes the hatch tight, and fastens it shut with the twist handle. The fresh air out here is a godsend after the turkey stench, and I see now that the roof is flat and clear. I'm on my feet again, knowing the ruckus will most likely have alerted others to something being amiss, but I need the auction to continue for just a little while longer...

We stay low, and trace along the roof, back in the direction of the office we were in just moments ago. There is a five foot drop to another platform, which looks to be the shape of the office itself, and on the other side of it is the larger barn roof, under which the auction must be underway. We climb across. I think of Jeremiah's men, watching us at a distance through scoped viewfinders, wondering what the hell we are doing.

Now, where is that hatch?

'Ben, what are you doing?' Amina asks, panting.

'I know it sounds bad, Amina, but I don't know what else to do,' I reply, breathing hard myself. 'Light footsteps here.'

We pad gently out onto the roof, in search of the hatch, but a better option presents itself, which I have missed before. There are large vents down the centre of the roof, one every ten yards, four feet across. Of course. I find the middle one and peer through. The outlets at the top here are slatted, and down between the slats, about ten feet below, is a whirling bladed rotor. I knew the air in these places would be carefully controlled. It's why I suggested it, after all.

I crouch by the vent and take my pack off, unzipping the side compartment. Down by my socks, and my underwear is another vial. This one contains Apex. The actual Apex, not the simple tap water I put in a spare vial that I pinched from Amina's pack, yesterday.

'When did you swap them?'

'After I had a whisky nightcap with Jeremiah last night,' I say. 'Thank you for covering the switch.'

'I'm not sure I would have survived this event if I hadn't,' she says.

'I'm sorry, Amina. This is the toughest thing I've ever had to do. But I *cannot* let any of those people take this.'

'What are going to do? You can't keep it, surely? What about Jeremiah, and William? What about your self-determined duty to your country?'

'I know, I know. I understand that this might seem like betrayal. I get it. But there is so much evil down below us that I can't bring myself to let them have it, especially when there is a way of ending it now, before this whole desperate thing goes any further.'

'You are not thinking…? You cannot seriously…?'

She takes a step towards me, her eyes on my closed left hand — the one that contains the vial.

'I will take the heat for this. You had nothing to do with it,' I say, as she holds out her hand.

'Don't,' she says, a simple word but one loaded with hope. *Her* hope.

'It was my call. Forgive me, Amina.'

She takes a step towards me, hand outstretched, her focus flitting between my left hand and my eyes. I wish I could submit to her.

'I set out to do good without compromise,' I say, but she's not hearing me. She takes my left hand at the wrist, which causes me to wince as the snake bite wound sings at the pressure. 'I set out to stop the innocent being taken for a ride by the evil.'

She looks me dead in the eyes, both hands on my wrist, imploring me, begging me, to change the course I have decided. 'I broke out of prison to make a stand for justice.'

'Justice?' she interrupts, as a scuffle begins. She is trying desperately to free the vial from my hand, but I stand firm. With a reluctant arm around her waist, and a sharp tug away with my left, I free my hand, but she is wriggling again and I can't hold her. She has her back close to my stomach now, with my arm out in front, while I try to hold her tight to me. I wish I could just let go, and let her have it... But I can't. This self-imposed oath I so foolishly follow is guiding me, and I am a reluctant yet obedient servant. We are edging ever closer to the vent in our near-silent battle.

She claws at me, hissing 'No, no!' into my neck. She then stops abruptly, as if realising she can't overpower me, not when I have the strength of my convictions on my side, and leans back into me very close. Her lips almost touch my ear as she whispers softly, in a moment of near blinding clarity, 'Ben, please, please don't.'

Her words creep under my skin and burrow into my heart.

It is almost enough.

But not quite.

'Yes, justice,' I say, and throw the vial down the vent. A tinkling glass crunch heralds the smashing of the vial on the fan, spraying the contents out into the barn below. Whether they know it or not, or heard it, or are blissfully carrying on with bidding for the damned substance, their coveted prize is raining gently down upon them, coating them one by one. To a man, they will be dead before sundown. Al Jahlel, The Chief, Bresciano, the Defence Secretary, the old lady. Dead, horribly, before this day is out.

Amina inhales sharply, her breath caught in shock. We take a few paces back from the vent, knowing precisely what dangers we are in if any of that stuff manages to find its way back out. I look at the floor, for a moment, listening. I don't know what I am expecting to hear. Screaming, perhaps? But it is as quiet as before.

I angled it this way the whole time — I suggested the controlled environment of a livestock facility for this very purpose. They are so precious about their animals, control of their environments is crucial, and that control means that whatever is in there is designed to *stay* in — even the air.

My head wants to burst. That's a whole lot of evil gone in one go. All those bastards and Apex with it. But it's a whole lot of nasty suffering I have just doled out, and when I came up with this idea, it has not sat right with me since. I have upped my game from vigilante to mass-murderer.

What have I become?

'We have to go,' says Amina. She speaks icily, and seems detached, but her eyes betray her horror at my actions.

'I'm sorry,' I say.

She doesn't reply, but it's not like there is any time to. A deep crunch comes from somewhere on the far side of the facility, and our necks snap round to the source. In the distance, towards the road, a tactical support truck has made short work of the security barrier, sending the guards spilling out of the way of the bouncing juggernaut. Shit-shit-shit-*shit-shit!* Those are Jeremiah's men, which must mean that he has seen me changing the plan without telling him, and has sent in the heavies to catch up.

Another black car appears, going the other way, exiting the car park at speed. It barrels through the mangled gap of the barrier. I don't need to guess who that is.

Masters is gone, and my chance at retribution with him.

Amina seems bewildered. I run to the rear of the building, to the edge of the roof, and I feel that she is following me. We lower ourselves down the service ladders in silence.

God knows what is going on inside, but it's wise not to stick around to find out. Now, at the back of the facility, there is thick woodland, dense and convoluted — just like my opinion of myself. I hate myself, but it was right, wasn't it? Surely?

'Amina, you can go back around the front, tell them who you are; they'll know, they'll look after you... and get a ride out of here, ASAP,' I say. 'Or you could come with me. I'm... I'm going underground for a while. I don't know what I'm saying... but you could come with me.'

She stares back at me, softly shaking her head. My actions have pushed her too far, I can tell.

'Please, just... Look, I don't know what kind of man I am, but I am trying. I only want to do good, but I've seen enough awful shit to know that good comes in many forms. I feel I had to do what I did there. I like you Amina. I feel drawn to you. I find myself wanting to protect you and I don't know why. If you'll come with me, please, I will never let anything happen to you again.'

I take a step towards her, my arms open, desperate to pick her up and take her anywhere she'll let me. Or even just to have her pressed close to me one last time. But she can barely look at me. I have let her down, I know it.

'No, Ben,' she says, solidly, tears forming. 'I can't... Nothing you can say will change the awful things I have seen you do. Nothing. I can't go anywhere with someone capable of the things you have done.'

My heart feels like it is tumbling down cold cellar steps, back to the place it started from. She was always forthright, with admirable conviction, and that is evident now, as she tells me what she really thinks of me.

'I'm sorry,' I say, and move backwards, towards the forest. 'I'm sorry for everything. Take care of yourself and get out of here.'

I turn and run. They will soon be on my tail. They will want me dead. I hear gunfire erupting behind me, a cacophony hidden behind buildings. I glance back, and see Amina walking around the corner of the facility, as an assault team arrives, well-trained hands pushing her roughly to the floor. *Don't you touch her.*

Their team leader catches sight of me, and points to me with a livid hand gesture. There is no time.

Go, Ben. Back to the foul anonymity you must be banished to. I run as hard as I can, the hill swallowing me whole and pitching me once more into the darkness of the forest, and my own despair.

24.

Some time later

The night is all encompassing, a cloak as black as my mood. There are no stars — well, there might be, but here in the forest I can't see them, thanks to the canopy. I have been on the run for a couple of hours, my pursuers never far away, except for the last thirty minutes. I think I have given them the slip.

There is one more thing to do. As I crunch through an earthy, musty clearing, I call Jeremiah via Cryptocall. He answers immediately.

'What the fuck were you doing on the roof?' he asks. He's got me there. I'm both embarrassed and sheepish; I'm a man who has debased himself fully. The awfulness of my deed may not have been discovered yet, but it won't be long now...

'I'm sorry Jeremiah, I'm sorry if you find this some kind of betrayal. I promise that it was never meant that way.'

'What did you do?' he asks, dread dripping from his words.

'I admire you, Jeremiah. I admire you very much. But my position has given me the opportunity to do good outside the rules, and I thought this was the best way.'

'Ben. What. Have. You. DONE?'

'What is the status there?'

'A standoff. A team of mercenaries is defending the facility, with the auction attendees all barricaded inside.'

'And Amina?'

'She's safe, but she's in no fit state to talk,' he replies with a thick sigh. I take heart at that, but only a little.

'Leave them to it. Leave them inside. You don't need to try to take them down. You need a chemical strike team, draft them in now. They will know what to do.'

An ominous block of silence descends between us. I have left a serious fucking mess for him to clean up, and I feel genuinely terrible about it.

'You...' Jeremiah whispers.

'No one is leaving that place with Apex. At least, none they can do any harm with.'

'What have you *done*?'

'What I thought was right. I know how stupid that sounds, given whatever it is you know about me. But letting those sons of bitches in there have any chance of doing the kind of evil that that substance was capable of, well... I just couldn't allow it'.

'Ben, you have elevated a situation that was being resolved, albeit unsatisfactorily, in a way that was non-violent, to one that could spark all-out war. If I'm following, you have killed some of the most important figures in the world with your little pang of conscience. Where do you think their financiers will come knocking for answers? On whose soil did this happen? OURS!'

I keep pressing on, through the undergrowth, hoping to leave it all behind. A distant, despicable memory.

'I know, but this will be covered up. We both know that. Do you think the Ministry of Defence will allow any word of this to get out? No chance! And with no suspects to hand, this will go down as a tragic accident. And who do you think is more to blame, the team who put the event on, the party who initiated the sale, or the country it happened to take place in? I bet you anything you like that it won't be the third.'

'Jesus,' Jeremiah says, partially conceding the point. 'The intel we could have amassed with catching them in the act...'

'Jeremiah, they will be dropping like flies as we speak. By midnight you'll be able to stroll in there yourself and send these bastards off to whichever morgue will take them. But ignore the details for a moment. This situation, this event, my actions... it's about justice and good. You can only do a finite amount of either, given the legal, bureaucratic handcuffs you are held by. The same goes for Grosvenor. Me? I am autonomous. I've made my choice, and I'm prepared to die executing it. I was given an option today, to wipe out a lot of evil, to make a statement to those smart enough to listen. That statement is: not on my watch. Not if I can help it. You come to this country with the intention to do harm, or you betray your country's people like Kirsten Sweetmore, then you are entering another domain entirely. *My* domain. They wanted Apex, I gave them Apex, at the hands of an Apex predator. You fuck around in this country, you will pay for it. I can promise that. I have set my stall out. I repeat. *Not on my watch.*'

Jeremiah is stunned into silence.

'Like I said, Jeremiah, I admire and respect you. I hope we can have that pint one day, and I hope you can forgive me for my actions and see the reasons behind what I have done. I have to hope that the world will be a better place because of it.'

I shut the phone off, and crush it under my foot. Goodbye, my trusty smartphone. It's time to start again from scratch. Whoever was backing Sweetmore, will have known about me. It won't be long before questions are being asked, when my body doesn't turn up. And they'll come running, for sure. I need a head start. I wish Amina had come with me, but I understand why she felt she couldn't. Goddamn it.

Mentally, I feel defeated and flayed, splayed on the spikes at the bottom of a dark pit. My instincts and duty have again dragged me to places I didn't think possible. But my abiding memory of this will be that I have to trust them, if I want to keep surviving.

ENDEAVOUR QUILL

Endeavour Quill is an imprint of Endeavour Media.

If you enjoyed *Morte Point* check out
Endeavour Media's eBooks here:
www.endeavourmedia.co.uk

For weekly updates on our free and discounted eBooks
sign up
to our newsletter:
www.endeavourmedia.co.uk/sign-up

Follow us on Twitter:
@EndeavourQuill

And Instagram:
endeavour_media

ENDEAVOUR MEDIA